Tenney's Landing

Stories

CATHERINE TUDISH

Scribner
New York   London   Toronto   Sydney

SCRIBNER
1230 Avenue of the Americas
New York, NY 10020

Some of the stories in this collection have appeared elsewhere,
in slightly different form: "Pigeon" in *Hunger Mountain* and
"The Infusion Suite" in *Green Mountains Review.*

SCRIBNER and design are trademarks of
Macmillan Library Reference USA, Inc., used under license by
Simon & Schuster, the publisher of this work.

For information about special discounts for bulk purchases,
please contact Simon & Schuster Special Sales:
1-800-456-6798 or business@simonandschuster.com

Designed by Kyoko Watanabe
Text set in Bembo

Manufactured in the United States of America

1   3   5   7   9   10   8   6   4   2

Library of Congress Cataloging-in-Publication Data

Tudish, Catherine, 1952–
Tenney's landing : stories / Catherine Tudish.
p. cm.
1. Pennsylvania—social life and customs—Fiction. I. Title.
PS3620.U34T46 2005
813'.6—dc22
2005042038

ISBN 0-7432-6767-2

for my grandparents:
Mary Black and Walter Carr
Anna Gale and Paul Tudish

Contents

I know more of rivers than merely where
ferries cross.

—Sung Tung-P'o,
"Seven Thousand Miles Away," 1094
(translated by Berton Watson)

Tenney's Landing

Prologue:
How Tenney Landed

B y April of 1765 the white fur trapper known as Big Hat could come and go as he pleased among the hills and waterways south of the demolished Fort Duquesne. The Iroquois and Shawnee left him alone now, amused by the sight of his peculiar headgear—not an ordinary hat but a beaver hide complete with head, feet, and tail. After drying the hide, the trapper had stitched it so that the animal seemed to perch on his head, front paws clasped across his brow, rear paws and broad tail hanging down behind. It kept the rain off, and the snow.

Big Hat had been in and out of the southwestern Pennsylvania Territory since 1754, when he was seventeen. The first time, he came with Lieutenant Colonel George Washington's Virginia troops and thus shared the embarrassment of being driven out of Fort Necessity by the French. Indignant, he returned as a militiaman in General Braddock's army the following summer, intending to take part in the capture of Fort Duquesne. He and a few others escaped that battle with their lives, if not their horses. On foot he made his way back to the Shenandoah Valley, where he was known as Lucius J. Tenney, son of Lawrence and Madeline Tenney. He came home without his brother.

That winter, Lucius brooded. He pictured snow falling on William's grave, so hastily dug near the path of their retreat that steamy July afternoon. There had been no time to mark the place, except for an *X* scratched into the bark of a nearby tree. As the Virginia skies darkened with cold, his father turned bitter. "What has this got to do with us?" Lawrence had shouted when his sons came riding up the lane wearing red coats and black tricornered hats, anxious to retrieve their muskets from the grain shed and be off. "What do we care if the French take over the whole blasted Ohio territory? Haven't we got land of our own under our feet?" Out of earshot, riding away again, the boys had laughed, attributing their father's generous attitude to a sprinkling of French ancestors.

No glory for Lawrence Tenney in losing his oldest, a fine

son of nineteen, and none for Madeline either. Lucius never told them about the drunken British officer who had slapped William across the face and called him "a stupid dog" for no reason, except that the British troops looked down on the colonials. That officer was dead too.

From time to time, Lucius rode over to a neighboring farm to sit with his brother's fiancée, Merilee Harding. She had impressed him by fainting, spiraling rather gracefully to the floor, when he went to deliver the news. Lucius hadn't said a word. When Merilee saw him alone at the door, her face turned white as milk and her eyes rolled back in her head. Suddenly Lucius was kneeling beside her, calling for help.

One of the things Lucius brooded about that winter was the way his brother and Merilee, friends since childhood, had loved each other. He himself had always been put off by her birthmark, a purple stain at the nape of her neck that crept up into her hair. Never before had he wondered about the point of origin. Where did it begin, then? He let himself imagine the downy softness of her back, his nervous fingers undoing the impossible hooks and eyes of her dress, tracing a path down the bumps of her spine to the gentle swelling at its base. Such imaginings would make him leap up suddenly from the chair near the fire where he appeared to be dozing. He would stalk out to the back porch and douse his head in a bucket of cold water, berating himself as a craven beast, a thief. The next evening, he would ride over to visit Merilee.

They were married in September, three months to the day past the date set for her wedding to William. Within a couple of years, Lucius was farming his own land, and on the eve of his twenty-first birthday, Merilee gave birth to a son they named Jordan. It was a strange and unexpected sight, then, when Lucius and his cousin Prosper Eastman set off in the little wagon with their traps and a few provisions in the fall of 1758, headed for the southwestern Pennsylvania Territory. While fleeing Fort Necessity and dodging French musket fire on the road to Fort Duquesne, Lucius had not failed to notice the lush wildlife living in the forests. He'd seen beaver dams in the streams, deer wandering everywhere, the tracks of rabbits, bear, and coons. Even though, as Merilee argued, the place had already killed his brother and tried hard to kill him too, something about it drew him back. Perhaps, he told her, he could find his brother's grave and put up a proper cross; perhaps he would spy the shaky X he'd scratched with the tip of his bayonet.

When the cousins returned to Virginia the following spring, Lucius was wearing the beaver hide, claiming it worked as a charm to keep him safe from the Indians. Prosper showed the scar a musket ball had left in his right hand and described how the shot had come just as he was opening the trap that held the animal now adorning Lucius's head. Both of them were gaunt and filthy, their hair and whiskers growing wild. But they had real money, silver and gold coins.

From April to October, Lucius farmed. And then he loaded up his traps, kissed Merilee on the back of the neck, and went off to the frigid northern hills for the winter. Often Prosper went along, and occasionally another cousin or two. They were shot at, and sometimes hit, but never killed. Every spring they returned to Virginia, thin and tough as wild hares, their leather pouches full of coins.

One April day in 1765 Lucius was alone, drifting down the Monongahela River on his raft, baring his chest to the sun. By then the French troops were gone, having destroyed their own Fort Duquesne before retreating to Canada. A Shawnee hunting party, catching sight of the raft, remarked that it was the time for Big Hat to go south. Most of the winter's furs had been sold. Prosper and Steadfast Eastman had already set off for home, eager to get their crops in. But Lucius, who had come to love the hills and rivers up this way, lingered awhile. Melancholy at the thought of leaving, he finished off his precious store of whiskey as he watched the high green banks passing by, the river swollen with spring rains. And so he fell asleep on the water, in the warm sun, safe in the shade of his big hat.

He woke some time later to a dizzy sensation of spinning and dug his fingernails into the rough bark logs of his raft, holding on until he finally bumped up against the shore. Standing on his trembling legs, Lucius looked around. He'd been caught in an eddy and carried onto a sandbar beneath the river's west bank. After he'd pulled himself up to dry ground, he took in the great curving sweep of water upstream, where it rounded a bend, and the long, wide expanse below, flowing off as far as he could see. Deciding to spend the night there, he built a small fire on the sand and fell asleep again, thinking of his brother, William, and the grave he'd never found.

In the morning, sober, he liked the look of the place even more and started walking up the hill to find the spot where he would build his house. Within a few months' time, Merilee and their four children had joined him, and by the next spring,

Eastmans, Hardings, Moffats, and Kramers were plowing the valley's rich bottomland. Lucius opened a trading post, nailing his lucky beaver hide over the door.

The following year, his friend Jonathan Rownd made the long trip from Virginia. Preferring the point of land upriver, Rownd moved his family there. Lucius liked the joke of it—Rownd's Point, as the settlement came to be called. As for the town named in his honor, only Lucius knew the joke of Tenney's Landing.

Awake or not, Lucius had chosen well. As Pittsburgh grew on the site of Fort Duquesne, some sixty miles upriver, the Monongahela became a well-traveled trade route. Because the Indians liked him and traded with him and protected his settlement, Tenney's Landing prospered. By 1820, the year Lucius died at the age of eighty-three, an Englishman named Trevor Sparrow had begun building a hotel on the riverbank—a hotel with a ballroom, people whispered. Not much later, Lucius's grandson Martin began to run the first ferry across the river to carry horses and wagons between Tenney's Landing and Lynchtown. From the beginning, the dark soil drew many out into the surrounding countryside, so that hill farms fanned out in both directions. There were other riches in those hills, too: oil and coal, yet to be discovered.

Today, the oldest residents of Tenney's Landing can remember the 1920s and '30s. On a Saturday night, the old-timers say, Front Street was jumping. You could go to a movie and then down to the Mon-View Lounge for a steak dinner and the latest tunes on the jukebox. You could get something strong to drink, too, they add with a laugh. If you knew the password. There might even be a showboat tied up at the landing, and strangers from places like Baton Rouge strolling arm in arm down the sidewalk in their fancy dress and makeup.

The town is smaller and quieter now—the movie theater boarded up, the hotel burned down, the showboats long gone. An occasional arrowhead found while digging a garden is all that's left of the Indians. The coal and oil are starting to peter out, and the farming families are dwindling. It's a pretty town, though, with its clapboard and brick houses built close to the river and spreading up the hill above—a few standing empty, paint peeling and front yards weedy. There's Paula's Café and the Good Food Market and the newspaper office on Front Street and Bright's Dairy on the road out of town. Then there's the new bed-and-breakfast, where people from Pittsburgh come to stay for the weekend. You can see them out on the porch in nice weather, reading the Sunday paper and drinking coffee. So maybe the town has life in it yet.

The house Lucius Tenney started building in 1765 was declared a state historic site in 1972. On a table inside the front door, visitors can pick up a slim pamphlet describing the life and times of Lucius J. Tenney, Patriot. At age thirty-eight, the pamphlet explains, Lucius, a veteran of the French and Indian War, had gone off to fight in the Revolution, taking his son Jordan with him. Both had returned home eventually, Jordan missing a leg.

Furnished as they were when Lucius and Merilee lived there, the modest rooms are cordoned off with velvet ropes. Framed charcoal drawings of the couple hang over the mantel in the parlor. The drawings are not very good—perhaps they were done by one of the children—but the Tenneys look alert and happy in their middle age. Whoever drew them captured something real. Every April, schoolchildren come with their teachers to see the rambling stone and wood house near the top of the hill. It's always raining in April, so these little pilgrims hop off the bright yellow buses wearing green and blue and red slickers. "Oh, look!" they cry, catching the first glimpse of the river from this high ground.

Where the Devil Lost
His Blanket

As the plane taxis away from the gate, I see Gordon standing with our children, Jamie and Sarah, at the big plate-glass window. And even though I know they can't see me, I press my hand against the tiny window next to my seat. The plane lurches along, with alarming creaks and vibrations, and gradually picks up speed. I watch the trees and the Air National Guard hangar whizzing past, and at the moment we leave the ground, I nearly cry out. Partly it's the unreality of taking flight, but mostly it's knowing how far away from them I will be when the plane touches ground again.

We rise above Pittsburgh, circling over the bridges and the three rivers that look motionless and glistening from above, and turn west, climbing into the clouds. Bogotá. I say the name to myself. It conjures up nothing.

Somewhere beneath me, in the plane's luggage compartment, Margaría Flores lies in her funeral box. And her husband, Arturo, in an urn, packed in a little crate. I know so little about these people whose remains I have inherited, but Margaría wrote in her will that I should be the one to take her home. "My friend Elizabeth Tenney," Jackson read from the pages he was holding. Gordon and I sat together on the sofa in his office while Jackson read the will, and Gordon held my hand, as if we were hearing the news of my own terminal illness.

Margaría left me a pair of silver candlesticks—I remember seeing them on her dining room table—and money for the trip to Colombia and back. "I want my friend Elizabeth Tenney to have some remembrance of me and take me to my final resting place," she had written. Jackson held the will up for us to see, several sheets of lined paper filled with very precise, sloping handwriting.

We sat there looking at those pages for a minute or two, and then Gordon said, "I'll be damned."

Watching me, Jackson tipped his head to one side. "I didn't realize you and Margaría were friends."

"We weren't close," I said. "It is kind of surprising." I tried to think of who else she might have asked instead, but I couldn't come up with anyone.

Jackson straightened the papers on his desk, looking amused. "Of course, you don't have to go. I can arrange to ship the casket."

"That wouldn't be right," I said, a feeling like shame curdling in my stomach. "I think I do have to go. She chose me."

That evening we called at the Cantwell Funeral Home, where Margaría was laid out. It's the only funeral home in Tenney's Landing. Our town has one lawyer and one undertaker. And one aging priest we share with Rownd's Point, a town nearby. Father Rollins stood beside the casket, a velvet-lined mahogany box that was too big for Margaría. She wore a black dress with a white silk flower at the neck, and she looked as if she had only closed her eyes for a moment, preparing herself for a photograph. A strand of her hair had come loose and trailed across the tiny pillow beneath her head. Instinctively, I reached out to tuck it into place, remembering how Sarah as a baby had been fascinated by Margaría's dark, glossy hair, the way she would reach up from her stroller and stroke it when Margaría bent down to speak to her. "Pretty," Sarah would say, her small hand patting Margaría's cheek.

Both of my children liked her. Jamie would call out "Hello, Mrs. Flores," whenever he saw her. Once she had given him a small jade carving of a turtle and told him it would bring him luck. He carried it in his pocket for a long time.

Father Rollins was speaking with Margaría's next-door neighbors, Aggie and Jasper Moffat. They were the ones who found her, lying in her back garden with a rake still in her hand. She'd been mulching her rosebushes, getting ready for the winter.

"I guess it's not such a bad way to die," Aggie said. "Except that she wasn't very old." The Moffats themselves were in their mid-seventies.

"Heart attack, it must have been," Jasper added.

Gordon stood next to me, his hand on my shoulder. Since leaving Jackson's office, he had been moving through the day reluctantly. When we had lunch in Pittsburgh while we waited for my passport, he took forever to choose a sandwich and then left half of it on his plate. As we were getting in the car to come to the funeral home, he decided that he needed to change his tie and spent another ten minutes picking out the right one. It's not like him.

"I'm glad you came," Father Rollins told me in a near-whisper. "You're the only ones from town, besides Aggie and Jasper, and just three or four from the college. Margaría told me she was grateful to you for your kindness last year when her husband died."

Because we are Presbyterians, I don't know this priest very well, so I did not say, "But all I did was take her a vegetable casserole on the day of the funeral," even though that was the extent of my kindness. Sometimes I'd see her at the post office or the grocery store and ask, "How are you, Margaría?" On those occasions, I would rattle on about the children, our busy lives, suggest that we get together—maybe next week. But the days would roll by, and I would forget about Margaría until I saw her again. Each time, her expectant glance caused a guilty shiver down my spine.

One thing I do know—Margaría was afraid of fire. That day last year when I stood in her kitchen clutching the steaming casserole between a pair of hot mitts, Margaría said, "It was

Arturo's wish to be cremated. I do not wish it myself—such a hellish way to die."

I hadn't pointed out that Arturo was dead already. Instead, I put the casserole on the table and, not knowing what to do next, hugged her clumsily with the hot mitts and said, "I'm sorry for your loss."

"You are a kind woman," she replied as I pulled away from her.

She asked me to stay and have a cup of coffee, but I told her I had to take Jamie to the doctor; he had an appointment for his school physical. I promised to come back soon. At the time of Arturo's funeral service, I was reading a magazine in the doctor's waiting room.

Margaría and Arturo appeared in Tenney's Landing so quietly, we hardly noticed them at first. One day they were living in the old Kramer place at the end of Pinkham Street, hanging curtains and sweeping the front walk. They were small, dark-haired people with unfamiliar accents, and because they seemed reserved we pretty much left them alone.

The morning Gordon stopped to help him fix a flat tire, he found out that Arturo taught Spanish at McClelland College, a small, expensive school of graceful red-brick buildings about twenty miles downriver in Fayette. No one from Tenney's Landing went to school there, and no one who taught there, except Arturo, lived in our town. It seemed odd, Gordon said, that Arturo would have come all the way from Colombia to teach at McClelland College. Although Margaría and Arturo lived there for years and had the house painted a new color, we always called it the old Kramer place.

As the plane levels out, I open my purse and find one of

the memorial cards printed up by the Cantwell Funeral Home. Margaría Flores, 1931–1982, it says at the top in black letters. Underneath is a short poem:

> *God hath not promised*
> *Skies always blue,*
> *Flower-strewn pathways*
> *All our lives through;*
> *God hath not promised*
> *Sun without rain,*
> *Joy without sorrow,*
> *Peace without pain.*

On the back is a picture of a sheaf of wheat in warm tones of tan and gold. Most of the little cards were still stacked on the table by the door when Gordon and I left the funeral home last night. For some reason, I gathered them up and took them with me.

Who picked out that poem, I wonder, and who wrote it? I read it again, as if it might have a message for me as I set out on my strange journey. Except for the two years I went away to college, I have never been far from home. I peer out the window again. We are above the clouds now. Around me, the other passengers appear unconcerned, flipping through magazines, chatting with each other. I tilt the seat back and close my eyes, imagine my family driving home from the airport, the leaf-dappled light on the river as it flows past our town.

The Monongahela runs fast and green most of the time, with thick, ropy currents out in the middle, so you'd think it was constant. In the coldest winters, though, when we were kids, it would freeze over. The first warm night of March, lying in our beds, we'd hear the ice start to creak and moan in some kind of water agony. By morning it would be cracked into big, ragged pieces that slid up over each other, trying to push their way downstream. Townspeople walked out and stood on the banks, looking it over and checking their watches, making bets on what time it was going to break up and let loose.

In the flood of '52, when I was nine, the river went wild, rising and rising until it ran down Front Street—the sixth day of a seven-day rain. My cousins who lived in the house next to the post office came up to stay with us because they had river water running through their downstairs. They kept saying, "Two feet of water right in the living room." They couldn't get over it. My little sister, Ruthie, gave her bed to these boy cousins and slept in with me and pressed her knees into the middle of my back as I imagined the river washing up against our second-story windows.

The first morning of the flood we walked down the hill to see if it was true that houses and goats and chicken coops were floating downstream. But it was only dead trees and one old rusted-out truck that turned and turned in the current. Then one of my cousins yelled, "Hey, it's Gordy!" and I saw Gordon in the back of his dad's rowboat, coming down the street. He was wearing a blue jacket, and when they went past I could see his black-and-white collie, Skipper, in the bottom of the boat, soaking wet and shivering. Gordon looked right at me and raised his hand and said, "Hey, Lizzy." I remember that.

Walking through the gate at the airport in Bogotá, I am surrounded by a knot of people pressing forward to greet the
arriving passengers. Everyone is hugging and talking all at
once as they exchange greetings in Spanish. Then, quite suddenly, I am standing alone, watching the others stride away
down the long, fluorescent corridor. Why has no one come to
meet me? Through the plate-glass windows, I can see the
shimmer of heat on the tarmac, planes nosing along like docile
silver beasts.

I begin to picture myself wandering through the city
loaded down with my suitcase, the coffin, Arturo's small crate,
growing more and more tired, afraid to stop and rest. I hold on
to the back of one of the plastic seats in the waiting area and
try to think.

Then I hear a voice approaching behind me and turn
around.

"I think you are Elizabeth Tenney," says an odd-looking
young man coming toward me.

Something is wrong with his face. As he gets closer, I see
that one side of it is badly scarred. "How did you know?" I
ask, wondering if I should shake his hand.

He shrugs. "I am Margaría's brother Herman," he says,
looking at me quizzically.

I try to concentrate on his name, to avoid staring at his face.
In its Spanish pronunciation, the name sounds more mascu-
line—*Herr-mon*, with an emphasis on the end.

"The youngest brother," he adds, in response to my confused look.

"I'm sorry about your sister," I say quickly. "It must be very
hard for you, living so far away."

I almost expect him to explain his strange appearance to
me, as someone might do if he were bleeding, as if an explanation were necessary.

Instead, he guides me down the corridor with occasional
light touches on my back. "I apologize for being just a bit
late," he says. "I was detained in Customs, filling out papers.
It's unusual, the circumstance. And now I must take you there,
so they can look into your suitcase." He turns and smiles at
me, adding, "In case you are a desperado."

I can feel my face flush as I think of someone pawing
through my neatly folded clothes. "Is your home nearby?" I
ask him.

"Not too close. A drive of an hour, a little more. There is
also a hearse outside for Margaría and Arturo."

At Customs I am asked, in careful English, if I have anything to declare. The official nods at Herman as if he is used
to seeing him and stamps my passport. He does not open my
suitcase.

I watch the hearse behind us in the side mirror as we take
the expressway into the city. Herman's car is a kind I have never
seen before, and although it is square and serious looking, it
smells of leather and dogs. I have the impression he would like
to drive faster, but he has to go slowly because of the hearse.

I sip from a paper cup of coffee Herman bought for me at
the airport—dark, bitter coffee that is also sweet. Sitting in the
passenger seat, I can see only the scarred side of his face, the
pale skin taut and wimpled at the same time. His right hand,
too, is badly scarred. On the steering wheel, his two hands: one
the color of caramel with smooth, shapely fingers, the other a
livid pink, fingers ending in calluses rather than nails.

He mentions squares and buildings as we pass—many named after Spanish conquerors. The names flow like quicksilver, and I catch only a few. *Iglesia Santa Clara. Plaza de Bolívar. Chorro del Quevedo.* In the older sections of the city, where the heavy stone buildings are surrounded by brilliant flowers, it seems to me that I have traveled back in time hundreds of years. Even though my eyes sting from lack of sleep, I can't stop looking at everything.

When I ask Herman where he learned to speak English, he says he studied it in high school. "Also," he says. "I went to college at Stanford."

I try to think of all the words I know in Spanish. *Sí. Gracias. Conquistador.* Only three?

"I quite liked it," he continues, "but then I got homesick and came back after the graduation."

"So did I," I tell him. "I mean the homesick part. I never did get used to being away. So I quit after two years and got married."

"And you are happy with that decision?"

It seems an odd question, coming from a stranger. "I don't need a college degree to live my life," I say, taken aback at my own rudeness. I begin to suspect there's something devilish about him, as if he might enjoy taking advantage of his disconcerting first impression. "I'm sorry," I add. "I think I must be tired."

"Yes," he says. "I can imagine."

From the elegant and bustling center of the city, we pass through its rougher edges, where the streets are littered with paper and broken glass and rusted trash cans overflow at the curbs. When we stop for a light, two young women in tight-fitting leather jackets are waiting at the corner. The one with a butterfly tattooed on her cheek bangs her fist on the fender of the car as they start across the street, and the other one gives us the finger as they pass in front of the windshield. Herman rolls down his window and says something in Spanish, and the butterfly girl turns her head and grins as they reach the other side.

I expect Herman to tell me what he said, but he doesn't. Maybe they're angry because he drives an expensive car. Maybe they're prostitutes.

All at once, we are beyond the city and driving into sweeping grasslands—as far as I can see, deep green grass, thigh high, billowing in the wind. And hills in the distance, rolling hills that look like the rumpled edges of an immense green carpet.

"Our ranch is out beyond those hills," Herman says, pointing with his chin and stepping down on the accelerator.

"This must be pampas grass," I say. "I've heard of it, but I didn't know it would be so beautiful."

"No, this is sweetgrass. Our cattle graze on it."

"Oh," I say, a little disappointed. "I had visions of ostriches running through the pampas grass."

Herman looks over at me. "No ostriches either. I believe you are thinking of Argentina."

When I come awake, we are driving between two stone pillars and down a long, narrow driveway planted with trees on either side. I think they are eucalyptus, but I don't ask. The drive is covered with fine white gravel, which crunches pleasantly beneath the tires, and at the end of it a rambling two-story house with a red tile roof. I check the mirror to see that the hearse is still with us.

We cross the wide porch, and someone opens the door just as we approach. "*Gracias*, Tiva," Herman says to the small woman standing in the shadow inside. A house with servants, then. I follow him down a hallway darkened by closed shutters. Although the day is quite warm, the house is cool inside. Our footsteps clatter on the slate floor, and the hushed darkness reminds me that this is a house of mourning. Herman stops at another doorway and waits for me to enter. Inside, near an open window, three women dressed in black are seated at a low table set for tea. The furniture is heavy and dark, a small vase of pink roses on the table the only color.

The women watch us with no change of expression, their faces set in sorrow. They might be figures in a painting, they're that striking. Herman introduces me to his mother with a little bow, saying, "Señora Tenney, I would like you to meet my mother, Señora Márquez."

She takes my hand as if she were about to kiss it and says, "*Buenos días*, Señora Tenney. I do not speak English." As she holds my gaze for a moment, I can see the resemblance to Margaría. Señora Márquez must be about seventy-five. Even in grief, she looks as if her life has not been too hard.

The slender woman I took to be Herman's wife is his sister Dorothea, and the plump, less pretty one, his wife, Rosamond. Each takes my hand in the same formal way as we are introduced.

At dinner that night I am seated next to Señora Márquez, who is at the head of the table, and across from Herman, my translator. Unlike the other men, who wear dark jackets, he has on a white shirt with the sleeves rolled up. Where he is not scarred, his face and arms are very tan. Herman is probably in his early thirties, and as I have a chance to observe him, I realize that he must have been quite handsome at one time. Even though I can understand almost nothing of the conversation, I see how the others follow the lead of his good-natured, irreverent spirit. In such a family, perhaps it is possible to remain beautiful, come what may. They say Margaría's name often, and I'm struck by how different it sounds here. *Mar-ha-ria.*

Herman turns to me every few minutes and tells me what they're talking about. "Eduardo is telling of the time Margaría let his pet birds out of their cage because she thought they needed to fly. They soon flew out of sight, but she told Eduardo not to worry. She covered the cage with flowers and put fruit inside and sang to the birds to come home. And when they did not come back, she cried for two days." Eduardo, one of the older brothers, looks down the table at me and makes a flying motion with his hands. Then he shrugs, as if to say it didn't really matter.

Señora Márquez interrupts their reminiscing after a while to ask me what my husband does, and I try to explain what it means to be a riverman, pausing between sentences so Herman can translate. Using some forks and knives, I demonstrate how the locks work and tell them that Gordon is now the lockmaster. With a serving spoon I show how the big cargo boats and pleasure boats pass through the lock a few miles downriver from our town.

Gordon has spent his whole life on the Monongahela River—which is appropriate, I tell them, since his ancestor

Lucius J. Tenney, a fur trapper, was the first white settler along the section that came to be called Tenney's Landing. Lucius went ashore one day in the spring of 1765, his raft piled with rabbit and coon hides, and felt the need to stretch his legs. He so liked the look of the river from that spot—the way it curved around a bend upstream and then widened out—that he decided to set up his own trading post right there.

When Gordon was a boy, I continue, one of his older cousins, Fred Tenney, ran the ferryboat that crossed over from Tenney's Landing to Lynchtown, and Gordon rode with him whenever he could. He'd be down there after school and most days in the summer, and sometimes he asked me to come along. The ferry was little more than a large raft with a motor; it had wooden planks for a deck, a rope railing, and old car tires tied to the sides for bumpers. It could take six cars and of course a few people on foot or even a horse and buggy. Gordon collected the fifty-cent fare, while his cousin directed each car up the ramp and placed a wooden chock under one of the front tires. The crossing took about twenty minutes; the small motor chugged across the current and churned up a wake that made you dizzy if you stared at it all the way across.

I tell them how, one time on the Lynchtown side, Gordon showed me a heron's nest with two gawky baby birds inside. We could see the tiny bald heads and the dark pouches of their eyes, the long beaks jabbing the air above their nest. A couple of weeks later, they were perched on a limb, turning their heads this way and that, puffing themselves up. Even when he was young, Gordon could predict the weather by watching the clouds, I say, and sometimes he made up names for them. The ones he liked best he called "broom tails," those clouds that look like horses' tails galloping off in the distance. "You might not notice it unless you're out there," he'd tell me, "but the river is different every day."

"You love your husband," Señora Márquez says approvingly, and a glance at Herman's amused expression as he translates tells me I have been talking too much.

The Márquez family has a cook, who—along with a spry, elderly man who may be the cook's father—also brings the food to the table. We are served several courses: sweet panfried fish with pepper sauce, hot garlic soup, crisply browned game hens with orange sauce, polenta, ripe plums, and cheese. The energetic father of the cook keeps bringing new bottles of wine to the table, and finally brandy and the bittersweet coffee. The dining room is fragrant with cilantro and cinnamon, fresh-cut limes, other scents I can't name. From time to time, two or three of the men step through the open doors to smoke on the terrace. I am so tired and so charmed, I feel as if my chair is floating above the floor, as if I might tip out and float away into the darkness outside.

But the weight of voices keeps me anchored. Looking around at Margaría's relatives, the brothers and sisters, the aunts and uncles and cousins, I think of her quiet dinners with Arturo. And then her final solitary year.

It is close to midnight when I finally get to bed. I have a room in the upstairs at the end of the hall, and I listen to the sounds of hushed voices and running water, doors closing. I have a feather pillow and smooth, soft sheets. When the house goes quiet, I can hear the wind in the grass. As I fall into sleep, just as in the car, I see the endless grasslands and feel the sun on my face. I hear the tune Herman is humming as he drives.

All night a river flows through my dreams, our river. But I can't be sure of where I am, whether I am awake or sleeping . . .

————

Birdsong and the sounds of cattle pull me awake. Before I open my eyes, I try to picture Gordon and Jamie and Sarah at home, but I can't quite see them, place them in the day. I get up and look out the window. Beyond the lawn, where the fields start, the grass is still damp, and small brown birds perch on the tallest blades. The heavy shoulders of the cattle push the grass aside, and they twist their necks to bite it off near the ground. They stand chewing, long tufts hanging from their mouths.

Herman has explained that although it is unusual for the youngest son to take over the family place, he and Rosamond live on the ranch with his mother. His older brothers have gone into business in Bogotá and have no interest in raising cattle. As I'm thinking this, Herman appears on horseback with his small son seated behind him. They ride slowly through the grazing cattle and farther out into the grassland. Two brown-and-white spaniels follow them. Herman wears a Panama hat and khaki pants and again a white shirt. At a distance, he looks unreal, as if two different people have been joined together somehow. His son clasps his waist tightly and grips the horse's flanks with sneakered feet. I watch until I can just see the top of Herman's hat vanishing in the high grass.

I don't see him again until late in the afternoon, when he and his son slip into the pew beside me at the start of Margaría's funeral. Rosamond, who is sitting two rows in front of us, turns around, looking pointedly at her watch and giving

Herman an exasperated frown. He pretends not to notice. He smells clean; his hair and his son's are still wet from the shower, combed back in the same way. The little boy looks at me, smiling shyly, then ducks back behind his father's jacket.

The church is large but surprisingly plain, with its white stucco walls and tall, clear, leaded-glass windows. Behind the raised altar, a peaceful Christ hangs on a heavy wooden cross, his forehead pricked with thorns. Margaría's casket stands before the altar on a cloth-covered table. The air is heavy with flowers and incense, and underneath these, a lighter scent, something like chalk dust. I have never, even in a dream, found myself in such an extraordinary place.

I follow Herman's lead through the unfamiliar ritual, kneeling when he kneels, standing when he stands. The women carry white handkerchiefs trimmed in black lace. They cry softly and continually throughout the funeral. Dorothea has given me such a handkerchief, and I hold it bunched awkwardly in my hand.

During the priest's long sermon, Herman leans over and whispers, "Don't bother about this, he's just talking of life after death."

"Oh, that," I whisper back. It's easier, I admit to myself, to be on Herman's left side, the good side.

Margaría's brother Eduardo gives the eulogy, and when he mentions America, people turn to look at me. At the end, when Dorothea stands to sing, Herman says, "This was Margaría's best song when she was a little girl." The song is a kind of lullaby, maybe the song she sang to the lost birds. As Dorothea's clear voice begins to tremble, I feel tears come to my own eyes and try to blink them back and dab at them with

25

the crumpled handkerchief. When Herman reaches over to pat my arm in a comforting, brotherly way, my heart lurches in my chest.

The cemetery, a family graveyard on a small rise overlooking the house, is shaded by immense trees. I stand at Margaría's grave next to Dorothea; Herman is on the opposite side with Rosamond and his son. I watch him tuck a strand of Rosamond's hair behind her ear and kiss her on the cheek. Her face is streaked with tears, and something about his tenderness toward her makes me think she is pregnant. The priest reads from a small black book as Margaría's casket is lowered into the ground. She and Arturo are buried together, next to the grave of Margaría's father. Only now I wonder why Margaría didn't come home when Arturo died.

Dorothea turns away before the first shovel of dirt falls on the casket, and I walk with her down the hill toward the house. She is a young widow—Herman told me her husband was killed in a speedboat accident two years ago—and she lives with her mother too and helps manage the household. We walk around to the terrace, where friends of the family are already waiting and where drinks and food are being served again.

I don't see Herman for some time, then he comes out of the house with Rosamond. They go sit near his mother. Standing with Dorothea and a few of the cousins, I feel somewhat lost and unaccountably disappointed. After perhaps an hour, when the guests have started to go, Herman catches my eye and motions for me to join them.

"My mother wants to thank you again," he says, as I take the seat next to him.

Señora Márquez smiles at me tenderly and speaks to Herman.

"She says that you will miss her," Herman tells me. "Margaría."

"I will," I say, flustered. It begins to seem true.

Rosamond, who has been watching me intently, now leans forward and speaks. She seems to be asking a series of questions. Her tone is rather fierce.

Herman pauses before translating. "My wife is asking if you will be the one to send us Margaría's things, her personal belongings," he says. "Rosamond is not feeling well today, as you might notice."

At first I wonder if she suspects me of stealing things that belonged to Margaría, but then I realize they must be disappointed that I brought nothing of hers to give them—a picture album, a favorite book or piece of jewelry. All I have are the memorial cards from the funeral home. "I'm sorry," I say, embarrassed to have come so unprepared, "but I had to leave home quickly. Is there something special you want me to look for when I get back?" I address the question to Rosamond, but she is already getting up and moving away. I think she is the only one to see that I am not a real friend.

Herman's mother gives me a sympathetic look and follows her daughter-in-law into the house. When the two women have gone, I start to ask Herman why Rosamond is upset, but he looks at my feet and says, "You need some different shoes. Can you get a jacket? I want to show you something."

He meets me in front of the house, driving a very old Jeep

with faded paint and a dented door. I wonder if anyone is watching us. We drive past the stables and into the horse track where I saw him with his son this morning. Though we drive for more than half an hour, neither of us says anything. Where the track is narrow, the tall grass whips against the fenders. Otherwise, it is quiet and still, the end of the afternoon. Herman stops at the top of a low hill. When he gets out, I follow him a little way. We are looking down on a kind of basin, a bowl of flattened grass about sixty or seventy yards across. All around us, the grassland goes on forever.

"What is this place?" I ask him.

"Ah. This is where the devil lost his blanket."

I try to guess what a devil's blanket might look like. An old horse blanket? A scarlet cape? "What does that mean?"

"It is hard to tell someone from away—if you lived here, you would understand—but it means something like the edge of nowhere, a place where strange things might happen."

Herman is not looking at me; he's gazing across the basin. I feel a little nervous, though I'm not sure why.

"You were Margaría's only friend in America," he says finally. "And so I wanted to bring you here."

"The truth is I didn't know her very well."

"Not many people did. She stayed too much inside herself."

"What I mean is I didn't really try to know her. I wish it had been different."

Herman sighs. "Half of life is regret, don't you think?" He turns to me and says, "She knew you well enough, in any case."

I can see my reflection in the darkness of Herman's eyes, and once again his closeness is confusing. I want to reach across the space between us and touch him, to take hold of his slender brown wrist. I walk away from him and stand closer to the edge. "That grass down there—why is it so flat?"

"Wild horses sleep here at night. Come, I will show you."

Walking down the slope is difficult because the grass is slippery. Now it might be natural to take Herman's arm, but I avoid looking at him and keep some distance between us. When we reach the bottom, the grass is matted and twisted.

"This is the place where Margaría saved her own life once," Herman tells me.

"When was that?"

"Oh, it was a long time ago. I think Margaría was just twenty-four. She and Arturo had been married about a year, and she was pregnant then—maybe three months. The autumn that year was very dry. Margaría was out riding one afternoon when a grass fire started, no one knows how."

As he talks, Herman looks around as if he can still see the grass fields burning. Maybe he can, although he would have been a young boy when it happened, seven or eight. He tells me how Margaría's horse was running from the fire when it stumbled and fell, throwing her to the ground. They had just noticed the smoke from their house when the horse came galloping back, and everyone ran out to look for Margaría. The fire was so hot they couldn't get close, but they could see it was burning all through the place where she liked to ride.

"The flames were taller than a house," Herman says. "And they roared like a hurricane. Even at a distance, the heat was scorching. I remember that I kept touching my hair, to make sure it wasn't on fire."

"But you were burned."

"Yes. Sparks were blowing, and my shirt caught fire. I tried to run away from my own burning shirt. Finally, my father got hold of me and pushed me to the ground and smothered the flames."

Herman's father carried him back to the house, where Tiva covered his burns in aloe leaves and caked him with mud. Then she wrapped him in damp sheets and put him to bed. The others stayed out for hours, calling Margaría's name, driving and walking all around the edge of the fire. Exhausted, they went back to the house and watched from the terrace as the fire burned farther and farther away through the night and finally burned itself out. They were certain Margaría was dead.

"Arturo was wild," Herman says. "My father and brothers had to hold him back from running into the fire to find her. They kept saying, 'Think what happened to Herman.' I could hear them."

The next morning, where the fire had been, the ground was still too hot to walk over. So Arturo and the older brothers walked around the edges, calling Margaría's name. Finally, they could see a figure in the distance, limping along. A miracle, their father said. They brought Margaría into the house and pulled off her riding boots, which were scorched from the heat, and gave her water to drink. She told them that when her horse ran away she knew she was close to the basin, so she ran here and slid down into the gully where the wild horses go and hid herself under the ledge. When the fire came it jumped over and kept going on the other side. She stayed here all night and started walking back as soon as it got light. She had burns on her feet, but that was all.

"Arturo blamed himself," Herman tells me. "He said he should have forbidden her to go riding."

It got worse, Herman continues. Margaría had a miscarriage. The doctor said her baby was probably damaged when she fell from the horse. He also told them Tiva had saved Herman from a great deal of pain with her leaves and mud. And no, little could be done about the scarring that would come. "Besides," the doctor had joked to Herman, "you're only half ugly now."

"We shared a room, Margaría and I, for two or three weeks, while we recovered, side by side, in our beds. Arturo would come in and read to us, and Tiva would bring us special things to eat. My mother started crying every time she looked at me, and finally Margaría told her to stay out."

Herman starts walking again, and I stay beside him. "You see," he says, "it meant much to my sister that you would do this for her, that you would bring her back to her family. She believed that you would."

"I think she must have died of loneliness," I tell him. "And I remember how once when I was talking to her, she mentioned something about going to a concert at the college, and I envied her a little. I thought she had an interesting life."

"Margaría stayed in America because of Arturo," Herman says. "My father was hoping she would marry a rancher, but of course she fell in love with a scholar instead. Arturo was still in graduate school, studying political history, when they met. Then he got in with an antigovernment group when he taught at the university in Bogotá." Herman stops for a moment and fingers a blade of grass. "In a way they used him, because he was passionate and he could write. Such groups are really quite mercenary, you know; they don't care about one person. Eventually, they persuaded him to publish things that got him into trouble."

"You mean he had to leave the country."

"Yes. He would have been arrested, and perhaps Margaría too. One of Arturo's uncles got them out, and then a friend helped him get a job in America."

"How strange," I say, "to think that someone in your own family wouldn't be allowed to come home. Only because of politics."

"You say that because, truly, you don't take politics seriously in America. People die for politics in my country."

He sounds angry, but when we go out through the gully, he takes my hand and leads the way. It is so odd, the feel of Herman's scarred right hand. Though hardened from work, the palm is smooth, but the back is rough and crisscrossed with welts. In my nervousness I keep squeezing the tips of his fingers, which feel thick as horn. When we get near the Jeep, he lets go suddenly.

Herman opens the passenger door and takes out the jacket I left on the seat and puts it around my shoulders. "Forty is a good age for a woman," he says, looking me in the eye, smiling.

Before he can move away, I step closer and kiss him on the mouth and put my hands on his waist. When I lean into him, brushing against his scarred cheek, he takes my head in his hands.

"I can't feel anything on that side," he says. "Now you have to kiss me again."

I can feel his heart beating and hear the rustling of the grass all around us. The sensation is confusing and exhilarating, as in a dream of falling from a great height and discovering I can fly. Eventually, I let go of him.

Then he says, "Yes, we must go." He holds the door for me as I climb into the seat.

We return over the bumpy horse track, and after a few minutes Herman switches on the headlights. I look out the side window, fascinated by the blurry image of my face in the glass.

———

Tonight the house is quiet because many of the family have gone back to the city already, but I lie awake in bed, restless as a girl of sixteen. Herman and I said good-bye at the bottom of the stairs. He has to travel south early tomorrow morning to meet another rancher and look over some breeding stock. He has arranged for his brother Eduardo to take me to the airport.

Coming back in the Jeep, Herman asked me what I do when I'm at home. "I will want to think of you," he said. "And not just floating around in my head, like some spirit, but like a real person, doing things."

"I don't do anything very exciting," I told him. "I take care of my family. I have a garden in the summer. I teach people to read."

"You are a teacher, then?"

"Probably not in the way you think. But a few years ago, after my father died, my mother decided to start a program to teach adults who can't read and write. I help her with it. For the past couple of months I've been working with an older couple, Joyce and Bill Eberling, who both had to go out and get jobs when they were children. They're in their eighties now and reading Dr. Seuss out loud to each other."

"He's the doctor who wrote *The Cat in the Hat*. My son has that book."

"Do you know the first thing this old man wrote? It was a note to his wife. They've been married for sixty years, and he wrote her a note that said, 'I love you.' He even drew a heart around the words."

"You are a very romantic person, Elizabeth Tenney."

"I didn't tell him what to write, it was his own idea."

"Nevertheless . . ."

Then Herman decided that I should send his mother some of the roses from Margaría's garden. "You know," he said, "Margaría wrote to us that *you* had the most beautiful flowers."

"She wrote to you about me?"

"Quite often she would mention some small thing about you. A pretty new coat you had one spring, another time something funny you said. She told us that once you gave her a rosebush."

"The President Eisenhower," I said. "I'd forgotten that."

It came back to me clearly, though, the day I was walking Sarah in her stroller and waved to Margaría on her porch, how she came out to say hello. How in a rush of proud motherhood I'd responded to her admiration of Sarah by giving her the rosebush we were taking to my mother-in-law. "This will look so nice with your others," I'd said. "See, you have a little empty space right there." We'd both laughed, enjoying the bright June day, and I had invited her to come over for lunch the next week. Then I'd had to call and cancel because by then both of the children were sick with chicken pox.

"All the better," Herman insisted when I told him it was illegal to ship plants from one country to another without a license. "That means you will have to contrive some way to make it look like an innocent package."

When we said good night, he looked at me in that quizzical way I remembered from our meeting at the airport. Now I lie here thinking of Margaría's lost life. And Herman, my wish to touch him, the necessity of pulling away. I can imagine how the stuff of an ordinary day—buying a roast to cook for dinner, walking along the riverbank with Jamie and Sarah looking for herons' nests, reading *Green Eggs and Ham* with the Eberlings at their kitchen table—will take on a kind of luster because Herman might be thinking of me as I'm doing them.

I get out of bed finally and wrap myself in the robe Dorothea loaned me and open the door to the hallway. No one is up, but the house is washed in moonlight. I go down the stairs and through the dining room and out onto the terrace, where the stones are smooth and cool beneath my bare feet. Herman must be asleep by now, lying next to Rosamond. In the last hours of night, Gordon often talks in his sleep. Most of it I can't understand, but sometimes he says "Lizzy," very clearly, as if he were still the boy in the rowboat.

In this silvery light the grasslands ripple and shift like the surface of a vast lake. I can picture Margaría standing here, a young woman about to leave her home, composing a memory to take with her. All of it: the faces and voices of her family, the sounds of birds and cattle, the sweet smell of sun-warmed grass, the hills rolling on to who knows where.

Pigeon

Aggie Moffat threw open the front door with a flourish, as she did every morning. Her husband, Jasper, tipped his chair back from the kitchen table so he could look down the hallway and see her. It was Thursday, and he was waiting for his newspaper and his coffee.

"My, what a . . . ," Aggie said, stepping outside. Usually she said, "My, what a beautiful morning!" or if it was raining, "My, what a morning!" Today the sight of a pigeon lying next to

The Messenger at the edge of the porch stopped her. It must be dead, she thought, as she leaned down to pick up the newspaper. Its feet were drawn up close to its body, and its head pointed off at a funny angle. How peculiar.

"Here," she said, thrusting the paper at Jasper. "See if there's anything about a missing pigeon."

Aggie washed her hands with yellow soap, in case any mites had jumped from the pigeon onto the newspaper, and ignored her husband's question, "A missing what?"

She boiled two four-minute eggs for Jasper and toasted some cinnamon-raisin bread. When the eggs were done, she placed them in the delicate white egg cups her daughter had given her and arranged the toast, which she had cut into triangles, on the plate around them.

"How about a little dish of your apple butter?" Jasper asked. He held one of the eggs in the palm of his hand, knocked half an inch off the top with the blade of his clasp knife, and set it back in the cup as he wiped the blade across his pants.

Aggie didn't hear him because she was out on the back porch looking through the old Bright's Dairy box for her gardening gloves.

"Apple butter?" Jasper repeated when she came back through the kitchen wearing the flowered cotton gloves and carrying a paper bag.

"For heaven's sake," she said. "I'd have to get a new jar down in the cellar." She brought him a half-empty jar of Ann Page strawberry jam from the refrigerator. "You like this," she told him.

"I do not," Jasper said, spooning a dab onto his toast.

Letting the front door bang behind her, Aggie strode up to

the pigeon and lifted the bird in both hands. Its head fell awkwardly to one side. "Someone broke your neck," she said. The warmth of the bird drew at her sympathy. She couldn't tell if the pigeon had died recently or if it was warm from lying in the sun. She placed it in the paper bag and, as she walked around the side of the house toward the garage, its weight shifted with her motion. Startled, Aggie opened the top of the bag and peered in. Satisfied that the pigeon was really dead, she spoke to it again. "I'll bury you when Jasper goes out," she said, stowing the bag under the workbench next to the car.

"If he ever does," she added. It was beyond her why men were allowed to retire. They didn't know what to do with themselves and got underfoot and had to ask for things that were either up in the attic or down in the cellar. Since Jasper's retirement from the railroad a few years before, Aggie had started going out more herself. Tuesday and Friday afternoons she played cards with her friends June and Lucy and Rose Valencia. Wednesday nights and Saturday nights, right after supper, she went to bingo at the Fire Hall. While Jasper sat at home reading *The Messenger* and the *National Geographic*, Aggie had a life of her own.

And now she had the dead pigeon. Washing the breakfast dishes, she studied the large calendar above the kitchen sink. Beneath a color photo of Mount McKinley were the words "Cantwell Funeral Home, Tenney's Landing, Pennsylvania," then in smaller letters underneath that, "A Friend in Need." The pigeon might be a sign, she considered, the way it had been placed so carefully. A threat of some kind? Aggie decided to call on Elberta; she had to get some insurance forms notarized anyway.

Elberta Rosten received no friends, only customers. The nickel-plated notary public's seal in her desk drawer gave her an unassailable authority, something like a doctor's stethoscope, and clients came to consult her about toothache, corn weevils, infidelity. They always brought some document for her to notarize, for which she charged a dollar and expected a tip of five. As far as anyone in Tenney's Landing knew, she never went out of the house. Young Mike Eastman, whose parents owned the Good Food Market, delivered her groceries, and cousins from McKeesport visited every so often, bringing packages done up in brown wrapping paper.

A little troll, Aggie thought to herself when she saw Elberta behind the desk wearing a black dress so old it was turning green across the shoulders. The room smelled of paper and dust, with a sharp overtone of something like cat pee. Elberta was just pushing aside one of the scrapbooks she habitually tended. She kept three kinds: one for animals, one for people, and one for natural disasters. She hunted through newspapers and magazines for illustrated articles about two-headed pigs, babies that could talk at birth, or the mysterious appearance of a pool of quicksand in someone's backyard, and pasted them on the tan pages of her books. Having collected at least a hundred of these scrapbooks, Elberta was well acquainted with the bizarre and inexplicable.

Aggie chatted with Elberta about Rose Valencia's married niece up in Butler County, the one whose husband had lost two fingers in a spring binder the summer before and had refused to go back to work ever since.

"Must of unbalanced him," Elberta said. "Some people are more attached to their body parts than others."

Aggie nodded, slid six dollars across the desk, and refolded her insurance forms. She half rose in her chair, then sat down again. "Elberta," she said, "I found a pigeon on our front porch this morning. Dead. Looks like someone had wrung its neck and then laid it up on the porch."

"Dead pigeon." Elberta poked at her wiry gray hair with her pen, squinting at Aggie. "Someone might be sending you a warning. I've heard of dead animals used in that way."

"I wondered about that too," Aggie said. "But who would want to frighten us?"

"Hard to say." Elberta studied her pen for a minute. "What about Jasper, now? What's he been up to lately?"

"I wish Jasper *had* been up to something." Aggie sighed. "Seems like he hardly knows what to do with himself anymore."

"Mark you, keep an eye on that Jasper," Elberta said. "And better make a charm to keep away the bad luck."

"A charm?"

"Here's what to do," Elberta said, sketching a design on a piece of paper. "Take the three longest feathers from the pigeon's tail and the two longest feathers from each wing—that's seven in all—and bind the quills together with seven hairs from your own head. Wrap the hairs around seven times to make a little fan." She tapped the drawing with the pen. "Like this. Then nail it up over your front door."

"Well," Aggie said, glancing at the sketch as she got up to go. "Thank you, Elberta."

At home, Aggie looked skeptically into the bathroom mirror. The pigeon was freshly buried behind the garage, and seven of its feathers, dark gray with lavender tips, lay on her vanity table. She chose her hairs carefully, pulling only the coarse white ones, leaving the few soft brown ones undisturbed. "What foolishness!" she remarked, twisting the seven white hairs seven times around the feathers. She was grateful that, for once, Jasper had gone out somewhere and wouldn't be in the way asking questions. She carried her charm outside and found a hammer and a nail in the dairy box. Then she stood on the sidewalk in front of the house, looking up and down. No one coming. She ran up the porch steps, pulled a chair to the front door, and balancing on tiptoe, drove the nail in with four strong blows. "There," she said and disappeared into the house.

That afternoon her friend Lucy Dibbs stopped by and called through the screen door. "Aggie, you there?"

Aggie brought out two glasses of lemonade. She and Lucy sat in the porch swing, absently pushing it back and forth with their feet. They could hear bumblebees droning in the lilac bushes.

"Your porch is always so cool," Lucy said, fanning herself with a white handkerchief.

Aggie started talking about the Mackenzie family across the street. "Earl Mackenzie found out he has sugar," she said. "Doc Brooks showed Dolores how to give him his insulin shots, but the first time she tried it at home, she fainted dead away. Now their oldest boy has to do the shots."

"Goodness, I know that," Lucy said. About two minutes later, she pointed at the feathers. "What in the world is that hanging over your door?"

Aggie followed her finger. "That?" She shrugged. "Just some mess of Jasper's, I suppose. Maybe he was trying to make a decoration."

"It looks like those things the kids hang up. I think they call them dream catchers," Lucy remarked. "You know, Reed was up in Rownd's Point last Friday, at the barber. Said he ran into Jasper up there."

"Oh?" Aggie replied mildly. Had Jasper gotten his hair cut last week? She didn't think so.

Jasper came in while Aggie was cooking supper and washed his hands at the kitchen sink. "Smells good," he said, bending over the pot of chicken and dumplings simmering on the stove. She noticed how his hair curled over the back of his shirt collar and wondered where he'd been. He went into the dining room and sat down.

"A good twenty minutes before supper's ready," Aggie muttered to herself, stirring up the golden, fat-flecked broth. She left the spoon in the pot and stood in the doorway watching Jasper rearrange the silverware.

He turned around. "Something wrong, Aggie?"

"Of course not," she said and went back to her stove.

At the table, she stared into Jasper's plate as he broke up the steaming dumplings with the side of his spoon. "You need a haircut," she told him.

Jasper patted the back of his head. "I thought I might take a run up to Rownd's Point tomorrow," he said. "I want to have the car looked at." He smiled at his wife. "Maybe I'll get a trim while I'm at it."

All afternoon Aggie had been wondering about Eleanor Detweiler, widowed now and living in that little house on the outskirts of Rownd's Point. Aggie and Eleanor had been friends, and then rivals, in high school. Aggie hadn't even seen her for ten or twelve years. Was Eleanor the reason Jasper had

43

been sneaking off to Rownd's Point? Although she admitted to herself that "sneaking" was a bit of an overstatement, she decided to skip the card party the next day, borrow Rose Valencia's car, and take a little run up to Rownd's Point herself.

Rose Valencia wasn't as nosy as June or Lucy. She handed over the keys to her car and didn't say anything about it. Aggie had a lie ready, just in case. She planned to say that she had to go see her daughter in Greensburg, but since she wasn't asked, she decided to save the lie. "Thank you, Rose Valencia," she said instead. "I'll bring it right back in a couple of hours."

Sunlight danced over the ripples in the water as she drove along the river. She felt almost happy, out on her own, driving the big, clean car with the windows rolled down. And yet some little worry was working away at her. She thought about the times she and Jasper had brought the children out for picnics along the riverbank. Once they found a field of wildflowers, and she and Janie made chains of daisies and buttercups and crowned Jasper and the boys with rings of flowers. Her husband was the only one whose chin didn't reflect the yellow light when Janie held a buttercup underneath. "Daddy hates butter!" the children had chanted. And she remembered the pang of sadness she'd felt right then, thinking of how Jasper was always a little removed from the rest of them.

Slowing down as she drove past Dibbs Motors, on the highway just before Rownd's Point, Aggie could see their blue Pontiac near the service entrance. When she got into town, she parked her borrowed car in a side street and walked quickly, arranging her straw sunhat to cover as much of her face as possible. The Detweiler house was at the end of a narrow street, directly across from a weedy lot with a falling-down garage in its center. Aggie came up through the back of the lot and tried the small door at the side of the garage. The wood was swollen with dampness, but it was spongy and popped open when she gave it a hard tug. Inside, it was warm and smelled of old motor oil and mice nests. Aggie looked across the street through the dust-coated window, and as she had almost expected, there was Jasper standing in front of Eleanor's house. He held a pair of hedge clippers in one hand and wiped his forehead with the other. Taking a deep breath, he continued cutting the unruly boxwoods that enclosed the yard.

"Ha!" Aggie whispered. "Getting a trim, indeed." Hoping to see Eleanor, she watched until Jasper finished with the hedge. Finally, Eleanor came to the door and said something. Jasper followed her inside. As the door closed, Aggie gripped the edge of the windowsill and stared hard across the street. Jasper walked out in a few minutes with a bottle of Coca-Cola and sat on the top step. With her hat pushed back and her nose nearly touching the dusty pane, Aggie watched as Eleanor joined him, sitting on the next step down. Jasper said something, and they both laughed.

Desperate to know what they were talking about, Aggie left the garage and walked straight back through the lot so they wouldn't see her. Careful not to step on any twigs or dry leaves, she made a wide circle to come out on the far side of the house and sat down outside the hedge, a little way back from the front porch. Tucking her legs beneath her and smoothing down her skirt, she looked like a lady at an outdoor concert.

"The one place I've always been curious to go and see," she heard Jasper say, "is Lapland."

"Lapland," Eleanor repeated in a hushed voice. "I don't believe I know where that is."

"Well, if anyone asks you," Jasper said, "you can tell them it's up in northern Finland and the northwest corner of Russia. Way up," he added, "above the Arctic Circle."

"My!" Eleanor said. "And why would you want to go to such a cold place?"

"Just to see how people live there. And the reindeer. The Lapps herd reindeer, you know, big herds of thousands. Their antlers grow in funny shapes, tall and twisted and mossy-like. They look like they have tree branches on their heads."

"Oh my." Eleanor chuckled.

"The Lapps are good-looking people—I've seen pictures of them. Healthy looking. They dress in skins and furs to keep warm. And they wear bright colors too—red and blue and green. They decorate their clothes with ribbons and yarns. Vigorous people, always out in the weather."

Aggie shifted her legs and leaned forward to hear better.

"Artist fellow," Jasper went on, "I can't think of his name just now. He was a painter from Germany, and parachuted into Lapland during World War Two. Broke every bone in his body. This was at night, but some Laplanders had seen him coming down, and they went to get him. Smeared him over with animal fat and wrapped him in skins to keep him from freezing. Then they strapped him to a sled and set out for the nearest hospital. Took four days to get there, but he made it. They saved his life."

"Just think," Eleanor said.

"Back in Germany after the war, this fellow stopped painting regular pictures and started to put on happenings. He'd smear globs of bright jellies on the walls—the jelly was the fat they'd put on him, and the colors were the colors of Lapland—and drag sleds back and forth across the stage. He never got over that experience, you see."

"I imagine not," Eleanor said. "But why did he parachute into Lapland in the first place?"

"That I don't know," Jasper answered. "Maybe he was pushed."

"Jasper! The things you say!"

Aggie had heard enough. She stood up stiffly, freezing at the sound of her knee joints cracking into place. Oh well, she thought, heading to the car, those two are laughing so hard they're not likely to hear the creak of this old lady's bones. Back on the river road, she kept glancing in the rearview mirror, looking for Jasper's car. Where do those stories come from, she wondered. Since when does Jasper know anything about the Arctic Circle and painters breaking their bones in Lapland?

As she pulled up in front of Rose Valencia's house, it came to her. "The *National Geographic*," she said, smacking the steering wheel with her palm. "He probably got it all wrong, anyway."

"Awfully quiet tonight, Aggie," Jasper remarked over dinner.

She had cooked Swiss steak, one of Jasper's favorite dishes, but was too furious to talk to him. "I don't have as much to say as some people," she replied.

"When did this come about?" Jasper asked her.

Aggie watched him cut his steak and swirl each piece in the gravy. "I hope you got a good price on that haircut, Jasper. I believe it's a little longer than yesterday."

"Oh," he said, pausing with a forkful of steak and carrot halfway to his mouth. "I forgot."

"Yes, you did," Aggie said, and they finished their dinner in silence.

Later, as she lay next to the slumbering Jasper, Aggie went over and over the story she'd heard him telling Eleanor. Their own dinner table talk consisted mostly of bits of gossip she brought home from her various outings, comments on the price of groceries, speculations about the weather. Aggie tried, as Elberta had suggested, to connect the pigeon she'd found with Jasper. Had someone come in the night to place the dead bird as a warning, to say, "Aggie, wake up"? That didn't seem likely. But how long had Jasper been stealing away to see Eleanor, and why the secrecy if his only intention was to help her with the yard work? It was the Coca-Cola that got to her, and that story meant to amaze and impress—as if Jasper were a teenager again. Aggie had to admit it, she was jealous.

In the morning, she opened the door cautiously, relieved to find only the porch swing, the rocking chair, the welcome mat in front of the door. Everything looked as it had the previous afternoon when she'd finished her vigorous sweeping, right after she got home from Rownd's Point. Back inside, she brought a jar of apple butter up from the cellar and spooned some into a cut-glass dish that she set in front of Jasper's place.

"Jasper," she said, as he cracked the top off his first egg, "do you believe in UFOs?"

He looked up, surprised. "I've never seen one," he said, closing his knife and setting it down next to his plate.

"But do you think they might be out there, all the same?"

"Not really." He spooned a creamy white-and-yellow bite into his mouth. "Why, do you?"

"Oh, never mind." Aggie hoisted herself to her feet and started tidying up the kitchen. "I just thought we might have a conversation is all."

At seven-thirty that evening, she told Jasper good-bye and set off for her Saturday night bingo game. But then she circled the block, walked up the alley that ran behind their house, and let herself into the toolshed. From there she could see if Jasper went up the street in either direction or if he took the car out of the garage. Her breathing sounded very loud in the small shed as she kept watch. After about fifteen minutes, she could see Jasper moving around in the kitchen. He took a glass from the cupboard and filled it with tap water. Aggie watched him drink it straight down. He came out on the back porch and looked up at the sky. Then he closed the kitchen door and walked down the steps. She ducked as he passed the shed.

From behind the Wyatts' elm, she saw Jasper turn left at the end of the alley. It wasn't quite dark yet, so Aggie had to follow way behind, proceeding stealthily in her crepe-soled oxfords. In Mason Street, Jasper met China Quail, and the two men clapped each other on the back. They walked along to Reed and Lucy's house and rang the front doorbell. Looking around the corner of the Lucius J. Tenney Grammar School, Aggie saw Reed let them in. She waited until it was full dark before she crossed the street and approached the house. At the back, she noticed light coming from the narrow basement windows and crept up to the nearest one on her hands and knees.

Inside, Jasper, China, Reed, and Vernon—June's husband—
were playing poker. They sat around Reed's leather-topped
card table, each man with a stack of chips and a highball glass
at his place. Reed poured a round of whiskey, and Aggie sat
down in the grass to watch them. They were quiet as they
played, scowling and flicking the edges of the cards with their
fingertips. Between hands, they talked and sipped their drinks.
Once, when Jasper stood up to rake in a big pile of chips,
China leaned back in his chair and laughed, his teeth a bright
flash in his dark face.

China Quail was the only colored man in Tenney's Landing—half black and half Iroquois, he said. Before his mother
died, the two of them lived in the house at the bottom of Sterling Hill, where his mother took in washing. When she was
growing up, Aggie had liked to visit her. She would pick a
bouquet of flowers in her mother's backyard and take them to
Mrs. Quail as a present, then sit and talk with her as she ironed
the big white shirts. There were young Doc Brooks's shirts and
old Cantwell the funeral director's shirts and then the strange
black shirts of the priest with the place for the white collar to
slide in. They would smell like fresh air until Mrs. Quail
touched them with the smooth, heavy flatirons she lifted from
the kitchen stove, and then they smelled like heat and starch.
Aggie used to wonder how it would feel to slip her arms into
one of those stiff shirts, so white they hurt her eyes.

Jasper and China had been friends since they started first
grade together. Aggie could remember being afraid of China
when she was very young and a little afraid of Jasper too
because he was China's friend. At school they said China carried a knife in his boot and could cut you in a second if he felt

like it. Aggie didn't really believe it, though—if only because Mrs. Quail had such a gentle, lilting voice.

Watching China's elegant black hands and Jasper's blunt white ones as they shuffled, dealt, held up their cards like fans, Aggie thought they looked like young men again. They'd started playing poker in high school, hitchhiking down to Morgantown, West Virginia, from the time they were fifteen to watch the high-stakes games at the Aurora Hotel. They always played together, Jasper and China, and one of them would usually win. Some men in Tenney's Landing hinted that Jasper and China had worked out a secret way of cheating and would split the winnings after the game.

One night in the winter of 1936 they had gone to the Aurora with a dollar, hoping to work their way up from the nickel-and-dime table to the ten-dollar table. But they already had a reputation, and the men said only Jasper could play. China sat on the far side of the room, drinking bootleg whiskey out of a teacup until he fell asleep. Jasper woke him at three in the morning, and they spent the rest of the night in the train station, keeping watch. Jasper had twenty ten-dollar bills rolled up in his coat pocket.

"I'm lucky," Jasper had said, winking at her when Aggie asked him about it at school a few days later.

Aggie rose from her place by the basement window and started walking. The streets were quiet, and she didn't even look up to see the mass of stars overhead. She was wondering if Jasper and China *had* cheated. In those days, when everyone was desperate for money, who could have blamed them?

I did chase him, Aggie thought. The year she graduated

from high school, Aggie had begun to suspect that Eleanor was prettier than she was. Then Jasper let Eleanor wear his baseball sweater. That summer Aggie used lipstick for the first time and practiced what she would say to Jasper when she ran into him, which she managed to do once or twice a day. One afternoon she ran into him down by the river, where he was helping his youngest brother fly a kite. When the kite was safely above the trees, Aggie and Jasper walked off a little way.

"I had such a long talk with Eleanor yesterday," Aggie told him. "Seems like she and Andy Detweiler—that A & P salesman, you know—are getting pretty thick. She thinks he's the handsomest thing. I can't see it myself."

Aggie had more to say, but she stopped when she noticed Jasper's face. Her words had made him pale. He didn't say anything at all, just turned away from her and walked off through the thick grass that grew by the river. Aggie had to help Joe Ray reel in his kite and walk him home.

It wasn't exactly true about Eleanor and Andy Detweiler; Eleanor had only said that he'd been flirting with her. But I had to do it, Aggie told herself again and again, because I love Jasper more than she does. I'll be better for him. They had married the following summer, and Eleanor and Andy a few months after that. Aggie had won Jasper, with his dark eyes and his dark hair and his luck.

At home, she sat down in the porch swing and listened to the dry creak of the chains as she swung slowly in the dark. Across the street, one of the Mackenzie children was calling his dog.

"Dodger," he said softly, "come here now."

The half-grown puppy ran around the corner of the porch

and pounced on a stick in Aggie's front yard. He shook it back and forth, growling.

"Dodger! Come on!" the boy said, louder, and Dodger ran across the street with the stick in his mouth.

Not much later, Aggie could hear Jasper's steps on the sidewalk. Her heart did a funny thing, like a bounce, that made her smile.

"Aggie, you're home early," he said, coming up the steps.

"I guess I didn't feel like bingo tonight."

He sat beside her on the swing. She could smell the clove gum he chewed.

"You've been out, too," she said.

"Poker." He reached into his pocket and took out some crumpled bills, counting as he straightened them. "Six dollars," he said. "Must be I'm still lucky."

"Jasper, did you ever know of a dog to kill pigeons?"

"Some will. Some dogs will try to kill anything smaller than themselves."

"Well, I think maybe that Mackenzie boy's dog is killing birds."

"Keep your eye on him, Aggie," he said with a chuckle.

The swing was still, and they sat quietly, surrounded by the scent of lilac and the cool night air. Aggie glanced up at her bedraggled feather charm, which seemed almost luminous in the dark.

After a while, she said, "Jasper, if you could go on a trip somewhere, where would you like to go?"

Jasper took one of her hands and held it between his. "My dear Aggie, I'd be proud to go anywhere in the world with you. You just pick the spot."

Aggie rested her head on the back of the swing and closed her eyes. She saw a hilly country covered with snow and heard the brisk tinkling of sleigh bells in the sharp air. Then she saw the reindeer, six of them pulling the sleigh, antlers like mossy tree branches and bright red ribbons woven into their reins. They stamped and pawed at the frozen earth, tossing their heads and breathing out little clouds of steam.

The Dowry

I heard Ed coming up our hill. I couldn't see him yet, but he'd just hit the steep part about halfway, and I recognized the low growl of the engine as he downshifted. Ed was our closest neighbor, and he'd stop by to visit from time to time, maybe drop something off on his way back from town. I finished sweeping the oats where Starboy had kicked over the bucket that morning and hung the broom on the peg in the grain room and walked across to the house to wait.

I was standing on the porch steps when I saw his old blue pickup turn into our road, the dust swarming up behind it. The lane's about a quarter mile long, so at first I wasn't sure if someone was with him. As soon as I made out the girl, though, something about her made me think of back home, which was strange enough. Then there was the sky that morning—the mackerel sky we get in the early summer, a great sweep of pearly clouds that makes you think you're floating when you look at it. It was the same sky as the day I looked up and saw my father riding in on a pack mule. The lane was all ruts then, and him just a speck down at the end of it, but I knew him right away. He was the sorriest sight, never had ridden before and didn't like it much I could tell. So rumpled and dirty he was, coming on toward the cabin— it wasn't really a house yet—and hanging on to that pack saddle for dear life.

Ed hopped out of the cab, grinning. "Brought you a relative, Frances," he said. "Didn't know you had any." He hoisted a big brown suitcase out of the back. "Met her at the post office asking about you, and since I was heading this way, offered to give her a lift."

The girl sat there for a minute, taking me in. All I could think was, Good Lord, my cousin Hillary has died and sent me her daughter to raise, left me this child in her will. Then the girl climbed out and walked up to me, offering a handshake. When I saw her closer, I remembered that she would be too old to need raising.

"Aunt Frances?" she said. "I'm Carrie MacKemson."

"That's plain as day," I told her, taking her hand. "You look exactly like your mother and father put together."

Ed sidled up to the porch and plunked her suitcase down. He pinched the brim of his hat and said, "Be seeing you, ladies," and took off in another swirl of dust before maybe I could come to my senses and send this girl and her big suitcase back into town with him.

So there I was, watching the back of Ed's truck, elbow to elbow with Hillary's girl. It was like she had dropped out of the sky.

"Wait until Jack sees you," I said. "He's up in the high pastures, checking on the sheep."

"Jack's your husband?"

"Yes he is." Jack and I have been keeping house together for twenty-five years, which isn't a bad record. "We had two hundred lambs this spring. It's a lot to keep track of."

"I always imagined you had a sheep farm."

"Ranch," I corrected. "Anyway, come on up and have a seat."

She sat down in the rocker with a big sigh, like she had some bad news to deliver—which she did, before I could say another word. "Your father's dying," she told me. "He might be dead already. It took me nearly three days to get here."

"Well now," I said. "You aren't one to beat about the bush, are you?"

Starboy and Pan kicked up their heels all of a sudden and started prancing around the corral, sniffing the wind. I'd gotten a letter a couple of weeks before. My mother wrote to say that the old fellow had had a stroke, but he was out of the hospital, home in bed. She thought he might get better. The girl, Carrie, was staring at me as I watched the horses.

"Did they send you out here?"

"No, I came on my own," she said. "On the train."

"What's your idea?" I turned and tried to smile at her. "You planning on taking me back?"

"I wanted to meet you, that's all." She scratched her cheek and glanced over at the horses. "I was at the farm, visiting my grandparents, and I went into town with them to see your parents a few times. And then I just thought it would be good to find you."

She seemed like an honest, well-meaning girl, and I was sorry to be making her uncomfortable. I took a seat in Jack's chair.

We sat rocking on the porch, and she started talking about the town, Tenney's Landing, as if I would naturally want to hear all the news, such as it was. Her voice sounded the way Hillary's used to, a skittery young voice that ran up and down a couple of octaves in every sentence, a voice with a sense of humor in it.

She told me about going with her grandparents—my uncle Walter and aunt Marian—to visit and take dinner for my mother. While they were eating, my mother kept a plastic nursery monitor on the sideboard so she could listen in on my father. Carrie said they could hear him breathing.

"It was a huffing and puffing sound, a little weird. Anyway, one night last week, your mother put down her knife and fork and said, 'Aggie Moffat stopped by today, with a peach pie for Owen.' And she rolled her eyes at the ceiling. 'He can't eat anything like that,' she said. Really, it's pretty much soup and pudding for him. All of a sudden she looked around and said, 'You know what, I can't remember where I put it.' Right then there was this little chuckling sound on the monitor, and I imagined Uncle Owen sitting up in his bed, polishing off the last bite of pie."

Listening to that voice of hers, I could just about smell the linoleum in my mother's kitchen, the pink-and-gray-speckled linoleum she was so proud of. She used to scrub it twice a week with some pine cleaner my father said gave him a headache. By that time, Hillary's family had moved out to the farm, but she would come home with me after school on Fridays and spend the night. Her parents would pick her up the next day when they came to town to buy their groceries.

Hillary and I always asked if we could have fried chicken for dinner. We liked to watch my mother making it almost as much as we liked eating it. She'd get the Crisco smoking hot in her big black skillet, and while the chicken popped and sizzled in the oil, we'd set the table. Once my mother said, "I'll tell you a little secret, add some baking soda to your flour when you coat the chicken." When everything was ready, my dad and my brother Barrett would come to the table. My dad always said the same grace: "Thank you, Lord, for these gifts we are about to receive." He didn't joke around as much as Uncle Walter, who sometimes said, "Rub-a-dub-dub, thanks for the grub." After we cleaned up the dishes, we'd play gin rummy until bedtime. Hillary and Barrett always played as a team, because he couldn't figure out the cards by himself.

"Carrie," I said, "I haven't got any peaches, but how do you like cherry pie?"

"Oh, fine," she said, looking a little wary.

"It's Jack's favorite," I told her. "Come and help me pit these sour cherries."

Jack, he's something. He came riding in around five o'clock, all sunburned and tired out. When I said, "Jack, meet my cousin Hillary's daughter, Carrie MacKemson," he threw his arms around her and gave her a hug, as if her showing up here was the most wonderful thing in the world.

"I'm awfully glad to see you," he said. He asked about her trip and invited her to come along while he took care of his horse. The next thing I knew, they were out at the corral talking about this and that. Well, I considered, she must think I'm a cold fish.

We ate supper out back, under the trees, where it was cool. Jack rooted around in the cupboards until he found a bottle of wine, and then he made a big fuss over opening it and toasting our guest. She only drank a few sips, so I guessed this wasn't a regular thing for her. But the wine gave us a little glow, and it was pleasant having company. Except that it was so damn peculiar to see her sitting there. She did look like Hillary and Dan both. She had her father's dark green eyes and her mother's copper-colored hair. We weren't used to having young people around, either. Next to Jack and me she looked fresh and shiny, like a bright new penny dropped into a jar of old dingy ones.

"I used to wonder about Ludlow, South Dakota," she said, getting up the last bit of cherry juice on the side of her fork. She had an appetite, I have to say.

"Not many people do that," Jack said. "Wonder about Ludlow."

"I remember when I found it in my seventh-grade geography book. There it was, in the upper-left-hand corner of the state, just below Little Nasty Creek." She laughed. "The population given was ten, so I figured Aunt Frances had nine neighbors."

"That sounds about right," Jack said. "But I think we have a few more these days."

"South Dakota, the Coyote State. The part around Ludlow was colored tan for sheep raising, so I could see a problem there. I used to imagine Aunt Frances wearing a fringed leather jacket, taking aim with her double-barreled shotgun, coyote eyes gleaming in the dark."

Aunt Frances. She said it so naturally. And yet I could hardly believe that this girl back East had been trying to imagine my life while I was out here living it, no more mindful of her than of the Atlantic Ocean. I only knew she existed because Hillary wrote when she was born and mentioned her and her brothers in the yearly Christmas letter. Maybe I had some school pictures in a drawer somewhere.

"Frances has been known to take down a coyote or two," Jack said, "when they go after the lambs. With a rifle, though. Shotgun's not powerful enough." He winked at me and gave my knee a squeeze.

"You know," I said, "technically, I'm not your aunt. Hillary's my first cousin, so I believe that makes you my second cousin. Isn't that how it works?"

"Oh," she said, looking down at her empty plate. "I'm not sure. I've always called your mother Aunt Louise, so I just thought . . ."

"Well, I think Aunt Frances sounds fine," Jack said, squeezing my knee again, this time to suggest I mind my manners.

"There's one really nice picture of you in your parents'

upstairs hallway," she went on. "It's you and Barrett, wearing your skates, standing on the river. In my mind, I made you taller and gave you the fringed jacket and put a gun in your hands. Kind of dumb, I guess."

"I was twelve when that picture was taken. That was 1952, one year the river froze all the way across—before they dredged it. Can you imagine, having the whole river to skate on?" I remember that day because it was so cold our skates made a *skree* sound on the ice. I'm standing beside Barrett with my hand on his shoulder. We're both wearing heavy parkas with fur around the hoods, and Barrett looks like a tiny Eskimo, his face circled in fur. He's holding his arms out to steady himself on the ice. When we got the picture developed, I wished I had put my hood up too, because my hair was all windblown and tangled. Sometimes I think about writing to my mother and asking if I can have that picture, but then I don't want to stir things up.

"Well, Barrett," Jack said. "The poor devil."

"He did love to skate on the river, that's for sure." I stood up and started stacking the dishes.

Jack's snoring woke me in the night, and I couldn't get back to sleep. I kept thinking about Hillary and Dan's daughter right here in my house, practically a stranger. Finally I went outside and sat down at the table where we'd eaten. It was warm out and clear, the sky crowded with stars. When I first moved out West I couldn't stop looking at the sky, it was so big. It took me a while to get used to it.

The summer I was sixteen, the year before I left home, I used to sneak out of the house at night and go down to the ferry landing to smoke a cigarette. Hillary went with me a couple of times, but mostly I went alone. I liked being out on the streets after the rest of the town had gone to bed. The only lights would be in the Mon-View Lounge, a sort of greenish yellow glow. Maybe four or five men would be sitting at the bar, drinking beer and listening to the radio. I used to wonder about the "View" part, since from inside you couldn't see the river, just the houses across the street.

At the ferry dock I'd lie on my back and look up at the stars and listen to the water slapping against the wood, smell the river and the trees. The night sky was a comfort then. I'd light my cigarette, watching the fire ring burn around the end of the paper and the smoke spiral up in the dark air. I got to know Evan Sayers that way. He was the blind man who lived in our town, and he didn't have any friends to speak of. He got around pretty well—you'd see him walking down the street with his broom, whistling some tune or other. He earned money sweeping out the Mon-View and Chessie's Market and Wright's Pharmacy. He was neat as a pin, and people liked him, but his eyes looked like cloudy blue marbles and he made odd gestures with his hands. It could put you off.

One time I was lying there on the dock, and I started hearing a sound like the beginning of a dance tune when the drummer starts off easy, playing over the drums with those little wire brushes. Then I noticed steps in between, so the sound was *tch step step*, *tch step step*. I sat up and peered into the dark, and pretty soon Evan stepped onto the dock, using his broom as a cane, with the bristle end down.

"Hello, Evan," I said. "It's Frances Wyatt."

"Ah, Owen's girl," he said, sitting down near me. "You old enough to smoke?" he asked, but in a friendly way.

I took the pack of Pall Malls from the waistband of my skirt and lit one for him and handed it over.

"Nothing like a summer evening down by the riverside," he said. In the dark, his voice sounded deep and soothing.

After that, I met him down there lots of times, and we'd have a smoke and talk. He told me about being a soldier in the First War, as he called it. He'd been blinded by gas in the trenches and got sent home with a medal. Once he reached into his pocket and took the medal out and told me to have a look at it. I held it between my fingers and rubbed my thumb over its surface, tracing the outline of the heart and the profile of General Washington and the coarse grain of the tattered ribbon.

"I used to wish I'd been killed," he said. "It's a grand idea, dying for your country. But coming home without your sight, you're only a bother and a strangeness to other people."

One night, later on, I told Evan about Barrett, how it got hard looking out for him all the time. "Mostly, I worry about what kind of a life he's going to have."

"His life might be better than you know," Evan said. "There's pleasure of some kind in every day, if you notice." When he got up and left, I sat there listening to the *tch step step, tch step step* of his progress home.

That night, when I let myself in the back door sometime after midnight, my father was waiting for me. I saw him in the dark, sitting in his chair, and was about to make up some reason why I'd been out. But before I had a chance to speak, he said, "Enough of this, Frances," very calmly. "I will expect you to be at home in your bed at night from now on."

So I missed Evan's big moment a few nights later. Everyone was talking about it the next morning, how a car went out of control at the top of Sterling Hill and how it screeched all the way down, the air reeking of burnt rubber. The car, a 1947 Ford, belonged to Roland Dibbs, a boy from Rownd's Point. He and three of his friends—they were all about eighteen or nineteen—had gotten drunk and Roland was showing off. They shot over the crest of the hill at about sixty miles an hour, and the brakes failed. The car ended up in the river, right near the ferry landing.

Evan was out there, and he heard everything. As he told the reporter from *The Messenger*, he took off his shoes and dove into the water. He went deep, feeling his way along the bottom, until he bumped into the hot metal of the car. The doors wouldn't open. When he pounded on the windows, he couldn't hear anything from inside. So he went up and groped along the riverbank until he found a good-size rock. He took it down and smashed a window. One by one he pulled the four dazed boys through the opening and carried them to the top. By the time the volunteer firemen got there, three of the boys were sitting on the grass, coughing and sputtering. Someone had called Doc Brooks, and he got there in time to save the fourth boy by artificial respiration. The next week the town had an Evan Sayers Day with a picnic in the park and a bright red banner he couldn't see.

I managed to speak to him for a minute and explain that I wouldn't be able to meet him at the dock anymore.

"I understand," he said. "It's too bad, though. We had some interesting talks."

The sun shone through the bedroom window, warming my face, and I knew it was late. The aroma of coffee and bacon drifted up from the kitchen, along with stifled laughter and snatches of song. Jack and Carrie fixing breakfast. When Jack and I had gone to bed the night before, I told him that she'd come to tell me my father was dying.

"It's still a mystery, though, why she had to tell me in person."

"I'm sorry, Frances," he said, taking my hand and kissing the back of it.

If he had more to say, he had the good judgment to keep it to himself. Jack understood as well as anyone could why I had left my family. I had told him about it at the beginning, and then we'd gotten on with our life together. Every few years, he suggested making a trip east, but when I said I wasn't interested, he never pressed it. Maybe, being an orphan, he thought I'd been too extreme, but it wasn't a question I cared to explore. As I got up to dress, I wondered again why Carrie had brought such a large suitcase.

From the hallway I could see Jack stirring batter in our big yellow bowl and Carrie melting butter on the griddle. They were singing "O Susanna," harmonizing as if they'd been singing together for years. Jack would have made a fine father—I always thought so, but kids weren't in the cards for us.

"Hey," I said. "You two are busy this morning."

"Oh, darn," Carrie said. "We wanted to bring you breakfast in bed."

"And you were planning to serenade me too?" I watched as Jack poured blueberry pancake batter on the hot griddle.

"Sorry about the noise," she said. "We were trying to sing quietly."

"In case you don't know, that was one of your mother's favorite songs," I told Carrie. "My dad got the biggest kick out of singing it to her when she was little, because she'd always stop him. 'Wait!' she'd say. 'How could he freeze to death if the sun was so hot?' And my dad would laugh. 'What's the problem, miss?' he'd ask her. 'Do you think I got the words wrong?'"

"Little Hillary," Carrie said, and Jack raised his eyebrows at me.

About halfway through breakfast, Jack got the bright idea that I should take Carrie out for a ride and show her the ranch. "Take all day, if you want," he said. "Pack some sandwiches and go up to the high pastures. The sheep will be glad of a visit."

"First of all," I said, "Carrie probably doesn't know how to ride. And besides that, we have a slew of chores to do around here."

Jack looked at Carrie.

"I can ride," she said.

"And I can do the chores," Jack added. "So it's settled."

Carrie rode ahead when we started out, following the trail. How, I wondered, did this child who grew up in Philadelphia learn to ride a horse? I let her take Pan, who was a good old soul but cranky too, and she charmed him so that he was nuzzling her ear by the time she got him saddled up. From behind, she looked exactly like Hillary—sitting up straight, her copper hair tied back beneath the white hat I'd loaned her. She was on the skinny side, the way her mother had been at that age. I could see her shoulder blades sticking out, like little wings tucked inside her shirt.

When the trail widened, I caught up to her. "Where'd you learn to ride, anyway? I would have figured you for a city slicker, and you turn out to be Annie Oakley."

"I owe it all to my violin teacher," she said, laughing. "My parents had a rule that each of us kids had to learn to play an instrument. Well, I picked the violin for some reason, and my teacher lived in Merion Station, just outside the city. He used to have me play duets with a girl named Margaret, whose parents were horse trainers, and we got to be good friends. It made playing the violin a lot more fun, because I knew we'd go riding afterward."

"Now that I think of it, I suppose your grandparents had horses too. I remember your grandfather bought a Tennessee walker not too long after they moved out to the farm. Sandy, he called it. Lord, he was crazy about that horse!"

"My mother has a picture of him riding Sandy," Carrie said. "He was dressed up like a banker, and Sandy's mane was braided too. I don't know what the occasion was."

"You know what happened, don't you?"

"Shooting him, you mean?"

"Maybe an hour after that picture was taken, another horse kicked Sandy and broke his leg. My dad said the other horse was jealous because your grandfather was making a big fuss over Sandy, getting him ready for the county fair. And then he had to shoot him instead. He cried, Hillary told me, stood out in the field and cried."

"He said later he never should have bought Sandy, that's what my mother told me. He said he had no business with such an expensive horse."

I decided we shouldn't go to the sheep pastures but should

ride up higher. In our part of the state, the plains run into the northern edge of the Black Hills, and on a day as clear as that was, you can get up into the foothills and find a good view to the south. It's fairly dramatic, the way the hills in the distance look like ocean waves, their tans and grays gradually shading to smoky blue near the horizon. We found a spot of shade for the horses between two spruce trees and tied them there while we went to have a look.

"It's a different world out here, isn't it?" Carrie said, shading her eyes with one hand. "This could be another country."

"How old are you?" I asked her.

"Seventeen. Eighteen almost. I graduated from high school two weeks ago."

"That's how old your parents were the last time I saw them." I was having trouble picturing Hillary and Dan as middle-aged—thicker, grayer versions of the people I'd known.

"When you left home, did you know where you were going? I mean, did you have a dream of South Dakota?"

"Not exactly," I said. "But tell me something—what brings you here?"

She dropped her hand and turned to look at me, as if it were a rude question. "I could say I wanted to do something for your father."

She told me how they put him in Barrett's room, in the old sleigh bed, when they brought him home from the hospital. My mother was reading *Treasure Island* to him. She must have picked it off the bookshelf beside the bed, because that was the book I brought home for Barrett when he got sick.

"He can't really talk, you know," she went on. "He makes sounds, but no one can understand him. So your mother printed up cards with words like 'ice' and 'blanket' and 'bedpan.' If he wants something, he holds up a card to let you know. When I told him I was coming out here to find you, he picked out the 'ice' card. At first I thought he wanted some, but when I brought it to him, he shook his head. He pointed at me, and finally I understood that he was trying to tell me what to expect if I ever got here."

"I guess he wasn't far off," I said. The idea of my father asking for a bedpan made me flinch. The last time I'd seen *him*, he couldn't have been more than forty-five. "So how's my mother holding up?"

"I'd say pretty well. The Banashevskys—their Russian neighbors, maybe you didn't know them—help out a lot. Mrs. Banashevsky brings over her famous beet soup, and Mr. Banashevsky fixed their hot water heater last week. And my grandparents go in to see them pretty often."

"Oh, I remember the Banashevskys. I went to school with their sons, but they lived on the other side of town then. Anyway, I'm surprised your parents let you come. It's a long way, especially all by yourself." Besides, in their experience, people who came out to Ludlow never went back.

"They weren't thrilled about the idea, but maybe they're trying to give me a little slack to make up for the other stuff."

"What other stuff?"

"We're sort of fighting these days." Carrie took off her hat and fanned herself, sat on an outcrop of rock and looked down the valley.

I glanced at the horses, who were standing nose to nose,

nodding off in the heat. "Now don't take this the wrong way, but you're not thinking of staying here, are you?"

"I'm thinking of moving to New York." She sounded a little huffy.

"I see."

She turned and looked at me over her shoulder. "You might understand," she said. "I want to be a photographer, but my parents think I should go to Columbia and study English, then maybe journalism. I applied, to please them, and I got accepted, too. But I've decided not to go."

I went and sat near her, in the temporary shade of a passing cloud. "I wouldn't be so quick to thumb my nose at an opportunity like that. What's your idea? You're just going to show up in New York and start taking pictures of people on the street?"

"Hey, give me a little credit," she said. But she laughed, too, and seemed to relax. She told me about her friend Valerie, who was going to acting school in New York. They wanted to get a studio apartment in the Village, and Carrie would study photography. "I really want to try it out," she said. "And if I need to, I can earn money waiting tables."

"Now you've hit on something I know about," I told her. It was pointless to say how young seventeen is, how the world is not so anxious to bend to your will. "You should probably think twice about waitressing."

"Is that what you were doing—those two years you were missing, before you showed up here?" She put her hat back on and gave me a long look.

"Maybe you should become a detective," I said. "You'd be good at it."

71

She smiled at me and shook her head and leaned back on her elbows, as if she were waiting for me to begin.

"I'll tell you about the day my brother, Barrett, was born," I said.

He was born four years after me, in an upstairs bedroom on an afternoon in January. That morning, they'd put me in the parlor to wait and given me a stack of picture books and a doll to play with. My father came in to say hello a couple of times and to check the stove. They forgot to give me lunch, and I wasn't supposed to go out, so I passed the time following the flower path in the maroon rug, back and forth between the gas stove and the front window. Hot by the stove, where the tiny blue flames licked at the enamel cylinders. Cold by the window, where frost ran around the edges of the panes. I went from cold to hot many times and then fell asleep in the big green chair by the stove.

The baby's crying woke me, and I thought, Good, now they'll come and get me. But then it was quiet for a long time. Someone came downstairs and banged the front door shut and hurried across the porch. The next thing I heard was my mother crying, a sound so sorrowful that I wanted to go to her. I was standing there listening with my hand on the doorknob when Aunt Marian came in and helped me get into my coat and carried me across the street, where they were living at the time. She set me down next to Hillary on the rug in front of their fireplace. Hillary had a box of crayons and a new coloring book, which we shared until your aunt Marian called us into the kitchen for supper. Uncle Walter came in too. Instead of saying grace, he put his hand on my head and said, "You have a baby brother, Frances. And he's a nice little boy, but he isn't right. So promise me you'll be very good when you go home, and not give your mom and dad any trouble. All right?" I nodded, and he took his hand away.

At bedtime my father came to get me. He carried me straight upstairs to my mother and the baby. In the lamplight, her eyes looked shiny and her face was swollen from crying, but she smiled at me and drew the blanket back so I could see the baby sleeping beside her. He looked all right to me. I sat on the edge of the bed and studied his dark eyelashes and the bow of his upper lip and his small, clenched hands. When I pried one hand open, he shivered and sighed.

A couple of years later, right before I started school, my father explained that Barrett was a Mongoloid child. He was different from other children, I could see that, but he was sweet and gentle, easy to love. Barrett would always be different, my father said, because it would be hard for him to learn things, even things like talking. We would have to be patient with him, and extra kind.

Most people in Tenney's Landing were kind. One exception was a girl in my class named Alice Buford. Even then, I understood how hard her life was. Her father had been fired from the mine for drunkenness, and her mother tried to make a living by sewing and mending. I don't know why it was, but Alice hated me on sight. At recess once, playing dodgeball on the playground, she hit me on the side of the head so hard my ears rang for the rest of the day. She tripped me up whenever she could—at hopscotch and jump rope—and many times I went home with skinned knees. At last Hillary and I waited for her after school. When Alice came out, Hillary said we were going to give her "a good thrashing." She laughed at us, and then she started to run. We chased her for three or four blocks, and I thought that would be the end of it.

But she started picking on Barrett. She might come up behind him and pull his hat off and toss it in the air, things like that. She had a little gang of younger children she bossed around, and they'd all start screeching and making faces when they saw him on the street. Sometimes the boys would get close to him and shoot their cap guns, which made him panic. He'd cry and run off flapping his arms, and they would imitate him. From the time I was eight years old, I was always trying to defend Barrett, chasing these children away, shouting threats at them. They must have found it great sport. Anyway, Barrett became really afraid of Alice, and whenever he saw her, he'd start to moan—even if she was walking on the other side of the street. I despised her.

That skating picture, it haunts me. One Saturday, a few days before Barrett's thirteenth birthday, he was fretful all morning. At breakfast he tipped over his oatmeal, and sticky lumps of it dropped in his lap, making him so angry he threw the bowl on the floor and broke it. Hillary was at our house, and we told Barrett we'd take him skating, to cheer him up. Learning to skate had been one of his big achievements, so he was happy to be on the frozen river, wearing the red-and-green scarf Aunt Marian had knitted him for Christmas. A lot of children were out that day. Dan MacKemson and the Banashevsky boys—Andrew and Thomas—came along, and we made a chain, holding hands and skating in a line. I kept an eye on Barrett, who always skated very carefully up and down in the same place.

After an hour or so, Hillary caught the toe of her skate on a branch frozen in the ice and went down hard. I remember how she said, "Twisted my damn ankle," acting mad so she wouldn't cry. She took her skates off and limped away in her red wool socks, Dan on one side holding her arm. Andrew and Thomas said they had to get home too. I skated on my own for a while, practicing figure eights, and just when I'd decided we should go in, I heard Barrett's high-pitched *uh, uh, uh.* When I turned around, I saw Alice and three or four other children sliding on the ice in their shoes, forming a circle around him.

"He looks like a big, silly bird," one of the children shouted.

"Yeah, a dodo bird," Alice whooped, as she grabbed the end of his scarf.

"Leave him alone!" I was skating as fast as I could to reach him, and when they saw me, they backed off. But Alice had Barrett's scarf, and she tied it around her head and did a little swivel-hipped, mocking dance. When I got to Barrett, they were about twenty yards away, laughing and looking eager.

When Alice yelled "Bombs away!" they started pelting us with icy snowballs. They had a sled with them, piled high with hard balls of ice that stung when they hit, even through my heavy clothes.

I grabbed Barrett's wrist and pulled him along behind me. In his panic, he thrashed around and tried to get away. I fell down two or three times before we reached the riverbank. All I wanted was to get Barrett home, to stop the noise he was making. As we got to the bank, though, a hard-thrown chunk of ice caught me on the back of the head. I fell forward, and my right hand landed on a rock. It was dark and wet, about the size of my father's fist.

Without a thought, I turned and threw it. The rock hit Alice in the face with a sickening smack, and she staggered backward as blood welled up from a cut above her eye. She was gasping for breath and wiping at the blood with her mittened hand. "I can't see," she wailed. "I mean it, I can't see."

Alice staggered away, holding one hand over her eye, and the other children followed. Then one of them, her younger brother, stopped and shook his fist at me. "You'll pay for this," he said.

For some reason, this struck me as funny, and I nearly laughed, except that I looked at Barrett, sitting in the snow where I'd dropped him. His face was as white and solemn as a judge's.

After supper that night, Barrett went to stand in the hall by the front door. He wouldn't come away, even when my father called to him, but stood looking at the street through the narrow glass panes around the door. Around eight o'clock, we heard him moaning and footsteps coming up the front walk. My mother took Barrett upstairs to bed as my father opened the door for Mr. Buford and Alice. He led them into the parlor, and I followed. Mr. Buford refused the chairs my father offered. He and Alice stood in front of us, while we sat together on the couch. I felt sick to my stomach, but also curious about what was going to happen and what would be said.

Alice wore a huge white bandage over her eye. "I'm going to take this off for a minute," Mr. Buford said. "I want you to see." As he pulled the tape away, Alice cried out. The rock had cut her from above the left eyebrow to the top of the cheek. Her eye was swollen shut, and we could see the tracks of stitches in her bruised flesh.

"Doc Brooks says she could lose the sight in this eye," Mr. Buford said. "What about that?"

My father cleared his throat and leaned forward to speak, but Mr. Buford rushed on. "Even if she doesn't end up blind, look at this gash here. She's going to have a bad scar. Disfigured, that's what she is. What man is going to marry her now? She's got no looks, she's got nothing. Your girl has wrecked my girl's chances in life, and you've got to make it right. I want the money to give my girl a dowry. I figure you owe us that much."

I couldn't have seen this coming in a million years: not the damage I'd done, or the price they were asking. Suddenly my father was holding my hand. "I'm sorry," I said to them. "I truly am."

Mr. Buford replaced the bandage, only now the tape wouldn't hold so well. Alice kept patting at it, looking straight ahead.

My father said he was sorry, too, but he wanted to emphasize that Alice should know better than to torment a helpless child. He said he knew it wasn't the first time. When there was no reply, my father said he would think over everything Mr. Buford had said and discuss it with my mother.

My parents must have talked most of the night. I got out of bed once and stood listening in the upstairs hallway, but I couldn't make out what they were saying. I wanted to go to them and try to explain all over again, but I don't honestly know if I'd meant to hit her or not. I know I was surprised when I did. And the flash of joy I'd felt had vanished in an instant.

In the morning my father took Barrett to church. I found my mother alone at the kitchen table when I went down. She smoothed my hair when I joined her and asked if I wanted a cup of coffee, so I figured she was trying to prepare me for something.

"I wish it were different, Frances," she said finally, "but what you did was wrong, even if you were provoked. Throwing snowballs and making fun isn't the same as really injuring someone. We called Doc Brooks last night, and he told us that Alice could very well lose the sight in that eye. In any case, she will surely have a bad scar." As she stirred her coffee, I noticed the dark circles around her eyes.

So Alice Buford got her dowry, the money my parents had saved over sixteen years to send me to college. My father tried offering him half of what he was asking, but Mr. Buford said he would sue us in court if he didn't get five thousand dollars. If it came to that, my parents said, they believed he would win.

I thought then, and I still do, that my father gave in too easily. Somehow all the years of Alice's meanness should have been weighed against my one rash act.

Around that same time, Barrett started getting sick. He had bronchitis and then pneumonia. He had to go into the hospital for treatments two or three times, and each time he came home he was more listless, as if he were literally fading away. After school, I'd sit beside him in his bed, reading *Treasure Island* and then *Alice in Wonderland*. Not even Hillary, doing her Cheshire cat imitation, could make him laugh. Sometimes I'd catch him watching me with a look of utter hopelessness.

Our high school graduation was the twelfth of June, two weeks after we buried my brother. We filed into our seats boy-girl, boy-girl, the boys wearing sport coats and ties, the girls in white dresses. The Presbyterian minister and the school principal gave speeches about the golden future that lay ahead of us. From my place in the back I could see Alice Buford in the front row. She hadn't lost her sight, but she did have a nasty scar. It was purple still and looked like a welt across her eye. She seemed almost proud of it.

Dan gave the valedictorian's address, and I noticed how he kept looking at Hillary as he spoke. When I saw her blow him a kiss with a little flutter of her hand, I understood that they were in love. Afterward, we had sandwiches and punch and cake our mothers had made, and there was a band for dancing in the gym. I got home fairly late, and I remember sitting on the edge of the bed in my graduation dress, feeling as if the spirit had been kicked right out of me.

Then I went missing for two years. I left a note on my bed, and I called home from time to time to tell them I was all right. I just didn't tell them I was living in Norfolk, Virginia, and working in a coffee shop six days a week. I was on the first shift, from six to three, and wore a mint green uniform with a matching cap and a white apron. I took a room in a small boardinghouse about five blocks from the restaurant so I could walk to work. In the afternoons I usually went to the public library and read for a couple of hours. I'd often think of Hillary and Dan up in Philadelphia, her at Swarthmore and him with his scholarship at the University of Pennsylvania. I liked to imagine we were all reading the same books.

In the evening, I'd go back to the boardinghouse for supper with the three other boarders, two elderly ladies and a man in his forties, Mr. Parkhurst. He worked at the navy yard and always had black grease under his fingernails, but he was pleasant enough. Sometimes after supper we played Chinese checkers. On the weekends, Mr. Parkhurst went home to Richmond to see his wife and kids. Sunday mornings I'd go for a long walk, then spend the afternoon in the library. I had a favorite spot there, a big leather chair near a window that looked out on the street. That was pretty much my life the first year.

I had saved up a little money, and the next year I decided to take a secretarial course one of the other waitresses told me about. After work I studied shorthand and typing and business etiquette. I also got to know a few other girls my age and started going with them to Saturday night movies or maybe a dance. Lots of sailors came to the dances, and they could be fun to talk to. Afterward they might take us out for a soda. I didn't have any real friends, though. The other girls talked a lot about their families and invited each other home for holidays. Sometimes the sailors were lonely and looking for girlfriends, but I wanted to stay clear of all that. I tried to keep in mind what Evan Sayers had once said about finding some pleasure in every day, but I didn't find much. I was more or less passing time, that's all.

Evan had wanted to know if I had a plan. He said that was the most important thing. What happened was I was lying on my bed graduation night, and it started to rain. I was staring at the ceiling, wondering if I might be able to get a job as a clerk at Wright's Pharmacy and thinking about how I would feel if Alice came in and saw me working there. Or saw me any place at all, stuck. I just wanted to get up and get the hell away. And that's what I did.

I walked up the hill to Evan's house, and when I heard the radio playing I knocked on the door. He asked me a lot of questions and scratched his forehead and said "Well now" several times. At last he went into his kitchen and came back with a cracker tin full of money.

"Take what you need," he said, handing it to me. "Take some extra, too."

Inside I found rolls of bills, tens and twenties and fives all mixed together. I took out two hundred dollars, which seemed like a lot, though I soon discovered it didn't go very far. I told Evan I would pay him back, but he insisted it was a farewell present. We shook hands, and I left.

My clothes and my suitcase were soaking wet by the time I got a ride with a coal truck driver. He let me out at the bus station in Uniontown, where I studied the departure board and decided on Norfolk because that was the next bus coming through. Heading south, I tried hard to come up with a plan. By the time I got off the bus in Norfolk, all wrinkled and still damp, I had decided that I would make a lot of money and go back home one day driving a big car, an Oldsmobile or a Cadillac. Until that happened, they weren't going to see me.

As the second year went on, I knew I wasn't going to make my fortune in the coffee shop. I wasn't much good at shorthand or typing, either. My heart wasn't in it. But I finally got tired of dragging myself around like a sad sack, and it came to me that the problem was I had taken too small a step. I needed to take a great big one. I quit the secretarial course and my job and took the train west.

I couldn't get over the dining car with its white tablecloths and the heavy knives and forks worn smooth by the hands of so many travelers, the way a red-jacketed waiter would bring a big steaming cup of tea with a lemon slice and set it down just so in front of me. I didn't understand how the other passengers could read or sleep in the daytime when there was so much to see out the window: the farms and highways, the rickety back ends of towns, the Mississippi River brown and wide in the early morning light, the prairies flying past. At night I'd take my shoes off and prop my feet up on the seat opposite and close my eyes and listen to the reassuring *clack, clack, clack* of the wheels on the rails. For the first time in my life, I knew I was doing the right thing.

When we crossed the Missouri River in the middle of South Dakota, it looked as if we had just barreled into a Western movie. The prairies lay spread out flat and wide all around us, no trees in sight. I saw two men on horseback waiting for the train to pass, their shoulders hunched against the evening chill. When we got to the Badlands, deep purple in the last light, I decided it was time to get off the train. I spent that first night in a small hotel near the Rapid City station, and in the morning I got a bus north to Ludlow. I liked the sound of it and the fact that it wasn't close to anything. So that's how I landed here, a nineteen-year-old girl with a suitcase full of high school clothes and a few books and not much money.

I met Jack a few days later—saw him is more accurate. He and two other fellows came into Hyde's Saloon, where I was waiting tables. They took a table in the corner and ordered some beers and roast beef sandwiches. Jack didn't say anything to me, except to ask if they could get some horseradish. He didn't strike me as the shy type, though. He had a kind of swagger, I could see that when they walked out. His friends came in without him the next night, and I wondered if he was married or something. I might have asked Lor—she was the other waitress and rented a room upstairs at Hyde's, the same as I did—but I'd only been there a week and didn't want to embarrass myself right off the bat.

Lor was the kind of person my mother would have called "a study." She liked to set things straight. The first thing she told me was that her name was Lor, not Lorraine. The next thing was that her husband, Damon, had been killed in the Black Hills and she didn't want to talk about it, so never ask her about Damon. She told me a lot of things, like "Don't take any shit off these cowboys" and "Buy yourself a pair of jeans, for crying out loud." I guessed she was about thirty-five.

The next time I saw Jack, Lor had his table. I watched her smiling at him and swinging her hips. It burned me when she laughed and swatted him on the shoulder, partly because I didn't have a clue about flirting myself and would have felt ridiculous carrying on that way.

Three months later I moved into his cabin. It surprised me a little, but falling in love with Jack seemed as natural as breathing. He taught me how to ride and took me up into the hills and out on the prairie. He taught me how to shoot, how to shear sheep, helped me pick out my first pair of boots. He was only twenty-eight, but he'd been around, working the oil fields in Oklahoma and Texas, cattle ranches and sheep ranches in Wyoming. He said he was ready to settle down and work his own place for a change.

I sent my folks a letter to let them know where I was. Then, about a month later, I looked up from a lamb I was tending and saw my father coming up the lane. My father, who had never been west of West Virginia, had ridden the train to Buffalo, South Dakota, and hitched a ride into Ludlow, where someone had found him a pack mule and told him the way. He looked like some old-time explorer who'd veered off course and lost his conviction. But here he was, and I was glad to see him. He'd come to take me home, he said.

"I am home," I told him.

He got thrown into a jumble when I told him about Jack and didn't know what to say. But he didn't give up. He stayed three or four days, puttering around the cabin, fixing and cleaning things. In the middle of washing a window, he might stop, as if he'd just thought of something, and say, "You know, Frances, we're getting those bills from Barrett's illness paid off. We could probably get a bank loan to send you to school, if that's what you want."

It hurt me to keep turning him down, he always looked so eager. "Daddy," I'd say, not raising my voice at all, "that's not what I want. My life is here now, with Jack."

Then he'd look out the window and raise his eyebrows, as if I'd decided to live in a crater on the far side of the moon. Finally, our cabin was spick-and-span, all the door hinges oiled, the loose boards nailed down, and he'd run out of arguments. Jack and I offered to drive him to the train in Buffalo, but he was determined to go back the way he'd come. He mounted up and jolted down the lane, his back as stiff as a grenadier's. Near the end, he turned and waved to me, and I watched the dust settle over his passing.

"That was twenty-five years ago," I told Carrie, standing up and brushing off my pants. I'd left out a lot of the details, but I'd given her the gist of it. So much talking had left me feeling dry in the mouth. And empty.

"I had no idea," she said. "It's really sad, what happened."

"Some of it is." I held out a hand to pull her to her feet. "Anyway, we'd better head back. I know Jack will be looking out for us."

"He's a nice man. I like him a lot."

"Jack's the best piece of luck I ever had."

We woke the horses from their nap and walked them down to a little stream for a drink. By the time we started off, we were riding through the purple shadows of the hills.

"What ever became of Alice Buford?" Carrie asked after a while. "Do you know?"

"Oh yes, my mother wrote me all about it. She married a guy named Roland Dibbs and moved up to Rownd's Point with him. Not long after that he opened his own garage and started repairing cars. He calls it R. D. Automotive."

"Alice's dowry."

"There you have it," I said.

Jack was cooking supper when we got back, and while we ate, the three of us talked over Carrie's situation.

"To be honest," Jack said, "going off to New York City is about the scariest thing I can think of. I'd get lost the first day—and probably stay lost."

Carrie laughed. "A lot of people would say the same about this place. When I turned the light off in my room last night, I couldn't believe how dark it was. At least New York has streetlights."

"Columbia is in New York, if I remember correctly," I said.

"It's not the same, though."

Carrie called her parents that night, and after she'd talked a few minutes, she handed me the receiver. I thought it was a dirty trick, until I heard Hillary's voice—unmistakable, even in its new, deeper tones. The first few years I'd lived with Jack, we hadn't had a phone, so I'd gotten in the habit of writing my parents a couple of times a year. I'd never even written to Hillary, but every Christmas I sent a card signed "Jack and Frances," just to let them know I was still alive. I hadn't talked to Hillary since the night of our graduation, the night I watched so jealously as she and Dan stayed on the gym floor together, dance after dance. Now she and Dan were packing, as it happened, to go to my father's funeral.

"Here it is 1984," I announced to Jack and Carrie when I got off the phone. "And I have never been on an airplane."

We didn't get much sleep that night; there was too much to do. At seven the next morning, the three of us were in the cab of the pickup, heading down the lane. We'd booked a flight from Rapid City to Detroit, and from there to Pittsburgh, where Hillary and Dan would meet us. It would take about an hour and a half to drive to Tenney's Landing from the airport. I would be sleeping in my parents' house that night.

When we got on the highway, I was thinking about Evan Sayers. My mother had written two or three years before to tell me he'd died in the Veterans Hospital in Pittsburgh, at the age of eighty-nine. He'd been sent home blind when he was twenty-three, and by the time I knew him, none of his relatives were living. I had his Purple Heart. He'd given it to me the last time I saw him, insisted I take it. I still look at it sometimes, and it never fails to make my heart beat faster.

Dog Stories

When I see the name Eugene Eastman in the newspaper, I stop breathing for a minute. Right away I know it's him, not someone else with the same name. My eyes are suddenly brimming with tears, as if I have spotted a long-lost friend at the end of a long journey. "Hello!" I want to call out. "Remember me?"

In the blurry picture above the announcement of his marriage to Laurie Mathis, formerly of Ambridge, PA, Eugene is standing in the shadow of a church door, wearing a dark jacket and a tie. Although his face is hardly more than a smudge on the page, it is the face I remember. He has a little mustache now, and his hair is cut shorter. It looks as if some gray is creeping into both. The last time I saw him, he was standing at the top of our driveway in the bright sun. I had turned around to look out the back window of the car as my mother drove us away from the house where we had lived for eight years. Eugene lifted his cap and ran his fingers through his hair. When he saw me watching him, he waved the cap in the air. For a long time after that, I would picture him waving good-bye and wonder what we had lost.

I wish my sister, Emma, were here, instead of three thousand miles away at law school. I am the only person in this room who knows Eugene, and I don't know the people sprawled on the floor and the sofa, reading the Sunday paper, all that well. My friend Margo invited me to spend Thanksgiving weekend with her family in Pittsburgh. Otherwise, I would probably be sitting in the campus library back in Ann Arbor, looking out the window at the Huron River, feeling lonely. My mother and stepfather are in Montreal, visiting his son's family, even though the Canadians already had Thanksgiving in October. My father, in the midst of his second divorce, decided to head to Madrid. And Curtis, my first real boyfriend, is in Topeka for the weekend, playing the clarinet with his brother's jazz band. One of the good things about Eugene: you knew he wasn't going anywhere.

Eugene Eastman loved to tell dog stories. And that's how we got to know him, the summer I turned eleven, maybe the worst summer of my life. At first, I used to think about how different from our father he was, the way he'd take his boots off by the front door and sit down at our kitchen table, set his New Holland cap on the windowsill and run his hands through his hair. Eugene was a shy man, a farmer and part-time logger who lived nearby. He never really settled himself until he got a story going.

"Did you know that Bill Lambert, used to live up near the old Tenney place?" he'd ask, something like that, curling his big fingers around a mug of tea. "Had that nice bluetick hound—Jake, I think it was?"

He never waited for an answer, or expected one, but kept right on.

"Well, one morning Bill had to go to Pittsburgh. And he tied that dog to a tree out behind the house, stayed away all day. When he got home he found Jake over on his side, all swelled up. Dead. And you know why?"

He'd pick up his cup, sniff, set it down.

"Because there was a hornets' nest in the tree where Lambert tied him. And those hornets set on to Jake for one reason or another, and he couldn't get away."

He'd pause again and shake his head, contemplating the impossible carelessness of human beings.

"Now that's a shame," he'd say and finally gulp down some tea.

Most of his stories ended badly.

My mother, noticing after a moment that he'd stopped talking, would turn away from whatever she happened to be doing on the other side of the room and look at him in the blank way she had in those days and say, utterly without conviction, "That's terrible, Eugene."

I sat at the table drawing pictures of the dogs, while my mother and Emma made lunch. I was the only one who paid attention to Eugene's stories. In a funny way, they were soothing to me, even though I would always make up a new ending in my head. When he told the Jake story, I might imagine Jake chewing through his rope and getting away, then going and soaking himself in the brook to ease the hornet stings. When Bill Lambert got home, he'd find the empty rope and notice the hornets buzzing around. He'd feel bad and think Jake had run away. But just around sunset, Jake would come up to the house—soaking wet and wagging his tail, full of forgiveness. Eugene always looked puzzled when he complimented my drawings. He must have wondered, where did that wet dog come from?

Eugene was at our house nearly every Saturday that summer.

It started one day in the late spring when he stopped by and offered to help us. "I was passing your road," he said the first time, "and thought I'd see if you needed a hand with anything, any heavy work."

It was eight o'clock on Saturday morning, and there he was, practically a stranger, standing at our front door. We had to go wake our mother up, and we were a little embarrassed, knowing it was late by country time. She went to the door, tying the cord of her bathrobe and pushing her hair away from her face. "Thank you, Eugene," she said, "but we don't need anything." She went straight back to bed.

"Anyway it was nice of him," Emma said as we watched Eugene's truck heading down the hill, thumping over the ruts in our road.

The next week he came again and said he'd been wondering if we didn't want to put our garden in. He'd noticed that it was rototilled but not planted. We stood beside our mother's bed and delivered this message. "Tell him you girls want to do it yourselves," she said vaguely, as if we weren't really there. "Tell him it's only going to be a small garden." She closed her eyes and pulled the blanket up around her shoulders.

Emma and I were in the kitchen eating cereal when we heard Eugene's truck coming up the road the following week. We sat still and listened as he slid things out over the metal tailgate. After a while, we heard him digging and pounding. We finished our breakfast.

When we went outside, we saw that he'd made a row of skinny poles on the far side of the garden and was tying bailing twine between them.

"It's a little late to be putting peas in," he said. "But I brought these Alaskas over—they take hot weather pretty well."

We walked out to watch him, the dirt under our bare feet still cool and damp. Eugene made another row of poles, while Emma and I tied the strings between them. He hoed the soil until it was crumbly and drew a line down each row with a pointed stick. "That looks good," he said when we'd finished dropping the dry peas in the rows and patting a bit of dirt over them.

We went into the house and found the seeds we'd bought back in April. We planted lettuce, cucumbers, squash, and beans. My mother came out on the porch once, still in her bathrobe, and watched us for a minute, then went back in the house.

We walked with Eugene down to the brook, where we

found some good-size stones and carried them back two at a time to make a bed for the herbs. Inside the circle of stones we put the basil and oregano and thyme, parsley and dill. Eugene was very particular about placing the stones and deciding which seeds would go where. Even though it started to get warm, he kept his cap and flannel shirt on, only rolling the sleeves up over a long-sleeved undershirt. Up close I noticed that he smelled of bacon grease and woodsmoke, odd on a spring morning.

Eugene's dog, Georgie—an Australian terrier with one back leg missing—lay nearby and watched us work. The dog was slowly inching his way through the grass on his stomach; whenever Eugene turned to look at him, he lay stock-still and looked back innocently. "He's not allowed in the garden at home," Eugene told us. "It drives him crazy."

We didn't know much about Eugene, except that he lived with his cousin Marshall in the old family farmhouse up on Eastman Hill. "The last of the old-time bachelors," my father had said about them once, "a dying breed."

When Eugene went home that day, Emma and I were hungry and went inside to find our mother. She was sitting on the piano bench in the living room, looking out the window. She didn't play anymore, not since our father left.

"Well, it was kind of Eugene to help you girls plant your garden, wasn't it?" she said. "Did you give him something to drink, though? Did you offer him a sandwich?"

"We did give him a glass of water," I said, looking at the floor.

But Emma spoke up. "Look," she said, "we're used to grown-ups offering *us* things, not the other way around."

After that, Eugene showed up on Saturday mornings and did anything he could see to do. He fixed the lawn mower and mowed the grass; he replaced some rotten clapboards under one of the upstairs windows; he brought tomato plants and made a place for them in our garden. Emma and I always went out to help him, handing him tools or holding things in place while he nailed them down. Georgie usually stayed close by, watching us.

Eugene didn't say much while he was working, though he whistled sometimes or showed us how to do something. "Best not to tie the strings too tight around the vines," he advised as we staked the tomatoes. "Give them some room to grow."

We'd invite him to stay for lunch and make him a pot of tea, which was what he liked to drink even in the summer. And that's when he told the dog stories, sitting at the kitchen table waiting for lunch to be ready.

The saddest one was about his uncle's dog Spy.

"You know those dogs that herd sheep? Those Scottish collies with the pretty black-and-white faces? Well, my uncle Jordan had one he called Spy, and he was a beauty, that dog. He'd find a lost ewe in a snowstorm and bring her home, he'd spend the night out on the hill guarding a newborn lamb. A real beauty."

He stirred some milk and sugar into his tea, leaned down and sniffed it, let it be.

"There's such a thing as training a dog too well, though, and that's what happened to Spy. He did just as he was told. One night in the winter, January, my uncle was in the barn finishing up his chores, and he was trying to hurry because it was cold and a big storm coming. Well, Spy was pestering him—he liked to mooch around when they were milking because usually they'd aim a squirt or two into his mouth. But this night my uncle put him out the side door and told him to stay. And when he finished and went to the house he forgot about Spy outside there."

Eugene shifted in his chair.

"It snowed half the night and then it was freezing rain for a while. By morning it was below zero and everything frozen. Uncle Jordan found Spy right outside the barn door where he'd told him to stay, his coat full of ice and his nose and feet frostbit. He was still alive, though, so my uncle took him in the house and wrapped him in a blanket, and my aunt tried to get some warm beef broth into him. It was too late; he died before the afternoon was out."

I was drawing furiously—Spy on a green hill, guarding a new lamb.

"A real shame," Eugene said, looking down at his hands.

One Friday night Emma and I made brownies for the Saturday lunch, but when we got up in the morning it was raining. We stood at the window, watching great swirls of rainwater washing new gullies into our road. "I guess Eugene won't come," Emma said, and he didn't.

Late in the afternoon, though, we heard his truck. I ran to open the door. He came in dripping and seemed a little lost as he stood just inside, watching rainwater running down the sleeve of his jacket. Finally, he took a couple of steps forward and cleared his throat.

"I stopped by to see if you might like to go to the program at Chandler Hall, over in Tenney's Landing," he said with a glance around the room to take us all in. "There's a chicken supper and then music and dancing afterward."

We were all looking at my mother, hoping she'd say yes. But cool as anything, she said, "That sounds nice, Eugene, but I'm afraid we have other plans for tonight. Thank you for asking us, though."

Eugene retreated toward the door, looking more relieved than disappointed. "All right then," he said. "When I come next Saturday I'm going to bring some pipe and put in a drainage ditch up here at the top of your road. It's washing away."

Emma and I walked out on the porch with him and waved as he drove off. "Did you ever notice how he always sniffs his food before he eats it?" Emma asked me. "Like he thinks maybe we're going to poison him?"

"Kind of like a dog," I said, and we couldn't help laughing.

That night we had a fire in the woodstove to keep off the damp. My mother made popcorn after supper and played one of her tapes—the spring concert from her senior year in college. After she'd washed her hair, she sat in a chair near the stove while Emma combed it out and braided it.

"This is pretty exciting," Emma said. "Our big Saturday night plans."

My mother didn't answer. She had her eyes closed, listening to the music—listening for her own voice, I imagined. She had sung in the college choir and claimed she could pick her voice out of the rest. I said I could too, but Emma told me I was full of it.

Our parents had met in their early twenties, when my mother was taking voice lessons in New York and my father was in graduate school studying philosophy. "Your father came from this snazzy family that lived in Hastings-on-Hudson," my mother used to tell us. "And I was a skinny girl from Columbus, Ohio. I remember when his mother came into the city to meet me and took us to lunch at the Russian Tea Room. I couldn't think of anything to say, so I started telling her about my great-uncle Richard, who played Russian roulette when he got drunk. After a bit, I noticed your father looking asphyxiated, and I finally had the sense to shut up."

She liked to talk about herself that way, but we knew better. She was too calm, too sure of herself, we thought, to get truly flustered by a potential mother-in-law. Watching her now in the firelight, I could imagine her performing onstage—a beautiful, unhappy woman who took things as they came.

My father used to tell us how he'd stolen our mother's youth. "She'd just won the Belson Prize," he'd say. "She was supposed to go and study in Italy the next year. Do you have any idea what that means?"

He called their honeymoon in Venice and Milan the Consolation Prize.

My mother dismissed it all with a wave of her hand. "It wouldn't have been the right sort of life for me," she assured us. "I wasn't cut out for it, all the sacrifices."

In the year before he left, it seemed as if my father couldn't say enough about how he'd ruined my mother's chances. But she'd say, "Don't be silly" or later "Let's leave it alone, shall we?"

"So," I said, as Emma was finishing the long braid that

reached the middle of my mother's back, "how old do you think Eugene is?"

"Oh, I don't know," my mother answered after a minute, her eyes still closed. "Forty or fifty—or somewhere in between."

"More like forty," I told her, even though I had no idea myself.

The next day, when my father came over to take us for our Sunday walk, he stopped and admired our garden.

"We planted it with Eugene," Emma told him.

"Eastman," I added.

He didn't say anything else but ambled off toward the old logging road that cut through one corner of our land and led into the woods. My father is tall and thin and was already a little stoop shouldered. He lifted his feet very high when he walked, as if he were stepping through invisible puddles.

I took Emma by the arm and pulled her back so I could whisper in her ear. "Do you think he looks like a giraffe?"

She looked at me, then at him. "You're right," she said. "He does."

We caught up with him and let him tell us the names of the plants and wildflowers he pointed out with his walking stick. "Wild holly," he'd say. "Fairly rare, and hard to recognize without its berries."

Sooner or later he'd get around to one of his ethics problems. Today it was the life raft with one passenger too many. Who should get thrown overboard in order to save the rest? The nun, the man with a broken arm, the woman with a baby? We'd heard this one before, in the student discussion groups he used to have at our house. His students would always ponder the life and potential good of each person onboard before choosing one to toss over the side. They always seemed to take it hard once they'd decided.

"Get rid of the baby first," Emma said right away. "He doesn't weigh much, but he'll be a pain in the butt."

"Well," my father said, looking hurt. "If you don't want to be serious."

It was a good ten minutes before he broke the silence. He stopped and pointed with his stick to the top of a battered beech tree where an owl was sleeping. "Look there," he said. "You won't see that very often."

"What keeps them from falling off the branch when they go to sleep?" I asked him.

"Velcro," Emma said, giving my arm a little pinch and walking ahead.

"You're a saucy one today," he told her.

Emma had always been impatient with these discussions. I remember the first question he put to us—the famous "If a tree falls in the forest and no one is there to hear it, does it make a sound?"

"Of course it does," Emma had replied immediately. "Do you think nothing really happens unless some person is there to see it or hear it?"

I had tried to answer the question for myself. Yes. No. How do you know? It made me feel giddy—like a cat chasing its tail—trying to figure it out.

When we got back from our walk, Emma asked our father if he'd like a glass of lemonade. We'd made it fresh for him that morning.

"I can't," he said. "I have to get back and finish grading

exams. Can you believe it? The summer term is half over already."

"Yeah, right," I said as he started his car. We sat down on the steps and watched him go.

"If a tree falls in the forest and lands on your father's head . . . ," Emma muttered.

He was going home to Myra, the student he'd fallen in love with, the one he'd moved in with after graduation.

It was Emma's friend Heather who told us, right before we got on the bus the last day of school. Emma was standing with her up by the flagpole, and when she saw me come out of the building she said, "Christine, get over here." I didn't hurry.

"Okay, tell her," Emma said, pulling me in close.

"Your father," Heather said. She was staring at the folder I hugged against my chest, half a year's worth of drawings and work sheets. "He's got an apartment in Fayette with a student from the college. My mother found out her name. It's Myra Singleton, and she's only like twenty-one, she just graduated. I heard her tell my father that Myra's about six feet tall. My mother said she looks like one of those supermodels, skirts like six inches long, three earrings in one ear."

"I guess your mother got a nice close look," Emma remarked.

"I think you must be wrong, Heather," I said. I walked down the driveway and got on the bus and sat by the window. I had to keep blinking, because everything outside was blurring together.

Emma got on just before the bus pulled out and sat down next to me. "It's true," she said.

"How do you know?"

"Because it is. Don't be stupid."

We had been let off and were halfway up our road when Emma said, "What an asshole." She kicked a stone out of the way.

I'd never heard her swear, but it seemed entirely natural. Asshole, I repeated to myself.

When we got to the house, Emma ran up the porch steps. "Wait," I said. "Don't tell her." But she was already charging through the door and down the hall into the kitchen.

"I suppose you know about Myra Singleton," I heard her say.

My mother looked at me when I came in. She was busy making a picnic dinner for us, an end-of-school celebration that we were planning to have on the porch that night. She was wearing a light summer dress, and her hair was pinned up. "I didn't know her name," she said.

"So you *did* know about her," Emma practically wailed. "Why didn't you tell us?"

"I didn't think it was something you needed to know," my mother said quietly, holding on to the back of a chair.

"Oh, really?" Emma said, mocking her. "It does make a difference, you know. You're not 'just spending some time apart and sorting things out.' Are you?"

"I think that's the main thing we're doing."

"What? You've been telling us he's going to come home." Emma was pacing up and down the kitchen, waving her arms in the air, looking a lot like my father. "But that's not true, is it?"

"I thought he *was* going to come home," my mother insisted. "Now I don't know. Honestly, I don't know if I want him to. It's very hard."

"Hard?" Emma shouted. "It's impossible. I can't believe it." We heard her footsteps banging down the hallway, then the even louder bang of the screen door.

My mother covered her face with her hands, and I went and hugged her around the waist, holding on tight. I couldn't tell if she was crying. So it was true—my father had left us to go live with another person. Myra Singleton.

After a moment, my mother started stroking my hair and saying, "It's all right, sweetie," the way she did when I woke up from a nightmare.

"Emma's the asshole," I muttered into the cloth of her dress.

She took a step back, holding me at arm's length. "Christine," she said. "Don't talk that way." But she smiled at me and dabbed at my wet cheeks with the dish towel. I helped her finish up our dinner: fried chicken, potato salad, coleslaw, pickled beets, angel food cake and strawberries for dessert. "A real Ohio-style picnic," she said.

When Emma came back from her mad walk, she made iced tea and set the table on the porch. My mother asked her to pick out the music, and Emma chose a Mozart tape because she knew that was what my mother would have picked. We ate as if we were starved and sat out until way after dark. I was getting drowsy when the first fireflies of the summer came out in the meadow, tiny lights down in the grass at first and then higher and higher until they were flickering in the trees. I wondered if my father could see fireflies from his apartment in town.

"Emma," I said when we were in bed that night. "Do you remember how Daddy used to cook dinner when we were little?" She didn't say anything, but I heard her sigh and turn over on her back in her bed across the room.

"Remember?" I persisted. "How he used to pick us up from the babysitter and take us to the grocery store with him? How you always asked for Tuna P. Wiggle?"

"Look," she said. "I really don't feel like talking about Daddy. Besides which you should stop calling him Daddy. It makes you sound like a baby. Call him John." She turned back on her side, facing the wall.

John. And Myra.

It made me mad, the way things kept changing. Our life would be one way, a good way, and then it would be different. Like when we first moved to Pennsylvania, when Emma was five and I was three, because our father got a job at McClelland College. My mother had to wake up early to go to work at the insurance office in town, so my father would make us breakfast and drive Emma to school and me to the babysitter. We'd all be in the kitchen together making dinner when my mother got home, and my father would say, "You look tired," and kiss her on the forehead.

On the weekends my mother stayed at home with us when my father went to the library to work on his book. On Sunday afternoons the four of us would go for a walk together, and on Sunday evenings they'd invite friends to the house. They brought casserole dishes of brown rice and spicy vegetables—"belly burners" Emma called them—and jugs of wine. Afterward, my mother played the piano. Everyone would sing, old love songs and show tunes from the songbooks we'd found in the attic. "You're so lucky to live out in the country," the friends would say, lingering in the driveway and looking up at the stars. We lived near the Monongahela River, between two towns—Tenney's Landing, about four miles up the river, and Fayette, where the college was, about fifteen miles down.

My father got his promotion at the college the year I started second grade. That's when my mother left the insurance office and started teaching music at our school two days a week. She joined the Chamber Singers, a community chorus, and went to rehearsals on Wednesday nights. She also bought an Italian cookbook and learned to make pasta, which she dried outside on the clothesline in good weather. I liked to watch the long noodles waving in the breeze, and the orange plastic streamers that were supposed to keep the birds away.

I think that was the best time. My parents still kissed each other hello in the evening, and we could hear them talking in bed on Saturday mornings, making plans. They'd decide what color to paint the living room or where to plant some new bulbs or talk about a movie they'd seen the night before. We'd get up and make them breakfast, and when they came to the table their faces would glow.

Our father moved away from us so slowly we hardly noticed at first. He had to work on his second book, he had to go to meetings. He stopped inviting students to the house. It was Emma who badgered him about it, not my mother. "Heather's father does most of his work at home," she'd say. "Why can't you?" Or "Look, Daddy, too much philosophy is making you weird. Why don't you spend some time in real life?"

One Friday night he called at dinnertime to say he needed to stay at the office and read a senior thesis. When he wasn't home by ten, my mother called him, but there was no answer.

"He's probably at the library," she told us. "And you're up way past bedtime." From our room upstairs, I heard her trying to call twice more. A few days later, they sat us down and told us he was taking a student group to Edinburgh for the spring term. We were staying at home, my mother said, because a little time apart would be good for everyone. He sent Emma and me postcards of castles and bagpipers and wrote that he missed us.

I remember the first Saturday in May, just after he got back from Scotland, when he went to our neighbor's house and borrowed the rototiller. Everything was going to be all right, I knew, watching him hang on as the noisy machine bumped and skidded over the slick ground. I stayed on the porch while he went around the garden three times. When he came up to the house in his muddy rubber boots, I told him to sit on the step so I could pull them off. He went inside in his socks and washed his hands at the kitchen sink. Then he took his robe and mortarboard out of the hall closet and got dressed for commencement. Two mornings later, he left a note on the refrigerator and slipped away while everyone was still asleep. We didn't know it, but Myra Singleton was waiting.

Today is August 11 and also my eleventh birthday. Even though Emma says it doesn't mean anything, I think it's going to be a special birthday. So will twenty-two and thirty-three and so on. I plan to live to be a hundred and ten, because eleven times ten seems like a good life. Anyway, I can tell that

I'm getting smarter because this is the first birthday I didn't look in the mirror as soon as I woke up to see if I'd changed. I did look in the mirror, but only to comb my hair.

After breakfast I walk up the hill beyond the apple trees to look for the phoebes' nest Emma and Heather saw up here yesterday. Heather says we should take it down and give it to Mr. Madden, our science teacher, when we go back to school. I can't find the tree they told me about, and I'm beginning to wonder if they made it up, when I hear a truck in the road. It's Eugene, even though this is Sunday.

When I get down to the house, Emma is waiting at the back door. She motions for me to come in. "Be quiet," she whispers, and I follow her down the hall. We stand a little behind the screen door and see my mother and Eugene leaning against the porch railing. I gauge the distance between them: about two feet. They're watching Georgie rolling on his back in the grass under the big maple.

"That's probably the happiest dog I ever knew," Eugene is telling her. "He doesn't know he's only got three legs."

"What happened to him anyway?" my mother asks.

"I'm not certain," Eugene says. "I found him when he was just a pup, by the fence next to our road. One of our cows was standing down there bellowing—Grace it was. She's got a bad disposition anyway, so I didn't think much of it. But she kept it up, and finally I went down to see what the fuss was. Well, here was this poor fellow, curled up in a ball and whimpering, all dirty and bloody, his leg mangled some way. Might've been hit by a car. I'd never seen a dog like him around here, didn't know who he might belong to. I put him in the truck and took him over to Foster, the horse doctor. Turned out the leg was crushed, so he lost it. He was awful sick for a while, had to feed him baby cereal and milk with a spoon. Marshall—that's my cousin, you know—said he was done for, but he came around."

"Well, a story with a happy ending," my mother says.

"Oh, he's young yet," Eugene tells her, crossing his arms over his chest. "Sooner or later a dog will break your heart."

Georgie gets up and shakes himself, sits down and barks at them.

"I don't usually care for a little dog," Eugene says, "but Georgie's a corker."

"He looks like that dog in *The Wizard of Oz*," my mother says.

"Toto," I blurt out. Emma gives me a push, and we go out on the porch too.

"Eugene came over to wish you a happy birthday," my mother says.

"That I did." He picks up the two packages I noticed on the railing beside him and hands them to me. They're wrapped in white tissue paper and look sort of lumpy. They have fingerprint smudges where he taped them. "I'm not much of a hand at wrapping," he says.

The first one I open is *The Illustrated Book of Dogs*, which has color pictures of every kind of dog and tells their characteristics and how to take care of them. I look up Australian terrier and show them the picture. "There's Georgie," I say, even though it doesn't look much like him.

The second present is a thick notebook of drawing paper with a red cover and three drawing pencils tucked into its spiral binding.

"Eugene, these are wonderful presents. In fact, I love them."

I stand on tiptoe to kiss his cheek, and although he takes a step back, he's smiling.

"Well, I hope you keep up your drawing," he tells me, blushing. "That picture of Spy you gave me, I taped it up in the kitchen, and even Marshall says it's good."

We're all standing there, kind of beaming at each other, and then Eugene suddenly starts down the steps. "Well, I'm headed," he says over his shoulder.

"You just got here," Emma says. "Stick around for five minutes."

"Oh, I couldn't," Eugene says. "I have an awful lot to do today."

"At least come back tonight and have some birthday cake," she tells him.

He lifts Georgie onto the seat of the truck and starts to get in himself but stops with one foot on the ground. "Oh," he says to my mother over the truck roof, "my aunt Cam wanted me to ask you if you might think about singing in church next Sunday. It's the old Presbyterian church in Tenney's Landing, you know. Her father used to be the minister there, so she thinks she's in charge now. I told her you wouldn't want to bother, though. I'll tell her you can't do it." He swings his leg up and starts to shut the door.

"No, wait," my mother says. "Tell your aunt to call me. I'd be happy to talk to her about it."

He waves to us and guns the engine.

"Hmm," Emma says. "Eugene wasn't wearing his hat today."

"I think he looks good without his hat," I add.

"Do you know what I like about Eugene?" my mother says.

"No, what?" Emma asks, grinning at her.

My mother gives her a look. "He seems to be completely without vanity. That's a remarkable quality, you know. He is who he is, take it or leave it."

"So if Eugene invites you to a dance again, you'll say yes?" I ask her.

"You girls are getting the wrong idea," my mother says. "Eugene is our friend, and he understands that."

"I don't think so," Emma says. "Besides, I haven't seen him driving around with that bleach blonde for a long time now."

"Bleach blonde?" I say just as the phone starts ringing.

It's my father calling to say he might not be able to come over this afternoon. He didn't come last Sunday either. I hear my mother reminding him that it's my birthday, and then she hands me the phone.

"Hi, honey," he says. "Listen, I did *not* forget your birthday. Only I'm tied up this afternoon, so I'll have to come over later and bring your present. All right?"

"That's fine with me, John," I tell him.

At lunchtime, Emma and I decide to pack our sandwiches and ride our bikes out to Sweetwater Pond for the afternoon. We try to talk my mother into going with us, but she says she wants to take a nap.

"Mom," Emma objects, "you sleep practically all the time now."

"I know," she says with a little shrug. "Don't worry too much, I'll get over it."

It's about two miles to Sweetwater Pond, and the road is dusty and bumpy most of the way. Some people are there already—Heather and her mother and her brother Wesley and his friend Bryce. The boys are in the water, floating on tubes.

"Oh no," Emma says when she sees Bryce.

In the old days, he and his parents would come out to our house on the weekends, and he used to make Emma mad, teasing her and giving her monkey burns on the arm. He and Wesley are going to start high school in the fall.

Heather waves to us, and they make room on their blanket.

"Where's your mother?" Heather's mother asks. "How is she?"

"She's good," Emma says. "She's busy this afternoon."

"Yeah," I add. "She's practicing. She's going to sing in church next Sunday."

"What church?" Heather says.

"Look, never mind," Emma says. "I'm famished after that bike ride."

We unpack our sandwiches and help ourselves to the fruit salad and cookies that Heather's mother brought. When the boys notice that we're eating, they paddle in and toss the tubes up on the sand. Wesley walks right into the middle of the blanket and shakes the water out of his hair.

"You awful boy," his mother says. "Get out of here."

He and Bryce fill two paper plates with food and stand a little way off. We can hear them talking in whispers and laughing softly. We know they're watching us. Emma rubs sunscreen on my back, then I do hers, and we lay out our towels and look through Heather's *People* magazines, ignoring the boys until they go back in the water.

"You girls are so boring!" Bryce shouts after about ten minutes.

"Come on," Wesley says. "Let's play Marco Polo."

Emma and Heather groan, but they get up and smooth

their bathing suits as they walk down to the water. I follow them. Wesley dives in with a splash and says he's going to be it. "Okay," Heather says, drawing a circle in the sand with her toe. "This is where you go when you're out."

Wesley catches me first and then Bryce and then Emma. We're sitting together in the circle, and Bryce yells "Polo" every once in a while to throw Wesley off. Heather is hard to catch anyway.

Bryce suddenly looks away from them and says, "I saw your father yesterday."

We don't say anything.

"With his girlfriend," Bryce adds.

"So?" Emma says.

"So, have you met her?"

"Why would we want to meet her?" Emma keeps her eyes on a tractor at work in the hayfield in the distance, like she's not interested.

"Well, she's kind of a babe."

"Really? I heard she was anorexic," Emma says.

Bryce picks up a handful of sand and lets it fall through his fingers.

"Anyway," he says, lowering his voice and glancing first at me and then at Emma, "I hear one of those Eastman wood-chucks is trying to make it with your mother."

"Are you crazy?" I start to say, but Emma cuts me off.

"Trying to?" she says. "He *is*, you nitwit. Every Saturday night out in the shed. They think we don't know, but you should hear the way they carry on, moaning and groaning and knocking things around. It's awful."

She gets up and walks away slowly, as if nothing's wrong,

and just then Wesley comes out of the water with his hand on Heather's arm. "Got her," he says.

"Hey," Heather says. "Where's your sister going?"

I see Emma going down the hill toward our bicycles, so I go pick up our things, and when Heather's mother says, "Is everything all right?" I don't even answer.

Emma's pedaling fast, making a cloud of dust that gets in my eyes and mouth. All I want to do is knock her flat. I stand up and pump as hard as I can. My bicycle crashes over the bumps, and everything in the basket is bouncing around.

"Just keep quiet," she yells when I finally catch up with her.

"You're a liar," I yell back.

"You leave me alone," Emma says. She's still pedaling like a demon, her wet hair flying.

She looks wild, like someone I've never seen before. I let her pull ahead.

All of a sudden, right before we get out to the main road, she stops and lets her bike drop. She's standing there, catching her breath. I take her shorts and T-shirt out of my basket and hand them to her.

"What are you so mad about?" I say.

"Maybe the fact that everyone's talking about our parents' sex lives all of a sudden? Shit, Christine."

"I forgot your shoes."

"That's okay."

She gets dressed and picks up her bike again, and we walk them down the road.

"Bryce, that little pisser," she says. "That wiener. He thinks he knows something."

"Do you think it's true?"

"What is?"

"That he's trying to? Eugene?"

"How should I know?" Emma says. "Probably. I mean, people aren't usually that nice for no reason."

"Were you making that up, about the bleach blonde?"

"No. I see him with this woman sometimes. Once I saw them at the store together, buying beer. She was laughing a lot, I noticed."

"Maybe it's one of his relatives," I say. "He has about fifty cousins."

"Maybe."

When it's five-thirty, our mother asks us to start the barbecue grill in the backyard. She lets us cook the hamburgers by ourselves, because she's inside making French fries and a salad.

"This is one good thing about getting rid of John," Emma says to me. "We can eat red meat at home instead of only at our friends' houses."

"Emma, we didn't get rid of him."

"No, really," she says. "Didn't you ever get sick of all those vegetables, those kabob things? It was like, come on, John, a steak on the grill isn't going to kill us."

We eat on the porch every night now, unless it's raining too hard, on a table we made from four crates and a piece of plywood. With the cloth on, you can't tell. We keep a jar of flowers in the middle. Sometimes after dinner we play Scrabble, or cards. We're teaching our mother to play poker, and she's teaching us to play hearts.

Tonight, after we clear the table, Emma brings the cake out. As she's putting the candles on, we hear Eugene's truck in the road.

"Wow, he's coming," Emma says. "I didn't think he would."

"Hey, Eugene," I say. He's wearing a yellow shirt that looks new, and he smells of soap. I'm happy to see him, but now I feel funny about it too.

"I had to drive over this way, so I thought I'd take you up on that birthday cake."

"We're glad you did, Eugene," my mother tells him.

"Oh," he says, "I picked up some ice cream and left it in the truck. Just a minute."

He comes back and fumbles a carton of vanilla ice cream out of a crumpled paper bag—still his good, shy self.

They sing "Happy Birthday," and I get all the candles on one blow. Finally, we sit down with our cake and ice cream.

"Chocolate cake, my favorite," Eugene says.

"Have you ever been married, Eugene?" Emma asks.

"No," he says, surprised, and swallows a mouthful. "No, never have. I came close once—back when I was twenty-four. Decided against it." He takes another bite and chews carefully.

"What happened?" Emma says. "Who was she?"

"*Emma!*" my mother says. "That's Eugene's business. Let him eat in peace."

"I don't mind," he says, laughing. "Not that I intend to answer."

"Well, what about your cousin then?" Emma asks him. "Marshall."

"I wish he was here to answer for himself," Eugene says, looking delighted. Then he says, "Oh . . . Marshall would never get married, he's too set in his ways—has been ever since he was a baby."

We hear another car coming up the road, and everyone

stops talking. We hear it hit the gully about halfway up and jump out of second gear.

"That's John," Emma says. "Our ex-father."

"I'd like to tell you she isn't always like this," my mother tells Eugene. "But it wouldn't be true."

We watch my father park his station wagon behind Eugene's truck and walk across the drive.

"Well, well, this is festive," he says when he gets to the top step. He's smiling, but he doesn't look happy. "Eugene," he says, nodding.

"Evening, John," Eugene says. He sits up straighter and sets his fork down.

"John," my mother asks, "would you like a piece of cake?"

"No, thank you. I don't want to break up this very interesting party. I just came to give Christine her birthday present."

He sets the large shopping bag he's carrying on a chair and lifts out a box wrapped in bright green paper tied with pink ribbon. Everyone is looking at me. I try not to tear the paper when I open it, even though my hands are shaking. Inside is a pink felt hat with the brim turned up and a floppy purple flower pinned to it, the kind the younger girls at school—the second and third graders—like to wear.

I take it out and hold it up. "Thank you, Daddy. It's pretty."

"Put it on," he says.

The idea of wearing this hat is too humiliating. I know Myra picked it out. I can't help it, I start to cry.

"Now what?" my father says. "You don't like it?"

Eugene gets up. "I'd best be going," he says, touching me lightly on the head.

"That's a good idea," my father says to him.

Eugene starts down the steps and then stops and turns to my mother. "You can call me if you need anything," he tells her.

When he's gone, my father says, "What was that about?"

I look at the plates on the table with the half-eaten pieces of cake sitting in puddles of ice cream and keep on crying.

"What's the matter with her?" my father says. "Christine?"

"Maybe you should go too," my mother tells him.

"I don't think so," my father says. "I think we need to have a talk."

Emma gives him a dark look, but my mother holds a hand up before she can say anything.

"You two go upstairs," my mother says. "Get washed up. You can read in bed for a while."

We turn on a lamp in our bedroom and tiptoe into our mother's room and sit shoulder to shoulder under the window to listen.

"It's obvious you're turning the girls against me," my father is saying. "Emma has been hostile toward me all summer, and today on the phone Christine called me John. That's a bit much."

"Do you think it's possible that *you're* turning the girls against you?" my mother asks him.

Emma nudges me with her elbow.

"It's so easy for you to be smug," he says. "Can you imagine how difficult this is for me?"

"Difficult," my mother repeats. "I would hope so."

My father starts to reply, but my mother interrupts him. "That girl Myra," she says, almost softly. "I believe she was one of the students in the group you took to Edinburgh."

"Nothing happened in Edinburgh," my father says.

"Something happened somewhere, John."

We can hear the boards of the porch creaking and know that my father is striding up and down in his awkward way.

"What about that Eastman?" he says, his voice turning hard. "He keeps showing up, doesn't he? What's going on with him?"

"Under the circumstances, I'd say it's none of your business."

"Look out," Emma whispers.

"Is that right?" my father says. "Is that right?" He's still now, probably standing in front of her, close to her. "I can take this house, you know. The deed is in my mother's name. How would you like that? You want to go live on the farm with Eastman? Go ahead. You'll have a grand time, won't you, getting up and milking the cows every morning, taking care of the half-wit cousin."

"Marshall is hardly a half-wit, John. He sings in the chorus with us—as you might remember."

"What is it with you?" The words are hardly out of his mouth when we hear a crash and the sound of splintering wood. We peer out the window and see my father smashing our table, kicking the crates to pieces. He's already tossed the plywood top into the yard; the plates and candles and flowers are broken, strewn everywhere. At last he stops. He stands there with his hands at his sides, looking at the shattered crates. "God damn it to hell," he says, as if he means the table.

"Do you think we should call Eugene?" I ask Emma.

"No," she whispers. She sits down again and pulls me down too. "It's all right, he won't hurt her."

We can hear my father breathing hard. "What a mess," he says. "I don't know what to do."

"You've lost me, John," my mother says. "There's no way I can help you."

"No," he says. "I suppose not."

For a long time it's quiet again. I picture him standing there, still staring at the wreck of our table, our mother waiting for him to go away.

When we hear his car start, she comes inside and shuts the door. Emma and I go back to our room and lie down on our beds. We leave the lamp on.

"What do you think, Emma?" I say.

"I think you were right."

"About what?"

She props herself up on her elbow and looks at me. "This *was* a special birthday. It's a good thing you're only expecting one every eleven years."

"Yeah, well, I meant what do you think is going to happen?"

"He won't take the house away, he's just being a jerk." She considers. "But she won't live in it much longer, not after he said that. Maybe we'll move to Ohio or something."

"It might not be too bad, living on the farm with Eugene and Marshall," I say.

"Christine, that is such a screwball idea."

"Why? We could see Eugene and Georgie every day. And Marshall—he'd get used to us after a while."

"I suppose that's your idea of a happy ending," Emma says. "Hey, what did you wish for anyway?"

"What?"

"Your birthday candles, dopey. When you blew them out, what did you wish for?"

"I didn't wish for anything. I couldn't figure it out."

"Geez, Christine," Emma says. "That's kind of sad."

When I look at her again, she's fallen asleep, her head on her arm, facing me. Her feet are dusty from our ride home from Sweetwater Pond, and I realize that she still has her bathing suit on under her clothes. I get up and turn the lamp off and get back in bed.

Downstairs, my mother opens the piano and starts to play scales—slowly at first, as if she is just learning them—letting each note hang in the air for a second. And then she plays a little faster, running the notes together. I start to see pictures mixed in with them—shimmery, as if they were underwater: Eugene lifting Georgie out of the grass beside the road, my father pointing with his stick to the owl asleep in the tree, giant Myra in the store trying on the pink hat, Emma running away on her bicycle with her hair flying.

When I hear Eugene's voice, I think at first I'm dreaming, and then I know I'm waking up. He's standing on the porch, talking to my mother through the open window.

"I hope you don't mind," he says. "I came back to see if everything was all right."

"No," my mother says. "It was kind of you."

"I don't want to interfere or anything."

"Of course. I'm just . . . well . . ."

"That's okay," Eugene says. "I'm going to pick up this stuff around the yard. The girls would hate to see it like this in the morning."

"You don't need to," she says, but I hear the creak of the screen door. "Here, let me help at least."

I'm listening so hard I can hear their footsteps in the grass and then the sound of our broken dishes as they gather them up in the tablecloth. Eugene brings the plywood top back onto the porch.

"I can make you a new table. It won't be any trouble."

"That would be nice," my mother tells him.

I hear the scrape of the tabletop as he leans it against the railing.

"There," he says. "I can come back tomorrow afternoon and fix you up a new one. With legs."

"Maybe if you wouldn't mind, you'd stay and have a glass of wine with me. I guess I'm kind of rattled."

"Oh," Eugene says. "Well, if you're going to have one."

I can hear her going into the kitchen and rummaging around. When she goes out again, she says, "Take that chair there. It's the most comfortable. Just sit and talk with me for a bit."

There's a startled silence, and I know Eugene is looking down at his hands. What can he possibly say to her?

"This is good wine," he begins after a while.

"It's not too bad," my mother replies.

There's another long silence, and then Eugene says, "I heard a good one this morning. Did you ever meet my cousin Phil? He has this beagle he calls Bess, a rabbit dog. Best rabbit dog he ever had, he says, and he's had quite a few. Anyway, he took Bess out yesterday to set her on to a rabbit track—he does that to keep her sharp, even when it's not hunting season. He has this one place he likes to go, and when he got there yesterday the ground was damp. He said he saw the biggest rabbit track he'd ever seen in his life right in the mud there."

He stops, probably sniffing his wineglass, taking a sip maybe.

"So Bess took off, and Phil settled himself in his truck to

wait for her to drive the rabbit back. Phil had a beer. All quiet. He started to think about taking his shotgun out from behind the seat, he didn't believe anybody was around. He sat there and thought about it. Nice warm day, still quiet. He was wondering just how big that rabbit was going to be. Who'd know if he shot a rabbit way out there? He thought he might. Decided to take the gun out and have it on the seat beside him. Had another beer. Nothing happening. He still wasn't sure what he'd do when he saw that rabbit. Bess had been out an awful long time, though, and Phil started to wonder. So he got out to pee, and when he turned back to the truck, there was Bess underneath it, sound asleep."

Eugene has this laugh that starts out deep and then goes high like a giggle when he's really tickled about something. My mother's is surprisingly low, nothing like her singing voice. Hers rolls along, more steady, and kind of balances Eugene's. Hearing them together, I feel happy and sorry for them both.

As dog stories go, this wasn't one of his best. But still, it's the first time all summer I've heard the sound of my mother laughing.

Killer

Mrs. Wells got the idea in the television room. She wasn't sure at first if she would actually try to say the words out loud, but then her idea took such a pleasing shape that it began to rise inside her, a bubble of anticipation. It traveled from the scuffed toes of her house slippers up through her legs and eventually settled in her chest, bobbing there as if it were a child's birthday balloon.

As the morning went on, Mrs. Wells drifted in and out of

sleep, held securely in the wheelchair by soft white bands that attached her wrists to the metal arms and a wider band that encircled her waist. When she woke from these short naps, she wouldn't be able to remember, and then they would show the picture on the screen again, the face of the pretty little girl with dark hair. Each time she saw the girl's face, Mrs. Wells could feel her idea inside, tugging at its string, urging her to tell them about Allen.

If anyone had been paying attention to her that morning, they might have noticed the hint of color creeping into her cheeks, the way she sat up in her chair instead of lolling over on one side as if she were half dead. In the hour before lunch, when the meds had lost their full force, Mrs. Wells began to rehearse what she would say, picturing the words, the up and down lines of the letters, the hard *K*.

After her stroke, Mrs. Wells had longed to talk again, fearing the way her silence allowed people to forget about her. But she'd hated the round, sad face of the speech therapist—that goon! He sighed so mournfully when she couldn't say a simple word like "bed." In the end, it was easier to take the meds and get parked in the television room. That's where she usually was when Allen came to visit.

Oh, they thought Allen was a wonderful son, the aides and the nurses. He came every Sunday afternoon at two and stayed until three-thirty. Then Wanda, the new girl, would fuss over her, tucking the cotton blanket around her knees, saying how nice she looked. This same Wanda forgot to comb Mrs. Wells's hair for days at a time, and when she finally remembered, it would be so full of tangles that the old woman had to grit her teeth to keep from crying out.

The little girl's picture appeared on the screen again. Mrs. Wells understood this much of the story: the child had been shot and killed at school the day before. She wanted to see the boy's face too, the face of the shooter, but they never showed it. She practiced the words again, just a whisper.

At last, Wanda shuffled in to take her to lunch. When the aide released the brake on her chair, Mrs. Wells nodded toward the TV and cleared her throat.

"My son," she said as loudly as she could, "is a killer."

Her revelation didn't come out right. The shakiness of her voice disappointed her deeply, and Mrs. Wells knew the word had sounded more like "h-h-hill-urr," like an old engine trying to start.

Even so, Wanda stopped the forward motion of her chair and took half a step around to look at the old woman's face. "Excuse me?" she said.

Mrs. Wells noticed a smear of something that might have been tomato sauce across the pocket of Wanda's white blouse and closed her eyes.

"Did you hear that?" Wanda asked the skinny aide nearby. She had Mrs. Wells's chair moving again.

"Yeah," the skinny girl said, maneuvering Mr. Faccio and his walker toward the door and glancing back at Mrs. Wells. "She's a weird one."

Wanda pushed her wheelchair up to the table and undid the wrist restraints, cut up her meat loaf into bite-size squares, and went off to fetch someone else. That was a funny thing about Wanda, so sloppy in every other way. When she cut Mrs. Wells's food, it looked as if her plate had been prepared by a geometry teacher.

Her left hand, the one she ate with, was nice and steady today, but Mrs. Wells had lost that excited, bubbly feeling. The day had gone flat, because Wanda hadn't really paid attention. She now willed her right hand to move toward Mrs. Riley, who sat next to her, and watched as it flopped onto her neighbor's arm.

"Yes, dear?" Mrs. Riley said, turning reluctantly from her lunch.

Mrs. Wells leaned closer and looked Mrs. Riley in the eye. "My son is a killer," she said, very calmly. Mrs. Wells thought she'd improved her delivery, though it still sounded a bit slippery.

She watched with satisfaction as a cloud of confusion passed over the woman's face, as her eyes filled with tears. Her heart lurched as Mrs. Riley looked down at the table.

"See this?" Mrs. Riley asked after a moment, pushing at the food on her plate. "See?" she said again, sniffing. "The juice from my green beans is running into my applesauce."

When Wanda came around with the afternoon meds, Mrs. Wells took her vitamin pill but pushed the tiny blue one, the one that made her sleepy, under her mattress pad. Even though she could sense a headache coming, Mrs. Wells felt a glimmer of her former excitement. Through the window of her room she could see the ice-crusted snow on the lawn and the bare, dripping trees. She heard her chickadees—their *dee, dee, dee*— and imagined them hopping from branch to branch in the bright sun.

Maybe, if the walkways were cleared, she could get Allen to take her out on Sunday. It was easier for him when the weather was fine, when he could push her wheelchair around and comment on the shrubbery. Mrs. Wells knew it was hard for Allen to sit in the lounge, trying to talk with her. When he brought a book to read out loud, she would doze off within a few minutes. And when she woke, she'd see Allen staring morosely into space, waiting for his time to be up. Once, recently, she'd wakened to find him with Wanda. The aide had brought him a cup of coffee, and they were sitting at a table on the far side of the lounge, chatting away. They might have been on a date.

Allen wasn't bad-looking, still slender and tall with thick gray hair combed back over his ears. To no one's surprise, his wife had left him just after their twenty-fifth wedding anniversary, taking the furniture and their almost grown twin daughters and moving to Nevada. Since then, for nearly twenty years, he had lived in his house alone. In rare moments of lucidity and kindness, Mrs. Wells wished for some happiness for her only child. But that was unlikely, she had considered, watching him with the lumpish Wanda. He had such bad judgment.

What *was* surprising about Allen was how well he'd done with his insurance business. Once his youthful resentment had been worn down by the dull routine of making a living, he had prospered—as if he'd been grateful to discover that life required nothing more of him than pleasant manners and a clean shirt.

Mrs. Wells heard the squeak of brisk rubber soles in the hallway, and in a minute one of the nurses stepped into her room. Ann Plunkett, R.N., her name tag said.

"Mrs. Wells, everything all right today?"

"Yes, good," Mrs. Wells replied. Ann Plunkett seemed to be

watching her suspiciously. Maybe she knew about the blue pill.

"I expect Allen will be coming this Sunday," the nurse said, absently straightening her blanket.

It sounded like another question, and Mrs. Wells nodded. She was beginning to feel little pulses of worry in her chest, where the good idea had been.

"We think the world of him, you know. He's such a gentleman."

"Yes," Mrs. Wells said again. "Good."

"Has something upset you?" the nurse persisted. "Something about Allen?"

Mrs. Wells looked out at the snow-crusted lawn. She didn't have enough words, she realized, to make them understand. "No," she said.

After filling the bedside cup with water, Ann Plunkett left the room. Mrs. Wells listened to her shoes squeaking back down the hall.

That Wanda, Mrs. Wells thought. She told the nurse, and now they think I'm cracked, on top of everything else. They felt sorry for Allen, not for her.

The face of the small girl from the TV floated into her mind, and then the face of the other child covered it up. Stevie.

The smell of the grocery store came back to her, the oily scent of wax on the oak floor when she and her husband polished it on Saturdays after closing. That was a lovely time, locking up the store Saturday evenings, and then—before Allen was born—going out to a roadhouse. Yes, that was something, the dim lights and cigarette smoke, the feel of her husband's arm around her waist when he pulled her onto the tiny dance floor, the sweat and perfume of all the dancers crowded together. Mrs. Wells loved the wind rushing through the window of their old pickup truck on the drive home, the cool wind off the river.

When she looked back, those days seemed less than a minute. Almost without noticing, she and her husband spent more and more time in the store. They got up before dawn and fell into bed at night, exhausted, even on Saturdays. They would have worked through Sundays too, but they understood the importance of making a good impression. So they slept until seven and went to church, and when they got home, Mrs. Wells would make smothered chicken for Sunday dinner. In the afternoon, she listened to the radio while she cleaned up the kitchen and mopped and dusted their small rented house. She could look through the front window and see her husband in the store across the street, where he would be stocking shelves and making out orders for the new week. They missed each other on those afternoons.

When Allen was four weeks old, Mrs. Wells carried him to the store and placed him in his bassinet in the back room. He slept there, surrounded by cartons and bins, mops and brooms. Fortunately, Allen was an easygoing baby, content with an occasional feeding and diaper change. Sometimes Mrs. Wells took him into the store so that customers could admire him.

Allen stood up for the first time when he reached for a box of cornflakes on the shelf and took his first steps when he tried to follow another child out the front door. After he started walking, Mrs. Wells put a playpen in the back room near the door, which she left open. He showed no interest in his stuffed clown or wooden blocks but preferred to stand, clutching the bars of the playpen and watching the comings and goings in the store. When a customer paused to speak to him, he would bounce excitedly and laugh, hoping to be picked up.

Mrs. Wells felt guilty on Allen's account, but what could she do? It was the Depression, after all.

"We're a small boat in a rough sea," her husband reminded her as they went over the books at the end of each week.

They were lucky to have no serious competition in Rownd's Point, only Tim Furman's nasty little grocery, where the produce turned yellow and keeled over in the wooden bins and the canned goods were furry with dust. Furman's real business was moonshine, everyone knew that. And so Wells Grocery stayed afloat.

Just before his third birthday, Allen climbed out of the playpen by himself, and after that his parents let him wander around the store. He would build forts from oatmeal boxes or rearrange the cigarette packs next to the cash register. On Saturdays, Mrs. Wells let him choose one of the penny candies, and he spent half the day deciding whether he wanted a licorice whip or a chocolate drop. She often thought of things that would be fun to do when they went home, like making fudge or building domino houses, but she was always so tired. When better times came, she and her husband agreed, they would hire someone to take her place in the store.

Once Allen started school, Mrs. Wells hoped he would make friends with some other boy and visit that boy's home in the afternoon. Maybe they would build a tree house in the boy's backyard and eat cookies made by the boy's mother. She liked to imagine him coming home for supper with stories to tell, his cheeks flushed from playing outdoors. But Allen always returned to the store, going straight to the back room to do his homework at the cluttered desk. When he finished, he would tie on one of the blue aprons and find something useful to do. He might sprinkle fresh sawdust behind the meat counter or help his mother size the eggs brought in by farmwives.

One afternoon when they were sorting eggs together—Allen must have been in second grade—Mrs. Wells said, "You're very good to help me, but wouldn't you rather be outside, playing with someone your own age?"

Allen looked up, startled. "Not really," he said.

"But who are your friends at school? Who do you play with at recess?"

Allen stared at the egg in his hand. "I don't know."

"Is there someone you like, though? Someone you might invite here after school?" Mrs. Wells was trying to remember the name of a boy in his class. Robert? Rupert?

Allen stroked the egg in his hand as if it were a live chick. "No one would come," he told her.

Sixty years later, it pained Mrs. Wells to remember the boy sitting beside her at the counter, wearing a storekeeper's apron, weighing the spotted brown eggs on the tin scale. Allen had been tall for his age, with long fingers and bony wrists. He needed a haircut, but Mrs. Wells liked the way his curls fell over his ears. What if she had put her arms around him, told him he was a wonderful boy? But mothers were different then, not like the ones on TV these days, saying "I love you" every five minutes.

What Mrs. Wells had done was leave Allen to sort the eggs by himself. She had gone into the toilet and latched the door and cried, sitting on the floor with her knees up under her chin. She and her husband had grown up in the northern part of the state, where their parents tended rocky farms, and after nine years in Rownd's Point they were still treated like strangers. Oh, people were friendly enough when they came into the store, but the Wellses never got invited anywhere. Mrs. Wells would overhear other women talking offhandedly about card parties and luncheons and anniversary suppers. After church she sometimes struck up a conversation with these same women, hoping that the pleasure of her company would be requested one day, but Mrs. Wells and her family remained in some way set apart.

It embarrassed her sometimes to see shy Allen becoming a show-off as he got older. He started filling customers' orders by himself and even made change or marked down their charges. She noticed how, when teenage girls came into the store, ten-year-old Allen would make a point of being seen lugging a heavy sack of flour over his shoulder or climbing up the ladder to fetch a jar of pimentos from the highest shelf.

Mrs. Wells especially liked two of the older girls, Alicia and Penny Brooks, because they joked with Allen in a sisterly way. They pretended to be stumped when he asked "Why did the fireman wear red suspenders?" and laughed when he told them the answer. Often they brought their baby brother along and let Allen watch him while they went around the store to find what they needed. Their father, Stephen Brooks, was the doctor for Rownd's Point and Tenney's Landing, and kept an office in each town. Both parents struck Mrs. Wells as a bit snooty. Every day after school the sisters brought in a list written out by Mrs. Brooks, who never set foot in the store.

When the war came, the older sister, Alicia, one year out of high school, had a fiancé who went off to the army. She told Allen, then eleven, that he would have to be her boyfriend until the war was over. Penny said that wasn't fair, Allen had to be her boyfriend too.

"Two beautiful redheads fighting over you," Mr. Wells remarked from time to time. "What's your secret, son?"

Allen would blush with pleasure and look at his shoes.

Mr. Wells escaped the draft because of his poor eyes, and in spite of rationing, Wells Grocery began to thrive. They decided to add a small hardware section in the back and talked about putting in a soda fountain one day. Mr. Wells bought a secondhand Ford sedan and drove it to Pittsburgh on Friday mornings to pick up specialty grocery items for the weekend.

When he bought the gun, a nickel-plated revolver with a dull black handle, Mrs. Wells wondered if her husband was trying to make up for missing out on the war. She had grown up with rifles and shotguns left around the house as casually as jackets—her father and brothers were hunters—but she didn't like the look of this stubby thing.

"It looks mean," she said to her husband when he showed it to her.

"It's supposed to look mean," he said, laughing. "That's why we have it."

"And who are we trying to scare?"

"There's a war on," he said importantly. "And strange people moving around. It's good to be prepared."

Strange people moving around? Mrs. Wells supposed this was an idea he'd picked up in Pittsburgh.

While Mr. Wells took Allen out behind the store and showed him how to shoot, Mrs. Wells stayed inside, listening to the bullets exploding and the *pings* when they hit cans. Later, Mr. Wells made a point of showing her how to switch off the safety and placed the gun in the drawer under the cash register, shoving it behind a stack of envelopes.

"There," he said, clapping Allen on the shoulder.

For years Mrs. Wells had recalled these details vividly, replaying them as if they were scenes from a movie she didn't like but couldn't stop watching. After the stroke, these scenes had disappeared. But day by day, as she slipped the blue pills out of sight, here they came again—darting around the blunted edges of her memory.

Stevie's face, that started it. Like his sisters, he was a redhead, but he was only five and still had that tender, velvety look of very young children. Now she could see him coming into the store that morning with Alicia, wearing a shortsleeved shirt and cotton pants with the cuffs rolled up above his ankles. His feet were bare, his toes coated with dust from the unpaved street. Mrs. Wells hoped he wouldn't pick up a splinter walking across the floor. He asked his sister if he could get a root beer.

It was a Friday, so Mrs. Wells and Allen were minding the store. She recalled how she'd asked Allen to help Stevie find his soda in the cold case while she went back to the meat counter with Alicia to slice a pound of chipped ham, extra thin, the way Mrs. Brooks liked it. As she watched the pink slices, shavings really, piling up beneath the round blade, she pictured the Brooks family sitting down to lunch. She imagined them at a large kitchen table covered with a flowered cloth, helping themselves to chipped ham sandwiches with tomatoes and mustard and tiny pickles from a glass dish.

Mrs. Wells remembered someone screaming at the same time she heard the shot and Alicia running to the front of the store, dropping her mother's list and a handful of coins where she'd stood waiting for the lunch meat. Mrs. Wells ran too, barely glancing at Allen by the cash register, still clutching the gun in his two hands. Up front, the smell of gunpowder stung her nose. She paused for a moment on the threshold. Stevie had tried to get away, and his sister was kneeling where he'd fallen facedown in the street. Alicia was bent over him, wailing—an eerie sound like nothing Mrs. Wells had ever heard before. She saw the blood pooling beneath his chest and soaking into the ground.

It was Mrs. Wells who went to get the doctor, praying as she ran that she would find him in his Rownd's Point office. "Your son's been shot!" she cried as she rushed in, ignoring a waiting patient and pounding on the door of the examining room.

Dr. Brooks left a man half dressed on the table and raced off in his white coat. When Mrs. Wells caught up to him, he had reached Stevie and was turning him onto his back. Mrs. Wells could see the bullet hole in Stevie's shirt, right over his heart. Dr. Brooks felt for a pulse in the neck, then the wrist.

"Nothing," he said, smoothing his son's hair back and then brushing his eyelids closed. Alicia had gone quiet. She was holding Stevie's hand and stroking his palm, which was scraped from his fall in the dirt.

For years after, Mrs. Wells was haunted by the memory of Stevie's hands, the soft palms scratched and dirty, the way his fingers curled so that she could see the pearly disks of his fingernails. Somehow he had run away, made it down the steps and into the street, turned toward home. She watched as Stephen Brooks lifted his boy's small body and carried him the rest of the way.

She had no memory of going back into the store and facing Allen. Maybe she took the gun away from him, or maybe he had put it down by then. She remembered her husband returning and his confusion at finding the sheriff's car and a knot of people out front. A newspaper reporter from Tenney's Landing came and asked questions until the sheriff sent him away. She remembered the blank, stunned look on Allen's face when the sheriff asked him to tell what happened, the way he kept repeating, "I only wanted to show it to him." She wondered if Allen would be arrested. He was barely twelve.

Finally, the sheriff decided to put it down as an "accidental shooting." He didn't even take the gun away but handed it to Mrs. Wells after he'd looked it over.

Of course Stevie's death was accidental, Mrs. Wells told herself.

She had heard Allen and her husband talking the night of the shooting. She was half asleep on the living room couch, numbed by the sedative Dr. Brooks had, to her astonishment, thought to send over. She could hear their voices in the kitchen.

"Just tell me," her husband said for the third or fourth time. He sounded more weary than angry.

Allen mumbled something she couldn't make out.

"How do you shoot someone in the chest without meaning to?"

"He said the gun wasn't real," Allen replied finally.

Mrs. Wells heard that clearly.

"I don't understand," her husband said. "What were you doing with the gun in the first place?"

"I wanted to show it to him."

Mrs. Wells could hear a chair scraping on the floor and then the creak of linoleum as her husband paced back and forth between the table and the stove.

"You wanted to show it to him, and when you did, he said it wasn't real?"

"Yes."

"So you shot him?"

"I didn't mean to," Allen said again.

"What did you mean to do?" Her husband's voice was cold, flat.

"Scare him, I guess."

What she heard next made her stomach clench. It was the sound of her husband dragging Allen out of his chair and pushing him across the room. She heard her son hit the wall and then the ripe, fleshy sounds of slaps and punches.

"I thought the safety was on." Every time Allen said that, her husband hit him again.

"Stupid," Mr. Wells called him. "Stupid, stupid."

When she finally heard her husband going upstairs, Mrs. Wells knew Allen was probably down on the kitchen floor. She should have gone to him, but she wasn't able to move from the couch until later. Right then she hated her son, and not only for killing Stevie. She could already see their lives, all their hard work, falling to pieces.

She woke in the night and noticed the band of light under the kitchen door and couldn't understand at first why she wasn't in bed. Mrs. Wells got up from the couch and moved slowly toward the light and pushed the door open, afraid of what she might find. She was surprised to see Allen sitting at the table, asleep with his head on his arms, as if he had drifted off while reading a book. As she pulled the light cord, she wanted desperately to believe that everything might be all right in the morning.

The gun was there on the shelf in the hall closet where she'd left it that afternoon. Closing the front door quietly behind her and starting off down the street, Mrs. Wells jammed it into the pocket of her sweater. She walked past the store and turned the corner and saw the river swelling in the starlight. Without thinking, she hurried to the water's edge and took her sweater off and hurled it in, gasping as the arms flew up for an instant before disappearing below the surface. When she turned away, there was the whole town spread out along the bend in the river, every window dark. Surely, she thought, she was not the only one awake.

The morning of Stevie's funeral, the Wellses closed the store, but they didn't go to the service. The minister had advised them not to. Instead, he set up a meeting between the two families in his office the following week.

It didn't surprise Mrs. Wells when Dr. Brooks came alone and told them his wife wasn't feeling well, but the change in him was shocking. She'd heard of people's hair turning white overnight, but she had never believed it. Now here was Dr. Brooks, dressed in a rumpled suit, his sandy hair as white as chicken feathers.

Stephen Brooks listened patiently, his hands clasped around one knee, and nodded as Allen told his story. This time, Allen mentioned the safety right away, how he thought it was on.

He made it sound as if they'd been playing a game. As Mrs. Wells watched the doctor questioning her son, she realized how much Stevie had looked like his father. Stevie had told her once that his real name was Alexander, and Alicia had laughed, saying it was true but nobody could remember his real name.

When Allen finished his explanations, the small room was quiet for a minute. And then Allen, who had been coached by his father, looked at Dr. Brooks and said, "I hope you can find it in your heart to forgive me."

To Mrs. Wells, it sounded stagy, but the doctor rose from his chair and touched Allen briefly on the arm. "That's something I'll have to work on," he said.

The following day, a Monday, Mrs. Wells and her husband closed the store after lunch and drove Allen north to her parents' farm. She couldn't bear the thought of Allen hanging around the store all summer, the customers staring at him. And with her brothers grown and gone, her parents could use his help.

Mrs. Wells wrote every week, reminding Allen to be good and say his prayers. She often wondered what it would be like for him, lying in one of the upstairs bedrooms of the farmhouse at night, knowing he had killed someone. She tried to be cheerful in her short letters, including a little news—such as the arrival of their shiny red Coca-Cola cooler—when she could. She didn't mention the customers who stayed away. None of the Brooks family ever came back, and several others, too, had started driving downriver to the Tenney's Landing store to buy their groceries.

Still, the routine of her workday was soothing. Mrs. Wells

liked being in the store, keeping everything tidy, watching the street through the tall windows at the front. They were managing to make ends meet, and surely, in time, they would be forgiven for Allen's mistake.

Sundays were hard for her, partly because Mr. Wells had stopped going to church, and she had to go alone. When the service ended and people greeted one another, then she knew the full weight of their disapproval. Women who chatted with her in the store during the week couldn't quite see her on Sunday morning. Dr. Brooks, guiding his wife down the aisle with a hand on her elbow, was the only one to nod and say hello. To Mrs. Brooks, she was utterly invisible.

That Labor Day weekend, when she and her husband went to bring Allen back, she was struck by the changes of two months. Allen had grown an inch, at least. Mrs. Wells noted his sunburned arms, his new muscles. She listened with pleasure as he talked about hoeing corn, carrying water to the wilting tomato plants, learning to drive the tractor—all the things that had burdened her as a girl. Allen was happy to see her, she could tell, but he and his father remained cool toward each other.

Allen returned to his old routine, coming straight from his seventh-grade classes and starting his homework in the back room. He still wanted to work in the store, but now he avoided the customers and was likely to stay out back, trimming produce or washing bottles. Mrs. Wells remembered the things she and her girlfriends used to get up to at his age, like stealing cigarette papers from their fathers and trying to smoke dried corn silk. Once she'd singed her eyelashes lighting a corn silk cigarette. Later, when she'd looked in the mirror, her lashes were just powdery ash and fell off when she flicked them with her finger. She had kissed a boy named Jeremy Watkins, who pushed a half-sucked Red Hot into her mouth with his tongue. Everyone had laughed when she spit it out, a sticky red ball flying into the school yard snow. Solitary Allen, she couldn't imagine his school days.

One afternoon in late October, Mrs. Wells noticed something odd as Allen waved hello and ducked into the back. When she went to see about him, she found him soaking wet and muddy. He was bent over slightly, leaning against the desk and hugging himself, trembling all over. She was about to touch his back when he groaned in pain, and she pulled her hand away.

"What's happened to you?"

"They spit on me," he told her, ashamed. "They kicked me."

She lifted his sweater and saw the painful blue marks of fresh bruises, the red welts, one perfect heel print just below his ribs. It would have been some of the Brooks cousins, she guessed, the high school boys with their heavy boots. Maybe they had taken him off somewhere, or maybe they had done it in plain sight. No one would have stopped them.

Mrs. Wells put her husband's jacket around Allen's shoulders and took him out the back door. He held on to her arm as they crossed the street and went up the steps to the house. Inside, she ran a warm bath for him and laid clean pajamas out on his bed. She let him sleep for a while and later brought him a bowl of soup and a plate of crackers on a tray. Even as she pitied him, Mrs. Wells couldn't help thinking he had it coming.

By the following summer, they had sold Wells Grocery and made arrangements to buy a country store, a feed and grain store, close to where her parents lived. Mr. Wells hired a man with a truck to move their belongings, and they left Rownd's

Point the day after school was out. It was still early morning when they set off in the car, driving along the river. Looking at the fog swirling delicately over the brown water, Mrs. Wells could feel her neck prickling when they passed the spot where she'd thrown the gun in. Strange, she thought, that her husband had never once mentioned it.

They crossed the bridge a few miles upriver, and when they got to the top of the first big hill, she could see Rownd's Point below in the distance. Fifteen years down there, and not a single person sorry to see them go.

Mrs. Wells, bathed and combed, waits in the sunroom for Allen to arrive. She has been off her meds for six days now, a secret.

When Wanda comes to check on her, Mrs. Wells sees that she's wearing a clean uniform and pink lipstick. Such effort on the part of the frumpy aide makes Mrs. Wells slightly nauseated. Allen, of course, might feel otherwise. She's trying to remember something he said last week, a special thing about this Sunday, and she fervently hopes it does not involve Wanda.

The real question on her mind is whether Wanda will mention the word "killer." Mrs. Wells thinks not, she hopes not. What did Wanda hear, after all?

Up until her husband died, it was understood between them that Allen had ruined their lives. He was a hard boy to love, especially after he started high school and got in with some of those wild country fellows. Her son would come home at all hours, stinking of beer, and in the mornings, fixing his breakfast, she would see his skinned knuckles, his bloodshot eyes.

Then, for reasons she couldn't know, Allen stopped running around. Though his father had hoped to make him a partner in the feed store, Allen began selling insurance. A few years later, he married that string bean, that temperamental Mindy.

Mrs. Wells sees Allen walking up from the parking lot at last, and feels a flash of panic when she notices the girl with him. At first she thinks it's one of the Brooks girls, the younger one, Penny. But how could that be? And then it comes to her. It's his granddaughter. Allen is bringing her to visit; that's what he told her about last week.

There's something about Allen's walk, the way he lists slightly to the left, that makes him look as if he's always heading against a strong wind. Mrs. Wells first noticed this many years ago, not long after they'd moved back north, when she saw Allen and her father walking together across a hayfield. It was nearly sunset, and they had been out haying all day.

"My boy," she'd said, "looks crooked."

Her mother, standing beside her on the farmhouse porch, had merely waved at the two approaching over the stubbled ground before going inside to warm their supper.

Now Mrs. Wells watches the granddaughter laugh as she takes Allen's hand and skips along the walkway beside him. He looks like a nice grandpa in his thick gray sweater and red wool scarf, his rubber boots. Even at a distance, Mrs. Wells can see the look of anticipation on her son's face, as if he is bringing her the most extraordinary gift. The little girl swings his hand into the air and lets go of it, then catches it again, leaning close to him as they near the steps of the nursing home.

Jordan's Stand

The bells of Jordan Eastman's alarm clock cut through the darkness. I am out of bed at once, warm feet on the cold floor. Drawing the curtain aside, I see a scattering of stars in the sky, the silvery patches where frost has settled on the tops of fence posts. I find my clothes by touch, where I arranged them on the chair last night, and dress in the dark. The silk long johns are cool and slippery against my skin, and I proceed as Jordan has advised, adding a layer of cotton and one of wool. "It's the cold you have to worry about, being still like that," he told me yesterday afternoon. I could see that it made him uncomfortable, advising a woman how to dress. Then he pressed the clock into my hands—an ancient windup one with two brass bells on top. I go down to the kitchen for coffee, already nervous with anticipation.

Stepping outside a few minutes later, I'm met by a sharp tingling up my nose and across my cheeks. The moon is so bright that I slip the small flashlight into my pocket. Now I have only the rifle—Jordan's old Model 94 Winchester—to carry, and I balance its weight in the crook of my arm. The frozen ground scrapes lightly underfoot as I head into the trees, so I try to walk more quietly, even though the stand is well over a mile away. At the crest of the first ridge I stop and look back to find the steep roof of Jordan's house. Snug in the lee of the hill, the house is dark. Jordan will be asleep next to Marie, missing the opening day of deer season for the first time since he was a boy.

The moonlight spreads deep pools of shadow through the trees, and I feel like a figure in a fairy tale, half expecting some creature to appear in my path and lead me astray. Every few yards I must stop and place my hand on a solid tree trunk to get my bearings. Finally, I cross the corner of the open meadow and circle around the line of trees on the far side, keeping my scent off the deer trail, staying downwind. I reach overhead to slide the rifle onto the wooden platform within the arms of a tall pine and climb up the four boards nailed to its trunk. Standing on the platform, I see that the woods in front of me are still, bare branches gray in the waning moonlight. I press the tiny button that illuminates my watch face to check the time. It is eighteen minutes before five. I imagine the deer curled in sleep, noses resting on hind legs, in their beds of dry grass farther up the hill.

I'm rigid as a sentry, left hand curled around the Winchester's barrel, wondering what James would think if he could see me here, when I remember Jordan telling me to stay relaxed. "You should *sit* in the stand," he said, "and stay loose, otherwise you'll lose your reflexes." So far I have followed his instructions—part common sense and part superstition—to the letter. I doused the bottoms of my boots with vixen's urine from a small plastic bottle, nearly choking on the first whiff of its thick smell. I hung my wool jacket and pants and down vest out on the clothesline for two days to rid them of human scent. Jordan doesn't believe in scopes or buck lure, so I'm using neither. "Use your head," he advised. "Your eye, your brain, your trigger finger, preferably in that order." Jordan is seventy-eight years old and tormented by arthritis. He fights back every day, but this year he has decided not to hunt. I guess he has some faith in me, his neighbor of three years, for he has given me his tree stand and loaned me his rifle and his clock. I sit down to wait.

Jordan didn't bother to hide his disappointment when he drove over to meet me that first day. "Where's your man?" he asked as soon as he had introduced himself.

"He's dead," I told him. I hadn't talked to anyone in a couple of weeks.

"Kinda young to be a widow, aren't you?" Jordan said, looking me up and down. Then he glanced at the Kansas license plate on my car and wanted to know what I was doing in Pennsylvania.

"Good question," I said, smiling at him, having no ready answer.

He kept on looking at me, so I told him about my cousin Marcia, who had sent me postcards from her summer camp in Pennsylvania when we were kids, and how I was jealous because I only went to day camp, where we made jewelry boxes out of Popsicle sticks. "So when I came unmoored in Kansas, I was kind of naturally drawn here," I told him, finishing up. "Just drifted northeast," I added, "like a cold front."

"Unmoored, huh?" Jordan said, wandering off. He walked around the outside of the house, scratching the back of his neck.

I'd found the little farmhouse with six acres, plus or minus, in an ad on the Internet. "Three miles from historic Tenney's Landing," the ad read. "Rent with option to buy." Though I hadn't yet figured out the town's historical significance, I liked the sound of it. I liked having an option.

Before he left, Jordan squinted at the porch, which was listing away from the front of the house, and told me who to call to have firewood delivered. He said he would send his wife over.

I figured that was the end of it, but a few days later Jordan and Marie arrived together. She went straight to the kitchen, carrying a loaf of brown bread wrapped in a dish towel and a crock of baked beans. "Homemade. I make the molasses too," she declared, setting the food down on the table. Jordan crawled under the porch, and we could hear him banging and tapping beneath our feet. When he finally emerged, brushing dirt from his sleeves, he announced that he'd have to replace one of the sills.

"It's no small job, either," he said. "Maybe I can get a couple of my nephews to give me a hand."

The firewood was delivered, cut to stove length, a daunting hill of it at the side of the house, and I set about stacking it early one morning. I had just stepped back to consider my new woodpile after finishing about half a cord, when I heard Jordan's truck pull into the driveway.

"What are you doing?" he called, ambling over.

Now, I thought it was perfectly obvious what I was doing, so I stood there silently, waiting to see if he could find some fault with it.

He could. "You don't want the wood so far from the house," he said. "Why would you shovel a path out this far?" Noticing my blank face, he said, "Snow. You never get snow in Kansas?" He started demolishing my neat stack and tossing logs in the wheelbarrow. "If you put it around here by the kitchen door," he called over his shoulder, "you can get to it easy. And the wood will give you some extra windbreak at the back of the house—which you can use, by the way."

I followed with an armload, wishing he'd go back home, but he persisted in demonstrating his several theories of wood stacking. He was especially fussy about what he called the "three-part end columns," and made me do mine over several times, until all the logs were evenly spaced and level. After an hour of this, I began to suspect that he was making up most of his firewood lore on the spot. And when he claimed that his elbow was bothering him and sat down nearby to watch—to make sure I didn't do anything wrong—I wondered if I was being had. By the middle of January, though, with a couple of feet of snow on the ground and the wind rattling my back door, I saw his point.

I hear a rustling in the underbrush and raise the rifle to my shoulder. In the dim light, I see a squirrel scurry across to the base of one of the raggedy apple trees, and my breath trails off in a cloud of white as I lower the gun. Jordan's tree stand is situated at the northern corner of an abandoned orchard. The apples have grown bumpy and spotted, a faded yellow-green. A low stone wall runs through the woods along one side of the orchard, an old wall with stones worn by rain and snow. When we walked up here in the summer, Jordan showed me the cellar hole, overgrown with a thick tangle of vine. "Where these pines are was a hayfield a hundred years ago," he told me. "And right there, that's my stand," he said proudly, pointing out a weathered wooden platform in the largest tree.

The gun business started one afternoon a couple of summers ago. I was in their kitchen with Marie, waiting for the first jars of green beans to finish in the canner, when Jordan poked his head in the door and told me to come outside. He'd set up some bottles on a sawhorse behind the barn and said we were going to shoot at them.

"It's time you learned how to use a gun," he told me.

"Why?" I wondered, glancing back toward the house to find Marie watching us through the window.

"It comes in useful," he said. "And you can go hunting with me."

"Look, Jordan," I said, "I've never even touched a gun before."

"Watch this." He settled the smooth wooden stock into his shoulder and sighted down the long barrel of his shotgun. He squeezed the trigger, and at the same moment I heard the explosion, one of the bottles flew apart in a bright shower of glass.

All right, I thought, as he passed the gun to me, no harm in shooting at bottles. Even though he'd warned me, I wasn't prepared for the kick when I fired, and tears sprang to my eyes.

"Oh, now, don't cry," Jordan said. "Hurt a bit, did it?"

"No," I said. "Well, it did, but I'm not really crying."

Jordan went up to the house and came back with a heavy wool vest. "Put this on," he said. "You need some padding."

When Marie came out to watch, my T-shirt was soaked with sweat under the vest. "Don't let him bully you," she said, looking at Jordan.

"She's doing fine," he said. "She's hit two already."

There I was—too hot, standing in a haze of gunpowder with Marie and Jordan smiling at me—and all of a sudden I felt at home. Although I am nearly forty years younger than they, I think my widowhood draws us closer, as if the confluence of grief and old age were inevitable.

The one time Jordan and I talked about James, we were partridge hunting together. We'd been out for more than an hour, walking a parallel course through the woods without spotting any birds, and had stopped to rest at the top of a hill. That was my first time hunting, and it was a relief to stop looking for something to kill and to set the gun down.

"Don't you want to get married again?" Jordan asked me, right out of the blue.

"I don't know," I said. "I can't even think about it right now."

He sighed heavily, looking me in the eye. "You never will, either, if you keep stumping around the woods with an old geezer like me."

"Who's an old geezer?" I began, but Jordan interrupted with another question.

"You admired your husband, did you?"

I told Jordan some things about James then, the easy things—that he had one blue eye and one green eye, that he liked dill pickles, that when I met him he had a cat named Mister Baggins, who surprised us one night by giving birth to four kittens in the laundry hamper. I told him that James would be having a fine time right now if he were with us.

"You must be lonesome," Jordan said. He cleared his throat. "Marie and I know a nice fellow, name of Will, that we thought of inviting round to supper next time you're over. He's about your age—a bit shy, maybe."

I looked down at my hands, marked with little scratches from pushing through the brambles, and remembered the awkward good-bye hug I'd given James at our front door, the way the sunlight through the side pane lit up his hair. "I'd rather you didn't."

"There's my nephew Gene," Jordan said, as if he hadn't heard me. "He's a sweetheart, but probably a bit too old for you. He's in over his head with some professor's wife, anyway. The professor took off, mind you, leaving the wife and two little girls. But I'd say that's a doomed project."

I'd met Eugene Eastman a couple of times. He was a tall, awkward fellow in his forties, somehow charming in spite of himself. I remembered seeing him once at the gas station, helping two girls put air in their bicycle tires. I'd assumed at the time they were his daughters, the way they joked with him as they set off on their bikes.

After a few minutes, Jordan went on. "Marie and I have

had good luck. There was one time of trouble, though, when I decided to make some money. Marie was dead set against it."

He paused, and I thought he'd finished—it was a habit of his, laying out a story line and then not telling it for days or maybe weeks. But this time he continued. "I had to lie about my age," he said, raising his bushy eyebrows. "Lopped off five years so they'd take me." He told me then about working on the interstate highways in the 1960s. Their three children were big enough by then to help Marie with the farm chores, and they had talked it over, sitting late at the supper table.

"Marie couldn't see any good in it," he said. "Told me I'd only be helping to ruin the state, that kind of thing. We already had the turnpike, and why did we want to make it any easier for trouble to find us? She was fierce, I have to say." But he'd already made up his mind. "I just kept telling her those highways would get built whether I took part or not, said we needed the money to keep the farm up. I was restless, you know, afraid of missing out on something. So I signed on with one of the highway crews, got myself a pair of steel-toed boots and a yellow hard hat."

He traveled up and down the state, following the tree fellers, the drillers, the dynamiters, flattening the land from the high, protected seat of a bulldozer. It made him feel like a giant, he said. Most weeks he would be gone from Sunday night until Friday afternoon, sleeping in run-down motels, eating in diners. The evenings were hard. Usually he'd buy a newspaper and read it in his room until he got sleepy; sometimes he'd join the other men for a drink or two. When he got home on Fridays, Marie would be standoffish. He'd see that first glimmer of happiness in her eyes when he kissed her hello, then she'd tamp it down and get busy with the milking or fixing supper. Not even his first paycheck, which Jordan dropped triumphantly on the table, made her smile.

From early spring until Christmas, Jordan worked on the highway, then they laid his crew off for the winter. He noticed that certain things had slipped at home; his milkers didn't gleam the way they used to, shingles had blown off the barn roof and let the rain in. He spent the winter trying to set things right.

Marie had hoped he wouldn't go back to the highway the next spring, but Jordan packed his bag again as soon as he got the foreman's call. There was a moment one evening that second summer, Jordan said, when he climbed down from his bulldozer and looked back over a stretch of land they'd been clearing. When he saw the raw earth churned up and the trees with their roots in the air, the farmhouses and barns now so close to the roadway, he wondered for the first time what they were doing. Still, he stayed with the crew for three years and fattened his account at the local bank. With his last check he bought Marie a gold brooch that she hid in a bureau drawer beneath her nightgowns. "It was probably ten years before she wore it," he said.

"If I had it to do over?" Jordan concluded, anticipating my question. "Hard to say." He stretched and yawned, as if the story had tired him. "Change comes round, whether it comes on the interstate highway or some other route. I don't really think about it anymore—it's just there." He stood up stiffly, using his gun to hoist himself. "Come on," he said, heading toward a grove of poplars. I watched his back, noticing the slight stoop of his shoulders, the way he favored his right leg.

He missed his children, I knew. One by one they'd left on the interstate, looking for bigger lives. He had two sons in Scranton, a daughter in Akron, seven or eight grandchildren he didn't see very often.

We hadn't gone more than a hundred yards when we flushed a pair of birds. They tore the air with an excited whir of wings, and without thinking I drew a bead on the one flying left and fired. My bird and Jordan's fell at the same moment, landing with a *whump* in the dry leaves.

"I'll be damned!" Jordan said, and when I turned to look at him, he was grinning at me. He'd been telling me for weeks how hard it is to shoot a bird in flight, how the odds are pretty much in the bird's favor. I lifted mine by its feet and ran my hand over its feathers. I could feel the heat in its breast, but the eyelids, a cold gray, were already shut.

I carried the birds in a canvas bag slung across my shoulder, and as we went deeper into the woods the melancholy rhythm of their weight made me think of James and the porcupines. James had told me how, when he was sixteen and driving his father's pickup home from school one afternoon, he'd come across a pair of porcupines in the road. One of them had been hit by a car and was still alive, barely. A trickle of blood ran from its nose, and its sides were heaving with the effort to breathe. Its mate was trying to drag it off the road. When he stopped and got out of the truck, he realized that the sounds of pain were made not by the male, who had been hit, but by the female trying to save him.

"The only thing I could do," James said, "was get my father's rifle out of the truck and shoot him, the only kindness." He carried the dead porcupine away from the road so the female wouldn't get hit too and stood nearby for a few minutes, watching as she pushed at her mate with her nose and paws. "She was whimpering then, and she must have known he was dead, but it looked like she was still trying to make him get up."

James had looked away when he told me the last part. This was back before we were married, before we knew each other very well. It was easy to imagine him at sixteen, though, and as I put my arms around him for the first time, I thought to myself, I love this man.

Jordan's gun went off somewhere to my right, and I hurried to catch up with him. "Never get out of sight, or at least hearing," he'd told me when we set off that day. "It's important to know where the other person is." Jordan got two more partridges that afternoon, and I flushed another one but missed it, firing low.

While we were plucking the birds on the back porch, Jordan drew out one of the long barred tail feathers and stuck it in the band of my green hat, thereafter my hunting hat. "Jaunty," he said. Billie, Jordan's ancient hound, watched us from her bed in the corner and thumped her tail against the floor. "Billie's retired," Jordan had said when I'd asked if she was coming with us. "She stays home now and waits till the birds are cooked." The smell of Marie's plum sauce drifted through the back door. We could hear her opening and closing cupboard doors, humming a nondescript tune. In a couple of hours we'd be sitting down to a small feast, and the thought gave a holiday glow to the October evening and helped to ease the sorrow of killing.

I have been watching the sky lighten, the darkness seeping away like ink washed from a plate. The thinnest edge of sunrise, a deep bluish orange, hovers at the lip of the horizon. I've been sitting in this tree long enough to feel a part of it, an oddly shaped appendage where birds might nest. My fingers brush the bulge in my jacket, the pocket of extra cartridges, even though Jordan has told me that I need only one, one perfectly aimed shot. I have come a long way to be here in Jordan's place. He will probably be awake now and thinking of me in his tree stand. He must, I imagine, wish that I were someone else, one of his grandsons or nephews, perhaps. I am an odd choice to succeed him, and yet he has taken to me with good humor, as it is habit to use what comes to hand.

I would like to do the same—though mostly I feel unable to act, as if in crossing from my past life into the future, I were caught in between. On the one side, regret; on the other, dread. When I saw him last, James was all fire and impatience, waiting at the door. We'd been avoiding an argument for a few weeks—more than an argument—and we went through the motions of farewell, relieved by the sound of the taxi drawing up to the curb.

"Have you got Celeste?" I called down the walk just as he opened the taxi door.

"Of course I do," he said, patting the front pocket of his big blue pack, smiling at last.

He was flying to Montana to meet his friend Pierce for their annual climb. James had told me about it as we were cleaning up after a party for his birthday. "By the way, Pierce and I have a climb date," he said, filling the sink with hot water and soap. "We're going to Montana this year." He washed about a dozen glasses, rinsing each carefully, before he said, "We're going up the Iverson Glacier."

I dried a few glasses and put them in the cupboard. "*By the way*, you're going to climb the Iverson Glacier?"

"Right."

One thing I know is you can't just stroll up the Iverson Glacier whenever you feel like it. The climbing season is short, and you have to apply for a permit, which isn't easy to get. "When are you going?"

"Four weeks," James said.

"How long have you known?"

"A while. I mean, Pierce has been making all the arrangements from out there." He picked up some more glasses from the table. "I didn't say anything before, because I wasn't sure we'd be able to get a permit this year." Finally, he looked at me. "There's no reason to worry," he said. "It's as safe as any other climb."

"That certainly puts my mind at ease." I watched him at the sink, shoulders set, head cocked defensively. My James, who cried over helpless porcupines, who tended our garden and baked blackberry pies and liked to brush my hair. Every so often he had to leave all that behind and enter some pure risk zone—as if that were the only way everyday life made sense.

Over the next month, waiting for the climb date, we were uneasy together and got in each other's way. The morning he left, I found James hunched over a cup of coffee in the kitchen, looking morose, and when I touched his shoulder, he pulled away before he could catch himself. Watching his taxi make the right-hand turn at the end of our street, I was relieved to be alone.

That lasted about a day. When the phone rang in the

evening nine days later, I knew it would be James calling from the ranger station at the base of the mountain to say he'd be home soon. I could already picture him coming up the walk, sunburned and fresh, and ached to see him again. A strange voice said my name, and it took a few seconds to realize that it was Pierce's brother, David. He told me that James and Pierce hadn't made it back to the station that day but not to worry. There were storms in the mountains, and they would be holed up somewhere, waiting for the bad weather to pass. He would call back the next day to let me know what was happening, he said, or more likely James would call himself. David sounded confident.

I made myself a cup of tea and sat down with James's climbing albums. He'd grown up in Bellingham, Washington, and his parents had taken him on his first climb when he was only nine or ten. I looked through the familiar photographs, stopping when I reached my favorite—taken six years ago, shortly before we were married. It's James and Pierce in the Andes, although you can see nothing but blue sky and a snow-field in the background. They are vivid in bright blue and red anoraks and matching wool baseball caps, their noses and lips smeared with a thick white film of NosKote, their eyes hidden behind reflective sunglasses. They are laughing, and I wonder if the photographer has made a joke or if they're giddy from lack of oxygen. The head of Celeste the elephant queen peers above the unzipped pocket of James's red anorak. Celeste is new, a birthday present from me, and her trunk curves up at a perky angle.

I slept badly that night, waking several times because I thought the telephone had rung. In the morning I switched on the answering machine and dashed to the store for a bottle of wine to go with the welcome-home dinner. When I got back, I turned the ringer up to full volume before I went into the yard to cut some lilacs. One of James's students called from the university in the afternoon to ask about his grade in the introductory biology course. I wrote down his name and number and assured him that James would call back in a couple of days. While I heated leftover spaghetti for dinner, someone called offering a discount on magazine subscriptions. "For God's sake," I said and hung up. I watched the evening news on television while I ate and later fell asleep on the couch. The telephone woke me around eleven. David's voice again, telling me that the storms hadn't let up, that the ranger station would send a helicopter out in the morning to find James and Pierce if the weather cleared. "They'll be fine," he said. "They know what to do."

Less than two days later I was in the air with David, listening to the jangle of keys as he shifted them ceaselessly from one hand to the other. "Orange," he kept saying, looking down through the side window. "It's orange. Come on." I wanted to ask him to be quiet, but I just watched the white snowfields beneath us, afraid to blink. I understood all the bright colors now. Before, when I'd watched James pack his gear for a trip with Pierce, I'd thought they were only cheerful, the green-and-yellow braided nylon ropes, the red socks and shoelaces and hats. David started telling the pilot again how Pierce and James never took foolish chances, they were too experienced.

We'd gone up in the early afternoon, about an hour after I arrived, with a heavy load of fuel. As we flew back and forth over the glacier, the small plane vibrated constantly, and the smell of fumes filled the cabin. It got confusing, scanning the gleaming white surface below, uncertain where the sky was, the mountaintops. When I finally sat back in the canvas seat, trying to relax and rest my eyes for a minute, I could feel my entire body humming. Suddenly David grabbed my arm, and I jolted upright to see movement below. It was a herd of elk, startled by the sound of the plane. They fanned out behind the leader, churning up a cloud of snow as they ran. Even so, we could see the long running shadows they cast and the shadow of the plane looming over them.

"That would have been a beautiful sight," David said.

"It's getting late." The pilot turned to look at us. "I don't like flying so close in with the dark coming." He banked and started to ascend. "We can come back in the morning," he added, as David and I shifted in our seats and craned our necks to see beneath the plane, alert for the orange tent, for any flash of color.

The ranger had gone over it for me, spreading topographic maps across a low table, pointing with a pencil—the route James and Pierce had filed, their final campsite marked with a red X. Except that it wasn't there anymore. The site on the southern edge of the glacier had become an avalanche, tons of snow crashing into a canyon far below. No one could be sure that James and Pierce had gone with it. Maybe they hadn't reached the site before it broke loose; arriving afterward, they would have been confused and perhaps gotten lost. The search parties flew over the glacier and the surrounding area in airplanes and helicopters, and finally a team went on foot, as far as they dared. Certain that I would see something the others had missed, I had come out to Montana to join them. Every morning when I met David in front of the dingy hangar where we waited for the rescue pilot, he'd hand me a red-and-white-striped paper cup of coffee and say, "We'll find them today."

The search went on for seven days, and at the end of it we had seen nothing but snow and a few elk herds. It was a longer than normal search, well beyond reason, but James and Pierce were known out there, and everyone found a way to imagine that they had survived. And then everyone agreed that they had gone with the avalanche, swept off the mountain as they slept.

David and I flew to Bellingham together to attend their memorial service. He sat quietly on this flight, and every few minutes we would tell each other something we already knew, calmed by a recitation of familiar things. Strange that James, who loved the mountains, should have taken a job in the flatlands of Kansas. Strange that Pierce hadn't married. I told him I'd been angry at James for planning this climb—not a premonition, exactly, but I hadn't wanted him to go. James felt it as possessiveness and resented it, and we had parted coolly, I said. I wanted David to say it was all right, but we could manage only "strange," back and forth.

At the church, I sat next to James's mother, who held my hand so tightly I thought my fingers would crack. She cried quietly, wiping her wet cheeks with the back of my hand. James's father, on her other side, kept leaning forward to look over at me, as if he needed to tell me something. And while the minister talked about their great spirit of adventure, the legacy that James and Pierce had left us, I had the eerie feeling that James was back at home mowing the lawn or weeding the flower beds.

The same taxi driver who had taken James away brought me back to the house in Kansas. It was early June, hot and muggy already, a thunderstorm boiling up in the distance. I walked through the rooms opening windows and noticed some dirty dishes I'd left in the sink, a box of crackers standing open on the table next to the vase of brown lilacs. I went into the backyard, where we had shade trees. Looking into the greenish water of the goldfish pond James had built the summer before, I let in the image I'd been holding off: James and Pierce and Celeste caught in the snow, forever. I wondered if they had wakened to a great roar, if they had even known what was happening to them. I could only see them whole, as they'd been when they set out, James and Pierce flushed with health, Celeste tattered now from her many trips, her gold felt crown askew. The storm wind came up behind me, rippling the pond's surface, and I could see myself in it—my hair blowing and my hands covering my face as I started to cry. Rain fell on my shoulders, in the pond. I watched while the storm washed over me until I seemed to dissolve. Later, sometime after dark, I went into the house and wrapped myself in a blanket.

The next day I made an appointment to see a counselor at the university. Her name was Jackie Widener, and she wore a perfect blouse of yellow silk. She had a cobalt blue vase of irises on her desk next to a picture of her husband and two children. I saw her once a week for twelve weeks and watched her face intently as she talked because I hated her. She made me tell her things about James, and she told me about grief, and I would sit there thinking, You are so full of shit. Then I would go home and feel all the things she told me I would feel.

Three years later, I wait in a tree. It's true, life goes on—whether you care or not. I write for *The Messenger* now, mostly features and high school sports. The editor, Dan MacKemson, hired me in a pinch, and he's just about gotten over the fact that he has a woman on sports.

Then there's Will. He's shy, all right. Yesterday afternoon, when Marie and I ran into him at the grocery store, he gave me a peppermint but didn't think to offer one to Marie. When we left, she said, "As far as Will could see, you were the only person in that store." I ignored her, but she went right on. "It wouldn't hurt to fix yourself up sometimes, you know, take in a movie with Will." *Fix myself up?*

A shadow passes in the trees at the edge of the stone wall, and then I see that it is not a shadow at all. A deer takes shape suddenly but unhurriedly, as if materializing out of thin air. It appears not to have come from anywhere—a spirit deer. I watch it sniff the air, and I think it knows where I am. This is the six-point buck Jordan has sent me hunting for. I count the points again, and the buck flicks his tail. I stand up slowly, knowing that Jordan expects me to get this deer, that he's counting on me. Down below, a plume of smoke will be rising from the chimney of Jordan and Marie's house, and they will be waiting for me to join them for a late breakfast. As I raise the gun, I think maybe Jordan has asked for too much this time, and as I ease my finger onto the trigger, I feel my legs begin to tremble.

Jordan has told me about "buck fever," how at the crucial moment even grown men will shake so badly they can't shoot.

Or else they'll shoot wildly. My hands are steady, though, and I have a clear shot. My success would mean a winter of meat for Jordan and Marie, but I know what he really wants is someone to carry on in his place. I take a deep breath, steady myself. The buck pushes his nose into the dry grass, and when he raises his head he's chewing one of the spotted windfall apples. Such a simple thing, another creature eating an apple. He looks slightly comical, as if he doesn't care for the sour taste. When he dips his head again, I take my finger off the trigger, click the safety on. The deer cocks an ear but keeps chewing.

When I slide down from the stand, though, the sound finally startles him. He runs off, but not far. I can see the flick of his tail about sixty yards away, and I imagine he is impatient for me to leave. Sour or not, there are more apples to be had, and the early December sun is slanting through the trees.

The Infusion Suite

My daughter Adrienne, bald as a sumo wrestler, delicate as one of the blue fairies in the book she holds on her lap, begins to hum as we pass Bright's Dairy. She always does this. When I recognize "Amazing Grace," my heart falls, as if I'm pitching down into the dream that wakes me once or twice a week. Even in deep sleep, I'll know it's the one that starts happily and ends in terror. We set off, my three children and I, going for a drive in the country. Then something happens—maybe a dog runs in front of the car—and suddenly we're flying down an impossibly steep hill in a car without brakes. The dream's silence scares me as much as anything. No one speaks or even screams; there is only the *whoosh* of tires on the road, the thump of the fenders as we careen off one bank and then another while I fight to keep us on the road. Ray, my husband, is never in the dream.

Adrienne learned "Amazing Grace" last weekend at George Garvey's funeral service. George dropped dead while stacking firewood in the shed next to the kitchen. His wife and sons—his second family—were just inside, eating breakfast. They heard the rattle of falling wood, and when they went outside, there was George, sprawled across the plank floor with his hat lying next to him.

George's boys, Brett and Stanley, are in Adrienne's class at the Lucius J. Tenney Grammar School, and though they're identical twins, everyone in the second grade can easily tell them apart. "They have different force fields," Adrienne says, explaining why she likes Stanley best.

Adrienne insisted on going to the funeral when her older sister, Nora, offered to stay at home with her. It was one of the bad days, when she looks pale and flattened in her bed. But she got up and took a bath and put on her blue dress and then brought me a new flowered bandanna and asked me to tie it around her head. Her father and her brother, Cliff, waited by the door in their good clothes, and for once neither of them had the heart to make babushka jokes.

At the service, when we stood to sing, Adrienne followed the words on a printed sheet, and I noticed splotches of pink on her face and neck. Ray was watching her too and reached over to straighten the collar of her dress. When Stanley turned around from the front pew and caught her eye, Adrienne crooked two fingers at him, and he smiled back at her. In the vestry afterward, I watched Adrienne and Stanley filling paper napkins with cookies and going off by themselves to sit under a table in the far corner. Waving away a cup of coffee, Lillian Garvey said, "I feel like I've been run over by a truck."

Although the church was nearly full, most of the people at George's funeral were family members and old friends from far away. When those visitors left in a day or two, Lillian and her boys—relative newcomers to the little town of Tenney's Landing, as we were—would likely feel deserted. A retired teacher, George had come to paint landscapes, not to make friends among the locals.

I now think of the different tunes Adrienne hums as the "Infusion Suite." That's where we're headed. She hums for courage, because what happens in the infusion suite makes her weak and sick, a sickness that lasts for days and keeps her out of school. My therapist friend Jane, who's on the staff at McClelland College and lives in Fayette, tries to help by suggesting that Adrienne play games such as throwing tennis balls at pillows. "She has to find a way to release her anger," Jane says. "She's keeping it bottled up."

When I asked her to draw a picture of "leukemia," Adrienne sat at the table with a stack of white paper and her big box of crayons, drawing birds. Some were flying, some perched on branches—sheet after sheet of brilliantly colored birds. A few of them wore glasses, others bow ties or red sneakers. "These are not leukemia," she told me, finally. "They're just what I feel like drawing."

"Honestly, I don't think she's angry," I tell Jane, who squeezes her eyes shut and shakes her head. I'm the one who's angry. I can't clear the table after dinner without fighting down the urge to hurl plates at the wall.

Bright's Dairy is a clean, white clapboard building just before the turnoff for the highway. In the summer, we take the children to Bright's for ice-cream cones. Today, snowbanks rise on either side of the road, partly obscuring the cheerful yellow sign that lets my daughter know it's time to start humming. We're thirty minutes from the medical center, over the state line in West Virginia, and the car fills with funeral music. For the first time, I join in, singing the words to her tune.

"Mom?" Adrienne asks suddenly. "*Snares?* I don't remember snares."

When we park in the big open lot, Adrienne looks around and says "B16," reading the number attached to the nearest light pole. Assured that we will know where to find the car, and thus be able to get home again, she unzips her backpack and exchanges the fairy book for the purple-haired troll doll she calls Gizzy. The doll annoys me for some reason. I have to tell everyone who notices it how Adrienne found it in the grass near our mailbox one day, how she took it in the house and washed it and combed out its hair and decided it was her good luck charm. When Ray asks what I've got against it, I say, "It's hideous. Someone's mother probably tossed it out the car window." In her heavy coat and flowered head scarf, Adrienne trudges ahead of me through the snowy parking lot, clutching the plastic troll. She looks like a miniature old lady on her way to bingo.

She waits for me to catch up when she reaches the big

revolving door at the main entrance and takes my hand as we squeeze into one of the glass wedges that sucks us into the brightly lit rotunda inside. She waves to the ladies at the information desk, turns right, and leads the way again, down the long corridor that ends with the double doors under the sign for the Adelle H. Simmons Cancer Center. Before I get through the door, I hear Judy, the head nurse, asking how Gizzy is feeling today.

"Gizzy fell out of bed last night," Adrienne says in a serious voice. "Her head hurts."

I say hello to Judy, who replies, "We'll just get settled here." It's my cue to wait outside in the hallway until she gets Adrienne's IV going. I wander over to the bulletin board, where the staff has made a collage of photos of the children they've treated since the center opened eight years ago. "Most of those children are alive today," a nurse once told me as I studied the small, hopeful faces. Some of them are not.

I find the photo of Maxwell Goldman, who died last year, a few weeks after his seventh birthday. It's summer in the picture, and Max and his mother, Martha, are sitting at the edge of a swimming pool. He's wearing a Pirates baseball cap over his bald head and looking calmly at the camera as his mother shades her eyes from the sun.

Martha Goldman is graceful in a self-possessed way I envy sometimes. She is also quite funny, but that part of her personality is easy to miss unless you pay close attention. We used to call ourselves the "Chemo Moms" when we were in the support group together. I dropped out shortly after she did, and now we keep in touch mostly by e-mail.

She called me one afternoon last fall and invited me over

for a visit. She told me that she was learning to weave and showed me the huge loom and a basket filled with gray and tan and white yarn. "I haven't actually made anything yet," she said. As we stood looking at the loom, she also told me that she couldn't have any more children and that her husband, an anesthesiologist at the medical center, was thinking of moving to Houston by himself. I remember how thin she felt when I hugged her good-bye. Martha hasn't mentioned any of these things since, but she sends a message every couple of weeks, asking about Adrienne and usually closing with some little joke about her husband, who is still there.

I find Adrienne's photograph, above and to the left of Max's. I took it myself, one afternoon in the backyard, just after her hair had grown back the first time. She's standing between her brother and sister. Both Nora and Cliff are holding hands with her. Cliff, on her right, holds her arm in the air in a victory salute as Adrienne smiles uncertainly. Towering above her, her older siblings seem aggressively robust, as sleek and healthy as a pair of racehorses. Tiny Adrienne, her hair still short and spiky, looks as if she's just been liberated from a refugee camp.

I'm about to remove the picture and slip it into my purse when I hear the door open behind me, and Judy motions for me to come in. "All set," she says brightly, and I see Adrienne reclining in her usual chair. She has a flannel hospital blanket pulled up to her chin, and her left arm is strapped down, the needle taped to the back of her hand. The IV pole and plastic bag loom above her left shoulder. She pokes her feet out from under the blanket and wiggles her toes at me. She's wearing one blue sock, one yellow. The naked Gizzy stands guard on the plastic tray table beside her.

Judy takes my coat, and I unpack Adrienne's Walkman and tapes and books. "Great music or literature?" I ask her.

She says "Music" and pulls her feet back under the blanket. The chemicals make her cold at first, then later she starts to sweat. Jane has given her a tape with the sounds of a flowing brook and wind in a canyon and, I think, humpback whales, accompanied by flute and recorder. Adrienne says it's boring, but it helps her relax, and she's learned to close her eyes and picture the shapes in the music and let herself float, instead of being suffocated by the enormous reclining chair and the needle and the chemicals. I adjust her headphones and sit down in the hard plastic seat beside her.

The infusion suite is large and bright, with long, narrow windows that let in the outside light and offer slim views of the pines surrounding this wing of the hospital. The space is divided into alcoves, with a reclining chair in the center of each one, as well as a couple of chairs for the relatives and friends who come along for moral support. At the far end, a long bay is filled with a row of hospital beds, where the oldest and sickest take their treatments. The nurses' station at the opposite end—which Adrienne calls the "popcorn stand"— dispenses juice and soda and various salty snacks to help counteract the nausea. The nurses and aides are a cheerful bunch, and there's a lot of joking around, questions like "Regular or high test?" as they hook up the bags and tubing.

Six others have come in for treatment this morning, one a girl of thirteen named Kristen, who also has leukemia and seems now to be sleeping. Kristen's father always comes with her. He's an accountant, and he sets up a makeshift office on a folding table near his daughter and works away on tax forms.

He looks up and nods in our direction, then continues punching numbers into his battery-operated calculator. I watch Kristen for a while, to reassure myself that she's breathing. She looks ashen today, with dark circles around her eyes. The father's calculator keeps up a steady *click, click, click* as the clear liquid drips down her IV tube.

Kristen reminds me of Kathy Millay, a girl I knew when I was Adrienne's age. When the Millays moved into the house next to ours with an eleven-year-old, we thought at first she was their granddaughter, but she turned out to be their only child. They doted on her. Kathy was small and timid, and even though I was younger, she seemed grateful to have a friend of any sort. Sometimes we would dress up in our mothers' castoffs and have tea parties, but most of all she liked to write skits to perform for her parents and anyone else we might rope in. She always played the strong, heroic characters and left the weak, bumbling ones to me. In our skits, Kathy saved me from one disaster after another—pouncing tigers, quicksand, falling pianos. She said she was going to be an author and a famous actress when she grew up.

Most of the time, we played at her house, because my mother didn't tolerate children indoors for too long. Fair weather or foul, she'd eventually shoo us out the door and tell us to "go blow the stink off." When my brothers or other children came around to get up a game of softball or hide-and-seek, Kathy usually stayed inside, watching us through the window. Strangely enough, no one ever teased her or called her a sissy. And none of us was surprised when we learned she was sick.

At the time my mother told us about Kathy's leukemia—

about a year after the Millays had moved in—I thought it was like mumps or chicken pox, something that made you sick for a while and then went away. When I visited Kathy after school, she had to stay in bed, and then one day her mother said she couldn't have company anymore because it made her too tired. I remember the evening I watched as her father carried her to the car wrapped in a blanket. I knew they were taking her to the hospital, and I had a terrible premonition: I knew she was going to die, even if she was only twelve. That same night I woke up crying, possibly more from fear than from sorrow.

Kathy's parents stayed in the house next door for about six months after that and then put it up for sale. They had come to be near a good hospital, they said, but now they wanted to go back home.

A few days before they left, Kathy's father was waiting on our front porch when I returned from school. He wanted to buy me a parakeet, he said. I didn't even change out of my school clothes but got right in his car and rode downtown to the pet store. The funny thing was, I hadn't known I wanted a parakeet until I saw the small, bright birds lined up on a wooden perch. I picked out a light blue one standing a little apart from the green ones and named him Freddy. When I got home with my new bird and his round cage and his cuttle-bones, my two brothers went into such a sulk that my mother promised them new baseball gloves as soon as it was payday.

About a year later, just after Freddy laid his first egg, I wrote to Kathy's parents with the news, including a sketch of Freddy standing proudly next to the egg. They never wrote back to me, but when my parents got a Christmas card, one of them had written "with love to you and your little ones" at the bottom.

I realize that Adrienne is watching me as I daydream over the book I've brought, and I reach out to touch her arm. It's cold. The tips of her fingers are blue.

"Sweetie," I say, "you're freezing."

She raises her eyebrows at me.

"Why didn't you ask for another blanket? I'll go get you one."

Judy sees me coming and steps over to the closet to get a blanket and then walks back with me. She checks the IV drip and feels Adrienne's forehead. "There's a package of microwave popcorn over there with your name on it," she says as Adrienne reaches out and plucks Gizzy off the table. "Just let me know when you're ready for it."

Adrienne smiles at her and clutches Gizzy under the blankets. Judy has the unruffled manner of an airline pilot, the voice that says, "Folks, we may be experiencing some turbulence up ahead," implying that it's nothing for *you* to worry about. Sit back and read your magazine, the voice implies, let the experts take care of it. So you return to the article on Dutch tulip farmers or New Orleans nightlife and don't think about the fact that you're thirty thousand feet in the air, sitting inside a metal tube with wings.

I watch Judy as she walks the length of the suite. She stops for a moment with each patient, and I notice that she touches them—a pat on the arm, a brush on the forehead—as she asks how they're feeling. Everyone in here loves Judy.

About a month before he died, I met George Garvey one morning at Paula's Café to talk about our school board. He'd called the afternoon before to suggest it, saying he was upset about some changes they were trying to push through. He was calling me, he said, because he thought we understood each other. I agreed to meet with him, even though I wasn't sure what he meant. Maybe I'd been so preoccupied with Adrienne I hadn't been paying attention.

George was waiting when I arrived, sitting by a window and wearing a paint-stained blue shirt. I remember thinking that he often wore blue, which might mean he was vain, trying to emphasize his blue eyes. At sixty-eight he was quite striking, with his white hair and sparkly manner. But I also remember thinking that he shouldn't be sitting in the bright light from the window because it showed the lines in his neck and the sag of his jaw. For the first time, George looked old to me.

"It's great to see you," he said, leaning forward across the table as I sat down with my coffee.

I had the impression that he was about to clasp my hands, so I jammed them into the pockets of my jacket and said, "Yes, hi." I'd noticed the waitress at the counter winking at one of the regular customers when she saw me going to George's table. People in Tenney's Landing kept an eye on us newcomers—at least for the first ten years, they joked. Because Ray worked for the state extension service, he'd gotten to know a lot of the farmers and other locals, and they seemed to think he was all right. George Garvey, though, they weren't too sure about.

Setting aside the pressing issues at the school for the time being, George talked about Brett and Stanley and what it was like to be the father of twins, how their sameness was fascinating and also, sometimes, a bit creepy. He told me about a series of paintings he was working on, how he was trying to combine elements of realism and abstraction. I sneaked a look at my watch. Adrienne was at home that day, and I'd had to ask a neighbor to come in and stay with her for an hour. Eventually, he got around to asking me about Adrienne. It was one of the days when I felt sure she would never get better, and once I started talking, I couldn't stop. Even though I understood that George had asked merely to be polite, I told him I thought there was always a special tenderness for the youngest child. I told him how I tried to make Adrienne's life as normal as possible, how I worried sometimes about pushing her too hard. I even told him about the runaway car dream.

"Where's Ray in all this?" he asked, leaning back in his chair and fixing me with his blue gaze. "It sounds like you have to carry everything on *your* shoulders."

I've thought the same thing myself, but I didn't like hearing it from George. His saying so made it seem truer. "Well, we have this unofficial division of labor at our house," I said, trying to keep my tone light. "I'm responsible for all the living things, and Ray takes care of inanimate objects."

George started laughing. He laughed so hard he got tears in his eyes, and the other customers turned around to look at us. "That's great," he said finally. He was winding down, wiping his eyes with his handkerchief. "You have a great sense of humor," he added.

What I'd said wasn't all that funny, and so I realized then that George had a crush on me. Even as it occurred to me, I could feel my heart speeding up, the blood reacting without a speck of common sense.

"Oh my gosh!" I said, making a show of looking at my

watch. "I have to go. I'm sorry we didn't get to talk about the school thing."

George stood up with me and touched me on the arm. "We can get to that next time," he said. "I'm glad I had a chance to see you, anyway."

Driving home, I peered at myself in the rearview mirror, wishing I'd had time to shower and wash my hair. *Oh my gosh?* I kept thinking.

That night I gave Adrienne her supper on the couch downstairs because she was too weak to sit at the table. I made her soup and cheese toast and lemon tea and sat close to her, encouraging her to eat everything. She was starting a new round of chemo, and she seemed to be losing a couple of pounds every day. I was getting superstitious in the kitchen, believing that if I could put together the right combination of foods, Adrienne would get well. I sometimes thought of my daughter as a jigsaw puzzle of different kinds of cells. I'd cook kale soup for her blood and caramel pudding for her bones, dice raw carrots for her skin. I could imagine the headline: "Mother of Three Discovers Cure for Cancer in Her Own Kitchen."

Though she had once been a picky eater, Adrienne decided to humor me in this. I remember the time Jane was visiting, watching in amazement as Adrienne ate one forkful after another of a casserole I'd made from lentils, chickpeas, broccoli, and onions. "I have to tell you," Jane had declared after two or three bites, "this really sucks." Adrienne laughed but kept on eating.

I wondered, as I took Adrienne up to bed, if I should tell Jane about George Garvey. Probably not. She'd have some discouraging theory to explain it all—how I was in denial and reverting to my own adolescent past. Besides, there was nothing to tell. An older man—a handsome older man, actually, a painter—had flirted with me that morning. And? And nothing. End of story. I could see Jane rolling her eyes.

As if she can read my thoughts, Adrienne suddenly pulls off her headphones and makes a face at me. It's her signal that the nausea is coming on strong. Beads of sweat pop out on her face as a dark blush creeps up her neck and into her hair.

"Okay," I say. "I'll be right back."

I nearly collide with Judy, who's bringing her a glass of cold ginger ale with a straw. Judy hands me a small ice pack in a cloth wrapper for Adrienne's forehead. I watch the spasms pass through my daughter's body as she dutifully sips the ginger ale. In a few minutes, the worst is over.

"You're really something," Judy says, giving Adrienne's ankle a squeeze. "I'll go get you that popcorn."

Adrienne shuts her eyes, too weak for the moment even to smile. Judy has told me that my daughter has remarkable self-control for someone so young. She thinks it improves her chances for a "good outcome." That phrase, I've learned, covers a lot of ground. It doesn't necessarily mean that Adrienne will beat the leukemia and live to a ripe old age. It could also mean that she might live for another year or two.

Once, when I pressed her to be more specific, Judy had replied, somewhat fiercely, "You need three things right now: hope, determination, and a good attitude. Your daughter has all of those."

I felt rebuked. "Really, how can I have a good attitude when something is trying to kill my child?" I'd asked Ray that night. "Trying very hard to kill her, I might add." Uncharacteristically, the two of us were sitting up late, watching an old movie on television. I kept interrupting to ask his opinion about what Judy had said to me.

"It must be hard for Judy," he finally answered, keeping his eyes on the screen. "She sees people die all the time."

Later, it occurred to me that this was a reasonable and generous remark on his part. But at the time, I'd wanted him to get angry too.

"Exactly," I said. "And what's the point of having a good attitude if we're not willing to do anything to stop all the dying?"

"You can't stop people from dying," Ray said patiently, as if I were a blockhead. "It's a fact of nature."

"Look," I said, getting up. "We don't understand anything— I mean most people in this country. Our kids have shiny hair and straight teeth, and the money we spend on one trip to the grocery store could probably feed a medium-size village somewhere."

"All right," Ray agreed. "Most of us eat too much, but what have you got against good teeth?"

"It's an illusion!" I practically shouted at him. "All that glossy, high-protein health." I was pacing back and forth in front of the television, trying to figure out what I did mean. Since Adrienne's diagnosis, I'd been reading about common toxins—everything from pesticides to greenhouse gases and landfills choked with disposable diapers. Sometimes it surprised me that anything besides cockroaches was still alive.

"What I think," I said finally, coming to a stop in front of Ray, "is that we're killing our own children. Everything—the ground, the water, the air—is polluted with chemicals. And why is that? So we can drive big hulking vehicles and produce a lot of plastic shit that nobody in their right mind would want anyway?"

Ray sat there with his eyes narrowed, looking skeptical. I moved off to the other side of the room and looked out at the trees on the front lawn, bent over with snow. "Adrienne could be dying because she was poisoned by the milk she drank as a baby," I said more quietly. "It could have come through me, the thing that's killing her. I don't know."

I could hear Ray's footsteps padding across the rug, and then I felt his hands on my shoulders. "It's not your fault," he said.

I reach over and take the ice pack from Adrienne's head and touch her cheek. She's still hot but relaxed now, reading the blue fairy book and eating her popcorn one piece at a time. In another couple of hours, she'll be dressed in her coat and boots again, and Judy will push her in a wheelchair up to the big front door of the hospital while I go to get the car at B16. On the way home, she'll play with Gizzy's hair and croon to that ugly doll, and I'll try to have a good attitude.

Tonight her brother and sister will take her supper upstairs on a tray and sit with her on the bed while she eats and then play fish or old maid until Adrienne is too tired to play anymore. When they come back down to eat with Ray and me, I'll be thankful for their glowing health and the way they can rise, so sweetly, to the occasion. I will refrain, for the time being, from sharing my thoughts with them on our capitalist-consumer society bent on its own stupid destruction. Tonight all of us will be extra kind with each other.

After the rest of my family has gone to sleep, I will go and sit for a while beside Adrienne's bed. She will be sleeping on her back, arms outstretched, palms up, on top of the blanket. I will see Gizzy's tiny troll feet poking out from under the pillow.

As I try to make up the words to some prayer that might keep her safe, I will remember the time almost two years ago when I took Adrienne to visit Eugene and Marshall Eastman's farm during lambing season. Each of their six white ewes had produced a healthy set of twins, and Adrienne met each of them in turn, gingerly patting the curly wool on their backs as Laurie Eastman, a new bride at the age of fifty, led her into the lambing pens in the big, drafty barn. The seventh ewe, Brownie, was outside, standing in one spot and baaing, over and over again. Adrienne asked what was wrong with her.

"Her lamb was born dead," Laurie explained. "Right in that spot where she's standing. Eugene and I found her when we came home from church yesterday, and she's been carrying on like that ever since."

When we went into the house to get warm, Adrienne stood on tiptoe, clutching the windowsill, so she could watch Brownie. The small brown ewe was her favorite. Laurie Eastman and I were deep into a conversation on the merits of canning versus freezing when I heard Adrienne singing softly. It was a familiar song, and as I listened I realized she was changing the words to an old lullaby I'd sung for her.

"Hush, little mama, don't say a word," Adrienne sang through the window. "Baby's gonna buy you a mockingbird."

I will remember how Adrienne had glanced over at us shyly as she realized we were listening. Still, she kept on, singing even louder, as if her voice might pass through the glass now frosted by her breath and reach the heart of animal grief.

The Springhouse

"We used to be girls, too, you know," Mrs. Bana-shevsky said, taking the warm, white sheet from Carrie's hands, folding it against her generous front. With an amused look, she bent to place it in the basket.

Carrie had just said something about helping her grandmother on laundry days, when her grandparents lived in the country. She had said how she and her cousins, when they were girls, loved laundry days, the old Maytag on its sturdy legs agitating importantly in the kitchen, wheeled up to the sink for the occasion. Because their well was low in the summer, Carrie's grandmother washed two or three loads before she set the drain hose in the sink and let the dirty water run out. Waiting in the basket were the flattened, soapy pieces that had been through the wringer once. Back they'd go into clean water, slap around in the metal tub, through the wringer again.

The cousins were always reminded to watch their fingers as they fed the socks and pillowcases through the rubber rollers. At least once every summer, they were told the story of Avis Mackenzie, who wasn't paying attention, who lost her middle finger, crushed when her hand got pulled into the wringer. It was thrilling to see how close they could get, just bumping their fingertips against the rollers that clamped down on their grandfather's undershorts, the towels from their swimmers' baths at the creek. Their mothers had a joke, something about "tits in the mangle," but they whispered it among themselves, and the girls never quite caught it.

In a different way, it was thrilling to carry the heavy baskets outside, shake out the flat, flat clothes, and pin them to the lines with wooden pins, then prop the lines with long poles their grandfather had fashioned to keep the sheets from dragging on the grass. City children, Carrie and her cousins found that the arch of sky and the open green of ripening hayfields called them out of themselves in a way nothing else did. The air filled with the scent of clean clothes, and when they lifted the empty baskets to take them inside, grasshoppers the size of their thumbs whirred up to startle them. By afternoon, the squished socks had come to life again and flapped on the line like flags next to the puffed-up sheets that were big as sails.

When they were girls, their parents brought them to the farm to visit their grandparents every summer. In those days, they thought of things lasting forever—their families just that way, coming together year after year on the hill farm in western Pennsylvania. Carrie had two younger brothers and boy cousins as well, but in those days it was the girls who counted.

"Your grandmother must have told you about the time we sold Bill Gapen's apples back to him," Mrs. Banashevsky said, folding a pair of pillowcases together. After all these years, she had not lost her accent completely. *Muzd have told you*, she said. And then, chuckling, "Marian and I, we got up to some mischief in the old days."

She didn't bother telling the whole story again, how she and Carrie's grandmother, one fall day on their way home from school, climbed over the Gapens' stone wall, took off their jackets, and filled them with apples, then walked up to the front door and asked Mr. Gapen if he'd like to buy some. "He gave us thirty-five cents. He said they were good-looking apples."

Mrs. Banashevsky and Carrie's grandmother were the only girls in their high school class of seven. Each of them had a copy of the graduation photo taken on the steps of the gray wooden schoolhouse, the five boys wearing ties and ill-fitting, borrowed jackets, Mrs. Banashevsky—then Mira Galisch—and Marian Kramer standing in front with their arms linked, two bright figures against the dark background of their classmates.

Carrie picked up Mrs. Banashevsky's laundry basket and carried it into her kitchen. Automatically, she smiled at the black cat clock on the wall, still working, its big round eyes shifting left then right as the seconds ticked by. Mrs. Banashevsky took two glass tumblers painted with yellow daisies out of the cupboard and poured iced tea from a matching pitcher. The house, Carrie reflected, was furnished with the very objects she and her friends searched for in thrift shops. All of them had been cared for over the years and not replaced with newer things.

They took their glasses out to the front porch. When Carrie's grandmother moved back to town after her husband's death, she and Mrs. Banashevsky, also a widow, had kept watch from this porch, side by side on a sagging wicker settee. As they observed the local comings and goings, the slipups, they resumed the friendship that had been watered down by husbands and children and the nine miles from town to the farm.

"What's the news of the world then?" Mrs. Banashevsky asked as Carrie took her usual seat on the hard wooden chair reserved for guests.

Carrie drank some tea, looked up and down the street. "Gerald Dibbs thinks we should get the ferry going again," she said at last. "He's made up a petition. He's planning to go around door to door and talk to people about it."

"What a crazy idea!" Mrs. Banashevsky said, plunking her glass down.

"He already got nine or ten people to sign at the meeting last night."

"Well." Mrs. Banashevsky snorted. "Gerald Dibbs."

"Don't forget that new playground next to the ball field. That was his idea."

"Oh, one rickety swing set and a sandbox all the town cats do their business in! What does your father say?"

"I haven't told him yet." Carrie looked at her watch. "I'm sure he knows by now, anyway." Carrie had been in town for a few weeks, staying with her parents and trying to avoid discussions of her husband, Nick, who was back in Chicago. Now working for the weekly newspaper her father published and edited, Carrie reported on school board meetings and compiled the events calendar. She also covered the biweekly town council meetings, and in her opinion Gerald Dibbs, the new council chair, wasn't so bad. It had occurred to her at the previous night's meeting that he looked like an actor from the 1940s. Not one of the obvious heartthrobs, more of a sandy-haired cowboy type. The foolishness of the thought had made her smile, and Gerald, noticing, had smiled back.

"He's just showing off," Mrs. Banashevsky said. "That's the kind of person he is."

Carrie didn't know where she got her information on Gerald Dibbs but decided to let the subject drop.

Mrs. Banashevsky drained her glass, swirled the ice cubes around. "I might like to have a boat myself. Not a big, clumsy ferry, I can tell you. A graceful boat to go rowing in." *A graze-vul boad.*

"And you would row this boat where?" Carrie couldn't imagine Mrs. Banashevsky in a rowboat, she being nearly the size of a small craft herself.

"I have a place in mind," she said, rising with dignity and going into the house.

She was back in a moment with a piece of paper, a page torn from a magazine and folded many times. "This is the boat I want," she said, unfolding the page on Carrie's knee. It was an advertisement for a lakeside inn, with a stone building on the far side of the water and a small wooden boat seemingly adrift in the foreground.

"Very nice." Carrie looked at the picture for a while, then refolded it and tried to give it back.

"No." Mrs. Banashevsky held up her hand. "You keep it."

"All right, then," Carrie said, slipping the picture into her pocket as she stood up to say good-bye. She had the odd impression that Mrs. Banashevsky meant for her to go out and find this very boat.

"Come back soon," Mrs. Banashevsky called after her as Carrie turned and waved from the sidewalk.

Carrie set out for the newspaper office but took a detour past her grandmother's house. Although her grandmother had been dead nearly a year, Carrie hadn't gotten over the habit of believing she was alive. Several times a day, she thought of things to tell her. Just last week, she had almost bought a new jigsaw puzzle for her grandmother to set up on the card table in the dining room.

Now that she was gone, the house looked surprisingly ordinary, a white ranch with a green shingled roof, cement steps going up to the front door. So different from the big, noisy farmhouse. Bright plastic children's toys littered the yard, and Carrie saw that the new owners had dug up the mountain laurel bushes her grandmother had brought with her from the country. Mountain laurel would not transplant, everyone told her, but she had fed them with bonemeal and made them thrive. Every spring they filled with wild pink blossoms. Where they had grown in front of the house, a few scraggly junipers squatted in a bed of white gravel. Inside the house, a curtain was drawn back. Carrie turned away and crossed the street.

Without really thinking about it, she walked all the way to

the old ferry landing at the end of River Street, where the road dipped down to meet the water. The wooden dock was gone; the last rotting board had floated off years ago. Only a section of the railing remained along one side, iron pipes once painted green. She shook it with both hands to make sure it would hold her and climbed up to sit on the top rung. Perched there, she had a good view up and down the Monongahela River, flowing along peaceably in the June sun. The town was so quiet now, it was hard to imagine the days when showboats came from upriver and stopped in at Tenney's Landing. Her grandmother had once told her that, for a ten-cent ticket, children could walk up the gangplank and see the afternoon shows—a magician sawing a woman in half, men in blackface tap dancing and singing about the sweet old days on the plantation. The nighttime adult shows featured "scandalously clad women" and "slick crooners." Every man in town would line up to buy a ticket, she'd added.

Carrie's great-uncle Theo, her grandmother's brother, had run the ferry for a time. He built a three-sided shelter on each landing and tacked up a schedule. The ferry crossed back and forth five times a day. In the off time, Theo went home to work in his garden and exercise his dogs. It was Theo who saved Mrs. Banashevsky—Mira Galisch—from a bad reputation. Carrie's grandmother had told her the story, the afternoon of Uncle Theo's funeral.

Mira's father, Miroslav, arrived with his family in 1921, the year Marian Kramer turned twelve. They were just off the boat, Croatians who got out after the war. They had connections in Pittsburgh who directed them to the coal mines around Tenney's Landing. There, Croats, Czechs, and Poles could find work and people who spoke a familiar language. Mira was also twelve—"a tiny thing, if you can believe it," Carrie's grandmother said—the second oldest of five children. Her parents rented a house at the edge of town, which put them between the old settlement of Tenney's Landing, where the Kramer family and the other Protestants had lived for seven generations, and the miners' houses, where everyone was Catholic and no one spoke decent English.

"The Slavs, people called them 'hunkies,' I'm not sure why," Carrie's grandmother told her. "Dumb hunkies."

Because Mira was bright and quick, her parents sent her to the Protestant school, hoping to give her an advantage. The first day, she seemed terrified of the large American children and spent the morning sitting rigidly at her desk, looking straight ahead. She wore a faded blue dress with puffy sleeves and had a flowered head scarf tied securely under her chin. At recess, the children discovered the only words she could say in English were "Yes, please." Floyd Tanner, one of the older boys, asked if she would like to kiss his ass and pretended to take down his pants when she answered him. Other boys joined in, asking ruder questions, but Mira knew they were making fun of her and moved away. "I can still see her that first day at recess," Carrie's grandmother had told her, "a skinny girl with a scab on her knee, standing off by herself and trying not to cry. I was such a coward, I didn't go over to her."

That night at supper when she told her parents about the new girl, her eleven-year-old brother, Theo, surprised everyone by saying, "She looks like a little phoebe bird."

A couple of weeks later, Marian invited Mira to come

home with her after school. As they were working out math problems at the kitchen table, Mrs. Kramer came up behind them and let out a shriek. She called for Theo and told him to bring water and fill the big pot on the stove. She tossed more wood in the firebox. The girls watched her, bewildered, as the flames shot up.

"Head lice," she said, turning to them finally.

Starting with Theo, since he had the shortest hair, she cut it even shorter with her big kitchen scissors, then made him lean over the steaming pot as she poured hot water over his head and scrubbed his scalp with pine tar soap. When he tried to wriggle away, she held him firmly by the back of the neck. Next was Marian, who complained loudly as swathes of her auburn hair fell to the floor.

"Oh, God," Marian sobbed, looking into the pot, where Theo's lice floated like grains of rice.

"The Lord's name," her mother chided, dousing her head. "Anyway, they're dead."

Mira was more confused than frightened, possibly thinking this was some American purification ritual, and lowered her head quietly when Mrs. Kramer turned to her with the scissors.

"Don't cut so much," Theo protested, watching from the other side of the room with a towel over his head as his mother sliced through Mira's dark curls.

"It's the latest fashion," Mrs. Kramer said with a little laugh. "And don't be such babies, you two. Look at Mira."

In the evening, while the Kramers were still at supper, they heard heavy footsteps at the back of the house and one loud knock. When Mr. Kramer opened the door, Mira's father came in, pushing his daughter ahead of him. Her older brother was with them and stood beside his father, clenching and unclenching his fists. Mr. Galisch spoke angrily, with dramatic gestures, though they couldn't understand what he said. He seemed about to lunge at them and knock things off the table when he noticed Marian and Theo, wide eyed, newly shorn. He stopped with one hand in midair and stared at the Kramer children.

Mrs. Kramer got up and smoothed her skirt. She held out her hand to Mr. Galisch, who was not used to shaking hands with women. He held her fingers for a moment and made a slight bow. She indicated that Mira's brother should sit down in her chair, and when he looked questioningly at his father, Mr. Galisch nodded. Mrs. Kramer found a pencil and poked around in the boy's hair. "Head lice," she said as Mr. Galisch peered closely. She held up the pencil so he could see one or two squirming on the point.

"Hid lize," he repeated.

As she talked, she pantomimed cutting and washing, directing his attention to the stove to emphasize the importance of hot water. She tried to make him understand that hats and scarves, sheets and pillowcases, all must be washed. Finally, she got a new bar of her pine tar soap from under the sink, put it in Mira's hand, and sent the baffled Galisches back to their rented house.

Just after school ended that June, Mrs. Galisch had another baby, and Mira was needed at home to help out. Marian didn't see her until the middle of August, when Mira carried her new brother to their house for a visit.

"See this sweet boy," she said, unwrapping his blanket and

tickling the corner of his mouth to make him smile. "His name is Charles," she added. "American name. We call him Charlie."

Mira had grown taller, Marian observed, and she now had small but noticeable breasts. Her hair, which had grown out less curly than before, was tied back with a blue ribbon. She looked very pretty and relaxed as she sat in the porch swing, humming to her baby brother.

"Oh, hello," Theo said formally when he came around the side of the house with his dog and saw Mira. He stood looking at her for a minute but apparently couldn't think of anything else to say and so walked on, whistling for the dog to follow.

Back at school two weeks later, boys who had made fun of Mira now smiled at her and watched her from behind their books. Floyd Tanner, grown rougher and shaggier over the summer, tried to talk to her at recess, and when she showed no interest he took to growling at her, making low, threatening sounds in his throat whenever she came near. Mira and Marian started calling him Wolf-Boy behind his back and in their notebooks drew pictures of boys with wolves' heads and lolling tongues.

In mid-October, Mr. Galisch made another night visit, this time demanding the return of his daughter's underwear. Marian had stayed home with a cold that day, which gave Floyd an idea; he convinced his friend T.J. to help him trap Mira as she walked home alone. They waited for her in the scrubby stand of pines that grew along one stretch of the river. When she got close, T.J. ran up over the bank and told her to come quick, he'd found a snapping turtle. Mira followed him. Next thing she knew, Floyd had knocked her to the ground. She screamed once.

When Theo found them, Mira was on her feet. T.J. stood behind her, holding her tight against his body with one arm. With his free hand, he covered her mouth. Floyd stood in front, with her underpants in his hands, taunting her.

"Nice drawers for a hunkie girl," he said, rubbing them against his cheek. "Now you're bare naked under that skirt, ain't you?"

Theo told Marian later he wasn't sure what happened after that. He leaped from the bank and landed on Floyd's back. When they fell down together, Theo started kicking and punching every which way, slewing his fists around and yelling like a madman. And then he was alone. Everyone, even Mira, had run off. He picked up her crumpled underpants and put them inside his jacket. He said nothing about it when he got home but washed up as usual and went outside to feed his dog. No one even noticed the bruises on his hands until Mr. Galisch came.

Marian and her mother were drying the dishes, and Theo was at the table stitching a piece of leather to make a leash when Mr. Kramer escorted Mira's father in through the living room. This time, he'd knocked on the front door.

"Boy," Mr. Galisch said.

Theo stood up, his face white, and Mr. Galisch embraced him in a clumsy hug. Patting Theo's back, he turned to the rest of the family. "This boy," he said, "was save my Mira."

Theo looked mortified.

"Strange thing," Mr. Galisch said, stepping back. "Strange thing is, you take small clothes of Mira?"

"Yes," Theo said, his face going from chalk to crimson. "I did."

"Not good, that. You give. You give me now."

"I buried them," Theo said.

"Would you mind telling me what's going on?" Mr. Kramer demanded. "Theo?"

Theo held his hands out, palms down, as if the swollen and discolored knuckles would explain everything. "I buried Mira's underclothes out behind the shed."

"What is saying?" Mr. Galisch wondered.

Mr. Kramer took over. He lit a lantern, and everyone followed him through the backyard and watched as Theo got a shovel and found the spot where the ground was freshly tamped. Mr. Kramer held the lantern up high, casting Theo's shadow against the back of the shed. Marian kept her eyes on the shadow–Theo's jerky motions as he bent and straightened, over and over. He had to dig down nearly two feet before finding the soiled white ball that he handed to Mira's father.

"Why do this?" Mr. Galisch asked as he shook out the cotton underpants Mira's mother had made for her and trimmed with a pink bow. He looked at them carefully, then put them in his pocket.

"I didn't think she'd want them, after what happened."

"What *did* happen?" Mr. Kramer asked his son.

Theo, intent on filling up the hole, didn't answer.

"This boy good." Mr. Galisch clapped Theo on the back again before disappearing into the darkness.

Carrie's grandmother said that Theo related the events to his family in the sketchiest way. He wasn't sure what had happened to Mira before he ran toward the sound of her scream.

The next day, Mira told Marian about Floyd knocking her down and reaching under her skirt to pull her underwear off. She tried to kick him, but he rolled out of the way. Still, it gave her a second to get up and run. Then T.J.—the "little snake" Mira called him—caught her and put his hands everywhere as he struggled to hold her.

When Carrie asked what had happened to the two boys, her grandmother shook her head. "Nothing at all," she said. "My father went to talk to their fathers, and they told him to mind his own business. What did he care about those hunkies anyway? They never bothered Mira after that, though—or Theo, either. I guess he scared the bejesus out of them, even if he was half their size."

Carrie remembered her uncle Theo as a quiet man with a brown beard. She and her cousins used to say he looked like an artist, though as far as they knew he had never painted a picture. Maybe it was the hat he wore, a soft felt hat with a wide brim. She thought about a bright, windy day when he took her on the ferry. She was only four, excited to be out on the water. Halfway across the river, a sudden gust lifted the hat from his head. It seemed to flutter a moment, like a huge moth, and Carrie grabbed for it, catching the brim as it was about to sail over the side. Uncle Theo laughed and placed it on her head. Carrie held her hands on the crown, to keep it on, and though she could barely see from under the brim, she stood like that in the front of the boat until they docked in Lynchtown.

The sound of tires on gravel made Carrie jump down from the railing. Her legs felt stiff, and the metal pipe had left an impression across the backs of her thighs. She brushed the rust flakes from her shorts as she watched the pickup approaching. It stopped a few feet away, and Gerald Dibbs got out.

"I thought that was you," he said, as if they were friends. "Pretty day."

"Yes, it is." She felt jittery, seeing him so unexpectedly.

"You're Carrie, is that right? Dan MacKemson's daughter?"

"Right." She looked at him closely as they shook hands. In the sunlight, she noticed more gray in his hair than she had seen at the council meetings, and a faded smattering of freckles across his nose. He wore a crisp blue shirt with the sleeves rolled up and looked cool in the afternoon heat.

"Tell me something about the ferry," he said. "Wasn't your grandfather involved some way?"

They were walking toward the water's edge, their shoulders nearly touching.

"That was my uncle Theo. Actually, my great-uncle. He ran the ferry for a while." Carrie reminded herself to stop using the word "actually." It sounded so prissy. "It's funny," she went on, "I was just thinking about him."

"I'm still sorting out the old families here, being sort of a new guy in town."

"A new guy?" He came from Rownd's Point, a few miles up the river. He would have gone to the consolidated high school. "You must know a lot of people in town."

"Still, they resent you, coming in and getting elected right off." He sounded proud of himself, in any case.

They stood and looked across the river at Lynchtown, a town that mirrored Tenney's Landing in the way its wooden houses fanned out across the hillside above Main Street. Carrie pointed out Lenhart's Market, with its bright blue door. "I can't tell from here," she said, "but I bet they've still got the old Salada tea sign in the window."

"I've never been in that store," Gerald Dibbs said.

"I have. One time Uncle Theo let us ride over there—my three cousins and I—and told us to be back on the ferry in ten minutes. Well, we weren't, and he left without us. When we came out of the store, he was halfway across already. I remember how he waved his big hat at us. We had to wait two hours until he came back."

"That's a long time."

"When you're eight years old, it's forever. We had enough change between us to buy one comic book. We sat on the steps of the store and took turns reading it out loud. When we got to the end, we read it backwards. After a while, Mrs. Lenhart felt sorry for us and brought us a cold cream soda and four paper cups."

"I don't think they make cream soda anymore," Gerald said.

Carrie could smell his aftershave, a clean lime scent. Normally, she didn't care for aftershave.

"I miss the old things," he added. "But maybe you have to go away and come back to really appreciate a place, the old ways." He started telling her about joining the navy after high school, the ships he'd been on, the places he'd seen in his eight years away. He had gone to Japan twice. Once he was on a destroyer that sailed through the Seychelles. "Anyway, it was an adventure," he said. "And then I came back here to help my dad and my uncle Reed with the dealership. I'm the sales manager now."

He talked with a kind of urgency, as if it were important

for Carrie to know these things. She checked her watch. "I have to go," she told him. "I'm supposed to be at the paper, writing about last night."

"Be nice to me when you do," he said.

As she turned to leave, he said, "Wait, there's a mosquito," and she felt the tips of his fingers brush her neck as he picked it off.

In the newsroom, Carrie sat at her desk and stared at the blank computer screen, aware of her father watching her through the big plate-glass window in his office. She had waved when she went in, relieved to see he was meeting with his assistant editor. The three-section weekly, which covered all the towns in the county, would be on the stands in two days, and Carrie hadn't even started on the calendar.

She read through her notes from the council meeting. If her father got to know Gerald Dibbs, he might actually like him, might stop calling him "that nitwit Dibbs." They had something in common. Both of them had grown up here, gone away, and then come back. Only her father had stayed away longer, leaving Philadelphia to take the job at *The Messenger* the year after her younger brother graduated from college. Carrie had never really lived here. She'd always been a visitor.

It took her nearly three hours to write a piece perceptibly biased in favor of the proposal to reinstitute the ferry between Tenney's Landing and Lynchtown. She pointed out that there were no bridges within twenty miles. Upstairs in the archives, she found the article about the ferry's last run, nearly twenty-five years before. In truth, people had gotten used to being without it, but Gerald Dibbs said that, besides its historic significance, the ferry would be good for business. Not that there was a whole lot of business on either side, unless you counted Dibbs Motors, out on the highway. It was, as Mrs. Banashevsky had said, a crazy idea, and yet Carrie found it appealing, the way Gerald wanted to bring back something lost. Everyone else, it seemed, was content to let the town continue its slow decline, to take their business to the strip malls half an hour's drive away.

For the final paragraph, Carrie wrote about the ferry's history, starting with the pole ferries that began crossing in the 1820s to carry horses and wagons. She listed the ferrymen of the final half century, including Theodore Kramer and Fred Tenney, a descendant of the town's founder. She knew her father would take all that out, saying it was irrelevant. He would remind her that she wasn't writing an editorial, but she wanted him, at least, to read it.

Shortly before she died, Carrie's grandmother had made a comment about Gerald Dibbs's family. Carrie didn't know him at the time, but the vehemence of the remark had unnerved her, and it came back to her now.

She and her husband, Nick, had made a quick trip from Chicago to celebrate her grandmother's eighty-seventh birthday and had stopped by her house to say good-bye the morning after the party. When they arrived, her grandmother was reading the newspaper, and she set it aside with a look of disgust.

"Gerald Dibbs got elected chair of the town council," she announced. "That probably doesn't mean anything to you, but if he's like the rest of his family, he doesn't have the sense to pour piss out of a boot."

"I never heard of them," Carrie said, glancing at Nick and trying not to laugh.

"Well, you wouldn't," her grandmother said. "They're from over by Rownd's Point, hardly one step above white trash."

Nick brought it up as they were waiting to board their flight in Pittsburgh. "I've always thought of your grandmother as so open-minded, I mean for someone who lives in the sticks, and now she's talking about 'white trash,' that Dobbs family."

"I think it's Dibbs," Carrie said. "Probably some Dibbs a hundred years ago got the better of some Kramer—sold them a piece of swampy land or something. These people know how to hold a grudge."

"But it's a real class thing, too," Nick insisted. "If one of them did something clever, the reason it's so galling is because they're supposed to be stupid as well as poor."

"Maybe you're right," Carrie had said. It annoyed her that Nick, who had grown up in Chicago, took a sort of anthropological interest in her family's hometown.

Carrie filed the town council report, then got out the shoe box full of printed postcards and handwritten event notices for the coming week. There were nearly a hundred, as there were most weeks in the summer. She started typing them in under the calendar headings, beginning with "Art Exhibitions" and ending with "Miscellaneous." She wondered if Gerald Dibbs was married. He seemed like he would be. Or maybe divorced.

When Carrie got home, her father was already there, having a drink in the kitchen, keeping her mother company while she cooked supper.

"Burning the midnight oil?" he joked as Carrie sat down across from him and took a sip of his gin and tonic.

"Nick phoned," her mother said. "He'd like you to call back, but I would appreciate it if right now you'd make a salad. You can call him after we eat."

"How's our Mrs. Banashevsky today?" her father asked as Carrie started rinsing lettuce.

"What, are you a spy? How did you know I was over there?"

"I know everything," he said happily.

"She told me she wants a boat."

"A boat?" her mother said. "She's eighty-eight years old! Be careful, you're splashing water on the floor."

"She must be losing it," her father remarked. "What kind of boat?"

"Here." Carrie took the folded page from her pocket and smoothed it out on the table. "She gave me this today."

Her father squinted at it, took his glasses from his shirt pocket, and looked again. "Well," he said. "At her age, I suppose it's good to have a fantasy or two."

After supper, Carrie took a long time cleaning up, loading the dishwasher, wiping off the stove and countertops. The prospect of talking to her husband made her stomach hurt, and she decided to put it off.

"Don't forget to call Nick," her mother reminded her, switching off the kitchen light.

When Carrie woke in the night, she didn't know where she was at first and sat up in a panic. It came to her as her eyes adjusted to the light in the room. She was home again, but not home. This was not her childhood room, only the guest room in her parents' house. She hadn't even unpacked completely. Her two suitcases were under the bed, still half full. She and Nick had slept together in this bed a few months before, at Christmastime.

The house was quiet, but she heard wind stirring the leaves of the big elm in the front yard. She got up to look outside, shivering as a breeze came through the open window and lifted the hem of her nightgown. The moon was nearly full—waxing or waning, she wasn't sure—and thin clouds blew across its face like shreds of cotton batting. Carrie thought about the conversation at the ferry landing and made a note to find out where the Seychelles were.

She woke in the morning to the smell of burning toast. As she watched a spider make its way across the ceiling, it occurred to her that Gerald Dibbs very likely had "woman troubles," as her grandmother and Mrs. Banashevsky used to say. The absence of a wedding ring didn't mean there was no wife, ex-wife, girlfriend.

"What did Nick have to say?" Carrie's mother asked, pouring a cup of coffee for each of them and sitting down at the table. Her father, the toast burner, had already left for the newsroom.

"I didn't call him."

"Oh, Carrie." Her mother looked away.

"You seem to think I'm waiting for Nick to say he forgives me for something," Carrie said, picking up her cup and setting it down again. "It isn't like that."

"What *is* it like?"

"Nick is not a good husband," Carrie told her solemnly.

"You said that before. I have no idea what you mean."

"Maybe you could take my word for it and not insist on hearing the gory details."

"How gory could they be? You have some differences to work out. Everyone does." Her mother got up and poured her coffee into the sink. "I have to go now, but I do wish you would take this seriously. It's not like breaking up with some boyfriend because he grows a mustache."

Her mother was referring to Lawrence, a man Carrie had dated her sophomore year of college. He was a bicycle racer, a year ahead of Carrie at school. She'd considered him nice looking until he grew a handlebar mustache. She hated the feel of the twirly waxed tips against her face when he kissed her. One day as she saw him walking across the quad in his tight black bicycle shorts and his ridiculous mustache she fell completely out of love. Her mother had laughed when Carrie told her. Nick was a different story.

"I cut your town council report in half," her father said, tapping her on the head with a rolled-up piece of paper. They had nearly collided as he came out his office door.

"Imagine that," Carrie said. "Anyway, I was wondering if I could use one of the cameras today."

"Why? Got a fast-breaking story on your hands?" Carrie's father, who had worked as a journalist in Philadelphia for thirty years, once said of *The Messenger's* news, "House fires in winter, drownings in summer, car crashes and family mayhem all year long."

"I have an idea for a feature series," Carrie told him. "I'll do the first one on spec and see what you think."

"You know where we keep the cameras, I suppose."

"I do. And I need the tape recorder too."

Packing up the equipment, Carrie set off to walk the few blocks to Mrs. Banashevsky's house. The morning was still cool, and in spite of the unpleasantness with her mother earlier, she enjoyed the feeling of being a real reporter again, of walking along in a light, confident body. She wished that Gerald Dibbs might drive by and see her. A car salesman—or sales manager, as he'd told her the day before. And so what? What else could he be around here? A coal miner? An insurance agent?

When Mrs. Banashevsky didn't answer her front door, Carrie went around back and found her standing at the edge of her little vegetable garden, hands on her hips, as if she were mad at the lettuces going to seed, the radishes starting to bolt.

"Look at you," Mrs. Banashevsky said, turning around, one hand fluttering up to her throat. "For a minute I thought you were Marian, the way your hair goes red in the sun." She laughed like someone out of breath. "Sometimes, you know, I think Marian will come for me when my time is up. So I'm glad it's you instead, because I need to tie my tomato plants today."

"Do you have stakes?" Carrie set her bag down in the shade and went with Mrs. Banashevsky to look in the garage.

Mr. Banashevsky's car, a black 1988 Buick sedan, was parked inside. Its paint was still shiny, and the whitewalls gleamed. Mrs. Banashevsky, who had never learned to drive, saw to that. Like the house, the garage was clean and orderly with a slightly antique feel, but with the added smells of grease and gasoline. Mr. Banashevsky's tools still hung on the Peg-Board. A red oilcan with a long, thin spout sat on the workbench.

"Your father made these for me last year," Mrs. Bana-shevsky said as Carrie pounded in the pointed wooden stakes beside the tomato plants. "Such a nice man he is." Her sons, Andrew and Thomas, lived in St. Louis, had started some business there. One of Andrew's daughters was planning an October wedding, Mrs. Banashevsky told Carrie, and she hoped her son would send her a plane ticket so she could go.

Together they tied the tomato vines to the stakes with soft strips of rag. It should have been done earlier. The vines were headed everywhere and had to be handled carefully so they wouldn't break. The plants were covered with yellow blossoms, and a few hard, green fruits had already set. Carrie looked at Mrs. Banashevsky kneeling among the vines, her hands covered with fine green dust, and told her she wanted to take a picture.

"Not now," Mrs. Banashevsky said, touching the kerchief that covered her hair. "Not like this."

"Please," Carrie said. "This is perfect."

Her plan, she explained as she crouched among the tomatoes with the camera, was to do a series on town elders. She would get them to tell stories from their lives as a kind of historical record. She hoped to talk to people in every town in the county, as well as some who lived across the river.

"That's going to take a long time," Mrs. Banashevsky observed.

"Anyway, you're the first," Carrie said. "I'm going to use your story to convince my dad it's a good idea."

Mrs. Banashevsky smiled broadly and hoisted herself to her feet. "Come inside," she said, "where it isn't so bright."

Carrie set up the tape recorder on the kitchen table and let

Mrs. Banashevsky talk about anything she liked. She started with her wedding day, describing the groom, Alexander Banashevsky, as "a good, strong man." He had come from Russia at the age of eighteen and worked as a welder at the mine. Carrie wanted to take her back farther, to her family's early days in Tenney's Landing. The little she knew from that time she had learned from her grandmother. Most of all, she wanted to ask about Uncle Theo, but she didn't know how to begin.

It could have gone either way, Carrie speculated. The two young people could have fallen in love. Or there might have been an unease between them that kept them apart. If Carrie had the years straight, Mira Galisch would have married Alexander Banashevsky while Theo was away at college. How would he have felt, hearing the news?

Theo married fairly late in life. He was thirty-eight when he traveled south to visit an old college friend and met the pale, quiet woman named Grace Llewellyn. The best thing about Aunt Grace, who died when Carrie was fourteen, was her Kentucky accent. She came from Louisville and baked a Derby pie every year on Kentucky Derby day, possibly because she was homesick. They had one child, a son named Paul. Carrie had seen a picture of him, taken when he was about eight, a dark-haired boy wearing a snowflake sweater, standing on the front porch on Christmas Day. The lighted tree gleamed through the window behind him. Paul was killed the following spring when he fell from the roof of the shed and broke his neck. No one knew why he'd gone up there.

Mrs. Banashevsky had stopped talking and was looking at Carrie. After a minute, she said, "Young people think time goes slowly for old people. I remember thinking the same thing." She frowned, concentrating on the little wheels turning inside the recorder. "It isn't true. The day is over before you know it."

Carrie was taken aback. Was Mrs. Banashevsky asking her to leave? "Oh," she said, turning off the machine. "Maybe I can come back tomorrow."

"What about my boat?"

Carrie had forgotten, partly because it didn't make any sense. "Do you mean you want to buy a boat?"

"No, don't be silly. I want a boat to use one time, for a special purpose."

Carrie waited for her to go on, but Mrs. Banashevsky was staring moodily out the window, as if she had been insulted.

"Okay," Carrie said, repacking the equipment. "I'll see what I can find."

She went home first to get some lunch. Her mother was working at the library, so Carrie had the house to herself. She cut up chicken for a sandwich and took it out to the picnic table in the backyard. It was a little feast: besides the sandwich, she had a sliced apple, smoked Gouda, a glass of lemonade. Carrie was thinking of Nick, though. The last time they had talked, the week before, he'd pressed her to make a decision, pointing out that he was still paying for her health insurance.

"Health insurance?" she'd said. "What's that got to do with anything?"

"If you're not coming back, I can stop the deduction for your share." He'd said it matter-of-factly, the same way he might say he would go ahead and eat dinner without her if she had to work late.

"Is it so much?"

He didn't answer, and the silence piled up for many seconds, perhaps minutes. Cost wasn't the point, she knew. Finally, Carrie told him she would call in a few days. When he still didn't say anything, she set the receiver down.

Nick's silent spells had started about halfway through their six-year marriage. He would stop speaking to her for days, and she wouldn't know why. There would have been no argument, nothing to offend him that she could recall, and then he would come home stony-faced, look at her reproachfully if she asked him a question. He expected her to carry on as usual, to serve meals, to sleep in the same bed, while he acted as if she were invisible.

There were other things, too—little acts of unkindness, his sudden announcement that he didn't want to have children—but his withdrawals from her were the most puzzling. At first, because they seemed a kind of punishment, she would assume she'd done something wrong and torment herself trying to remember a careless remark or a forgotten promise. If she attempted to joke with him, he grew even colder.

Once, after a weekend of silence, when she had suggested he see a psychiatrist, he merely rolled his eyes.

"This is way too creepy," she'd finally announced one morning as he sat across the table from her, staring at his bacon and eggs. She had gone upstairs to wait until he left for work. As she stood by the window in their bedroom, it occurred to her that she was making a list of things to take. She heard the front door open finally. Breaking his silence, Nick called up to her. "Don't do anything stupid, Carrie."

Her parents, her mother especially, were fond of Nick. After a series of unsuitable boyfriends—the cyclist, a poet who wore a maroon cloak, a chemist who specialized in insect repellents—her mother was overjoyed when Carrie brought Nick home after meeting him at a friend's wedding. He worked for a financial firm in Chicago and made a lot of money, and was good looking besides. He also had interests: basketball, John Coltrane. "Almost a regular guy," Carrie's father said. "A godsend," her mother replied.

Nick was a different person with them, and with her brothers too. Both of her brothers liked to visit Chicago because Nick would get tickets to Bulls games, then treat them to beer and pizza afterward. When her parents came to visit, he took them to the jazz clubs. Surely, Carrie thought, Nick had wanted her to leave. And he wasn't asking her to come back now, only to make a decision.

She ate a slice of apple with cheese, annoyed with herself for not calling him and getting it over with. A clean break, wasn't that what she wanted? As if such a thing existed, as if fate might slip you a little silver hatchet and let you cut yourself free. Carrie had an image of the sycamore tree at the top of the hill on her grandparents' farm, the tree that grew around the barbed-wire fence. Maybe that was what old marriages were like. They kept on year after year, and eventually the barbs hardly showed.

Carrie left a few apple slices on the grass for the gray squirrel who would come to get them when she went in the house. Rinsing the coffee cup her mother had left in the sink, she thought about how it would sound to say, "Nick doesn't talk to me for days on end. He acts as if I've done something terrible, but I haven't." She suspected it didn't sound important enough. It wouldn't make her mother understand the cold, frightened feeling she got, the fear that she didn't belong anywhere.

As she looked around for Mrs. Banashevsky's boat picture, it occurred to Carrie that she could call Gerald Dibbs. He'd been in the navy, after all, so it was almost a legitimate reason. Of course, Mrs. Banashevsky wasn't looking for an aircraft carrier. Still, she could call him at work, keep it light. Ha, ha, guess what. If he were out on the lot, though, showing cars to a customer, he might be annoyed. As she considered the possibility, Carrie started to cry. She leaned against the sink, letting the tears run down her face. After a few minutes, when she became aware of the strange sounds she was making, she forced herself to stop.

Just as she was blowing her nose, the phone rang. She took a deep breath and picked up the receiver. She forgot to say hello.

"Carrie?" It was a man's voice, slightly familiar.

"Sorry, I was . . . hello?"

"Hi. It's Gerald Dibbs. Is this a bad time?"

"No, it's fine."

"I wonder if you might do me a favor, if you're not too busy."

Within five minutes, she had rinsed her face in cold water, combed her hair, put on lipstick, and was backing out of the driveway. Gerald needed a ride, he said, to pick up a car from an elderly man who lived over in Lynchtown. It wouldn't take more than an hour, but one of their salesmen was out sick and there was no one else who could do it. An obvious setup, which pleased Carrie and also made her feel like a furtive teenager.

Gerald was waiting outside when she pulled up to the showroom. He squinted into the car to make sure it was her, then opened the passenger door and said, "Wait one minute. I forgot to bring a plate."

When he got in, he was fiddling with the screws on the dealer's plate. "This gentleman said his expired a couple of years ago," he explained. Then he turned to Carrie and smiled. "I'm glad I found you at home. I wasn't even sure you had a car, since I see you walking all the time."

Carrie pulled back onto the highway, heading for the Lynchtown Bridge. It was ridiculous, the way her leg trembled on the accelerator. She took a deep breath and asked Gerald about his family, learned that he had four older brothers, that he and his father, one brother, and an uncle ran the car business. He told her he'd bought a piece of land on which he wanted to try growing wine grapes. It was hilly, he explained, with a southern exposure, protected on three sides by trees. He could imagine it covered with grapevines, he said, and then a small stone winery that he would build himself.

"I'm reading books about grapes," he said. "I know western Pennsylvania isn't exactly wine country, the climate's iffy. And then I don't have much time, between the dealership and all the town business. So maybe it's a pipe dream."

"I hope not," Carrie said, although it did strike her as farfetched. She told him about visiting a vineyard in northern Illinois, also an inhospitable place for wine grapes. She didn't mention that she'd gone there with Nick. Her voice sounded unnatural to her, as if she were trying too hard to say something interesting.

When they got into Lynchtown, Gerald directed her to the

street, and as they approached the house he asked Carrie how old she was. "I'm eight years older than you," he said when she told him she was thirty-six. He said this as if it were a good omen.

The man with the car Gerald was taking back to sell turned out to be old Mr. Lenhart, who had owned the market when Carrie was younger. He remembered her uncle Theo. "He was quite a fellow," Mr. Lenhart said. "I always wondered why he didn't get on out of here and make something of himself." Then he glanced quickly from Gerald to Carrie, afraid he'd said something wrong.

They were standing in the driveway next to the car, a nondescript but fairly new green four-door, freshly washed. Gerald asked for a screwdriver so he could switch the license plates.

"This car has only 7,800 miles on it," Mr. Lenhart told Carrie. "But my eyesight's so bad, I'm a menace on the road."

She wanted to ask about his wife, the woman who had given Carrie and her cousins the cream soda years ago, but she feared Mrs. Lenhart was dead. Instead, confident her father would give his approval, she told him about her series on town elders and set up a time to interview him the week after next.

"Yes, indeed," he said, absently twisting his wedding ring. "You keep a store, you see a lot. I could tell you a few things."

Gerald straightened up and gave Mr. Lenhart the old plate. As they shook hands, Mr. Lenhart said, "My daughter and her husband run the store now. They make their own ice cream. You should try it."

"Lead the way," Gerald said to Carrie. "I'll buy you a cone."

The store had changed very little, but now there was a small counter at the back where the ice cream was sold. A sign tacked above it read "Home-Made: Three Flavors Daily." A young woman in a white apron—Mr. Lenhart's granddaughter, Carrie guessed—waited on them, and they took their cones outside and sat on the steps. They looked across the river to where they had stood together the day before.

"Pistachio," Carrie said, making a face at Gerald. "Isn't that an old man's flavor?"

"You tell me."

He held the cone out to her, and Carrie hesitated before taking a small bite from the top, where his tongue had left an impression. "Not too bad," she said.

She was disappointed when she offered her cone in return and he said strawberries gave him an allergic reaction. But then he laughed and told her how he'd broken out in hives from eating strawberry shortcake when he was a boy, and he let his knee brush against hers.

"What brought you back here?" he asked, sitting up straighter so that there was a space between them.

It felt as if a cool shadow had fallen across her leg. "I seem to be leaving my husband," Carrie said. "It isn't that simple, of course."

"Do you love him?" Gerald had finished his ice cream already and was looking down at his hands.

Carrie noticed that he had a small bump on the top knuckle of his right-hand middle finger, as she did, as if he had gripped his pencil too tightly while learning to write. "I can't answer that," she said.

"None of my business, you mean?"

"Well," Carrie said, "I can't answer that either." She held the half-eaten cone out in front of her, trying to catch the drips with a paper napkin. "I should have gotten a smaller one, I guess."

"Here," Gerald said, taking it from her and walking over to a trash barrel she hadn't noticed.

When he came back and sat beside her, he took her hand in his and turned it over, as if he might read her future. "I was married once," he said, tracing the lines of her palm with his thumb.

Unexpected as it was, his touch sent a pleasant shiver up her arm, and Carrie waited for him to say more. When he didn't, she asked if he had children.

"No. We'd hoped to, but it didn't work out."

"I'm sorry."

"We got divorced almost ten years ago. I started seeing a lady from Rownd's Point, a girl I went to high school with."

Carrie instinctively pulled her hand away, but he held on to it.

"That didn't go anywhere, trust me," he added. "We sort of keep each other company is all."

Later, when he opened her car door for her, he kept his distance but said he hoped to see her again.

Driving home, Carrie understood that it was up to her to decide what happened next. She could let it drop, or not. She wondered what the woman from Rownd's Point would have to say about it. She pictured someone completely unlike herself, a woman like that teller at the bank with the puffed-up hair and shiny blouses and long, painted fingernails. The girlfriend of a sales manager.

The next morning Carrie got up early and went to *The Messenger*'s darkroom to develop the pictures of Mrs. Banashevsky. She chose eight to enlarge and was hanging them up to dry when her father looked in.

"Well," he said, squinting at each one. "Pretty good, aren't they?"

She spent the rest of the day in the newsroom, transcribing the interview with Mrs. Banashevsky, organizing her files, experimenting with a new format for the calendar section. At lunchtime, she went with her father and the assistant editor to Paula's Café for homemade vegetable soup and Parker House rolls. It was Thursday, the day *The Messenger* came out, so the two men were in no hurry. At her father's suggestion, they ordered a piece of lemon meringue pie and cut it into three narrow pieces for dessert. Carrie eyed the stack of brand-new *Messenger*s by the cash register with a sense of contentment. She allowed herself to think of Gerald Dibbs just long enough to pray he wouldn't come into the restaurant.

Her mother was in a good mood that evening too, as if the library's deep quiet had absorbed her grievances over the past two days. By way of apology, she had brought home a book she thought Carrie would like, a new anthology of Irish poetry. After supper, as she and her parents sat reading in separate corners of the living room, it occurred to Carrie that if there were no men in her life, she could be a good daughter—a help to her parents as they grew older, a competent spinster taking over the parental nest.

Carrie's attraction to Gerald Dibbs felt treacherous in every way. A line from her college French class came back to her, something Flaubert had written in a letter to his mistress, about love being merely a superior form of curiosity. There was truth in that. How else to explain the keen desire for a near stranger? But people talked about desire as if it were one thing—sexual longing. It was more, Carrie thought. It was also a longing for something that might carry you into the future and not leave you stranded.

When her parents invited her along to a movie in Morgantown the next evening, Carrie told them to go ahead, she didn't want to intrude on their Friday night date. They went off in high spirits, joking about how she shouldn't wait up for them. As they got older, Carrie noticed, her parents were more gentle with each other, as if their faults too had become precious over time. There was a period when Carrie and her brothers were growing up that arguments ignited between her parents without warning. Even a Sunday outing could become a disaster. They would return home early, the children sliding silently out of the backseat and filing into the house like defeated troops, a promised treat forgotten. The three of them would stand together at the window, watching their parents in the front seat of the car, willing them to stop what they were doing and come inside. Now it was impossible to remember what they'd been fighting about.

Carrie got out the phone book and looked up Gerald's number. There was his name printed on the page: Dibbs, Gerald, Blaze Hollow Road. She knew where it was, only a couple of miles outside town, and what could it hurt to drive out that way on a summer evening?

By the time she got up the courage to turn into the road instead of driving past, it was nearly dark. Blaze Hollow, Carrie recalled, used to be Blaise Hollow, until a fire burned through the valley on New Year's Day in 1938. Trees had grown back densely on both sides of the road, so the few houses would spring up unexpectedly in her headlights. Finally, she spotted his blue pickup parked near a neat white farmhouse at the end of a long driveway. Pulled up beside it was a small American car of the sort she imagined the bank teller would own. Lights were on in the downstairs windows of the house.

Feeling reckless all of a sudden, Carrie drove in and parked behind Gerald's truck. Up close, she could see that the house was cream colored with green trim, not as large as it looked at first. Probably it had been the farm manager's house on the Straight Up Dairy Farm. Carrie followed the sound of a radio around to the back, where the door stood open. Inside, a teenage boy sat at the table, listening to a Pirates game. She could see a woman standing at the sink, washing dishes, and Gerald beside her, drying them. Because of the baseball game, they hadn't heard her car. She was about to turn and go when the boy looked up and saw her standing just beyond the light.

"Hey," he said, startled, half rising from his chair.

"Oh, hi," Carrie replied, forcing herself to move forward.

Gerald didn't seem all that surprised to see her. "What brings you out this way?" he asked, draping the dish towel over his shoulder.

"Well," Carrie said, jamming her hands into the pockets of her shorts and discovering the folded-up picture of Mrs. Banashevsky's boat, a piece of luck that gave a little extra credence to the story she had prepared. "Someone in town told me you do woodworking. Also that you have an interest in boats." She could feel sweat popping out along her spine.

"First time I've heard of it," said the woman, who had been staring at Carrie. She stood with her hands at her sides, dripping soapy dishwater onto the floor.

"Maybe it was another Dibbs," Carrie said. "I thought it was you."

"You've got the right one." Gerald walked across the room to turn the radio down.

"He does all sorts of things," the boy said, as if the evening had just turned interesting. "You want him to build you a boat?"

"Not me, exactly. I'm trying to find a boat for a friend of mine." She was embarrassed by the crumpled magazine ad as she placed it on the table in front of the boy. "It's for Mrs. Banashevsky, actually," she told Gerald. "Maybe you know her, Mira Banashevsky? She lives on Depot Street."

"I don't think that old woman likes me," he said. "I stopped by her house last night to ask her to sign the ferry petition. She said its time had come and gone, and something like 'Best to let the dead dogs lie.'"

Carrie almost wished she had been there. The woman, she noticed, had gone back to washing the dishes. She didn't look anything like Carrie expected. She had glossy black hair pulled back and held in place with a silver barrette but otherwise seemed beyond caring about her appearance. Although she was rail thin, she'd still managed to find a pair of tight-fitting cutoffs, and her legs were covered with mosquito bites. Or maybe poison ivy. The boy, who had the same dark hair, was astonishingly handsome.

"Cool," he said, holding the picture at arm's length.

"I've never built a boat before." Gerald sat down at the

table and pulled out a chair for Carrie. "It's not an easy thing to do."

"You've never built anything, far as I know," the woman said, keeping her back to them.

"When I was a kid, I used to make pencil boxes," Gerald told Carrie and the boy. "My uncle Reed showed me how to cut dovetails and join the sides. They had a lid you could slide out, with a groove in the end for your finger."

"Oh, great, a floating pencil box," the woman chortled, banging a pot against the edge of the sink and splashing herself as she rinsed it.

"I had one of those," the boy said. "Only mine was plastic. In fourth grade, some fat kid stepped on it."

The woman dried her hands and began rummaging through her purse, which hung on the doorknob. She fished out a pack of cigarettes and a lighter and went outside.

"Would you like something to drink?" Gerald asked Carrie. "There's some beer, iced tea."

"It's the instant," the boy said. "I don't recommend it." His attention was caught by something on the radio, and he listened intently for a minute before switching it off.

"Not tonight," Gerald said, referring to the Pirates' chances of winning.

Carrie kept an eye on the shadowy figure of the woman pacing in the backyard. Every few steps she'd stop to draw on the cigarette, making the tip glow red. The wind seemed to be picking up—Carrie could see sparks flying in the air. "I don't think this is a good time," she said. "I should go."

"Hold on, let's get this figured out." Gerald put his hand on her wrist, as if to keep her sitting there.

"I'll sketch it for you," the boy said, going to the closet and taking out a grocery bag. He tore the back out neatly and got a pencil from beside the phone.

"Mrs. Banashevsky said she wants a boat you can row, a graceful boat. I believe she's thinking of something like a dory." Carrie leaned forward, toward the boy, and Gerald took his hand away.

"Maybe a skiff," he said. "That's more of a rowing boat." Gerald described it in some detail—flat bottom, square back, pointed bow—and the boy drew.

"You draw really well," Carrie told him, as he roughed it out with bold lines.

"It's kind of a hobby," the boy said. "This would be better if I had some charcoal, though." He drew in the lapstrake sides, the oarlocks, put in two seats—a long one in the back and a shorter one in the front. When he'd finished, he added his initials, "CW."

"Maybe we could just frame your drawing and give it to Mrs. Banashevsky," Carrie said. "You know," she added, turning to Gerald, "it would be a lot easier to find a used boat somewhere. I mean, how long would it take to build this?"

"Bending the wood's the hard part, isn't it?" the boy asked.

"My dad could help with that. When he was young, he used to help my granddad make barrels. Never mind for what," Gerald said, smiling at her.

So they were moonshiners, Carrie thought. No wonder her grandmother, who refused even a tiny glass of wine at Christmas dinner, hated them. Back at the farm, when Carrie's father and her uncles had wanted a beer, they had to go out to the barn to drink it. They kept it in a cooler behind the tractor shed, and her grandmother pretended not to know.

Gerald got up and looked in the refrigerator, appeared to change his mind. "If I can get some marine plywood, we can do this. It won't be quick, though. Is she in some all-fired hurry?"

The rain started before Carrie got to the end of Gerald's driveway, fat drops that hit the windshield with force. Even with the windows rolled up, she could hear the wind thrashing the trees. The smart thing would be to stop right there in the driveway and wait for the storm to pass, but she wanted to get away from the woman, who had stood silently inside the open garage door as Carrie left the house. When Carrie pulled onto the road, the rain fell so hard she could barely see ahead, even with the wipers on high. It came in sheets, washing over the car, and she could imagine the dusty road turning to a muddy stream.

All at once, headlights loomed up, appeared to come straight at her. Carrie turned the wheel right and felt her car skimming across tall weeds that whipped the underside. She stopped with a thump, tilted in a ditch. Not hurt, except for her right hand, which she'd thrust against the dashboard to brace herself. She could hear hailstones peppering the hood. Maybe the driver of the other car had seen what happened and would come back to help her.

It was a long time before the rain let up, and no cars passed. When Carrie decided to get out and have a look, the air had turned chilly. She had to pee in the worst way, so she squatted down on the far side of the car. From there, it looked as if her front bumper was firmly lodged in the bank. She'd have to walk out to the main road and find a phone or flag somebody down. As she zipped up her shorts, she saw lights approaching and stayed behind the car. It was Gerald's blue truck, but when it stopped, the boy got out. He was alone.

"You all right?" he called to her.

"Yeah," she said. "Considering."

"Don't worry. I have a flashlight."

She stepped up out of the ditch and stood beside him, trying to stop herself from shaking as he shone the light over her car. It was spattered with mud, but it didn't appear to be damaged.

"You're cold," he said. "Maybe I can find you something." He looked in the truck and came back with a gray sweatshirt. "It's Gerald's," he told her as she pulled it over her head.

The boy walked all around the car with the light. From the back of the truck he took a length of chain with a hook on one end and fastened it under the car's rear axle. "Get in the truck," he said, attaching the other end of the chain to its tow bar. "We'll pull your car out backwards."

Carrie turned to watch through the rear window as the boy drove forward. She could feel the hesitation when the slack in the chain ran out. The car didn't move at first, then all at once it pulled free and lurched back onto the road.

"There," the boy said. "Good thing I came along, I guess."

"I'm grateful," Carrie said, reaching for the door handle.

"I'll sit here until you see if it starts up okay." The boy's voice sounded flat, maybe disappointed.

"Well, thank you." Carrie opened the door and started to get out.

"He would've come himself," the boy told her, "except that my mom would've had a hiss fit."

"You mean you weren't on your way somewhere?"

"No. I don't have my license yet." He shone the flashlight straight through the windshield so that it sent a beam out into the mist. He twirled it around three or four times before switching it off. "Sometimes in these bad storms, trees come down across the road. He asked me to drive out here and check."

The rain started up again as Carrie drove along the highway—not hard now but enough to wash the mud off. She parked the car beside the garage and got a rag to wipe off the front fender. A clod of dirt and grass was wedged under the bumper, and as she pulled it out she could see that the headlight casing was cracked. She'd barely gotten into bed when she heard her parents come home. They were whispering as they passed her room. She listened to their footsteps going down the hall, the closing of the door at the far end. As she fell asleep, she wondered why she hadn't asked the boy's name.

"It's Chester," Gerald told her over the phone two days later. "He's called Chess."

Gerald had phoned Carrie at the newspaper office Monday morning to say he was sorry about her trouble in the storm. She had nearly convinced herself that she didn't want to hear from him, and she was dismayed at the effect of his voice. Her right wrist was bruised and swollen; probably she'd sprained it when she went in the ditch. She'd been covering it with long-sleeved shirts, in spite of the heat. "Do you get a lunch break?" he asked her.

"Not officially," Carrie said. It seemed like too much trouble to explain how *The Messenger* worked—the stringers coming and going throughout the day, the freelance photographers who took turns being on call. The paper had only three full-time employees. Carrie herself worked half-time and could pretty much set her own hours.

"I was hoping to take you out and show you that land I mentioned the other day," Gerald said. "My vineyard," he added with a nervous laugh.

"You know what—I'm pretty busy today." Carrie's father walked up and sat on the corner of her desk. "I'm trying to write something new. I can't really get away."

There was a pause on his end, and Carrie could hear people in the background, people looking at cars, perhaps. "Well," Gerald said finally. "We should talk sometime."

Later, eating a microwave burrito at her desk, Carrie was sorry she'd said no. But she didn't want to begin something when she could already see where it would end. Because, of course, they would go their separate ways. She tried to put Gerald out of her mind and concentrate on the story she was writing about Mrs. Banashevsky.

The day before, when she'd gone back with the tape recorder, Carrie had been vague on the matter of the boat, saying she'd put out some feelers.

Mrs. Banashevsky laughed her big, hearty laugh. "Feelers," she said. "It sounds like an insect."

Finished with the interview for the time being, they were out in the garden again, weeding in the shade of late afternoon. Mrs. Banashevsky now seemed a little embarrassed about the boat, and Carrie began to wonder if it had been some passing whim. If so, it would be a relief. For now, she was happy to be kneeling in the warm dirt, listening to the sound of Mrs. Banashevsky's voice as she talked about the gardens of her grandmothers back in the old country: the cabbages and turnips, the onions and parsley, the poppies and buttercups. Carrie was using a screwdriver from Mr. Banashevsky's workbench to root out the weeds that had sprung up after the recent rain and thinking about the woman at Gerald Dibbs's house.

She recalled the three people in his kitchen before she'd interrupted them, a family picture. There had been no outward sign of affection between Gerald and the woman, but surely it was there. Gerald and the boy were close. Best to stay out of it altogether, she told herself. And yet she felt sick at heart. Even ending the lives of weeds seemed wrong.

When she noticed Mrs. Banashevsky leaning on the hoe, watching her, Carrie blushed, as if she'd been caught talking out loud.

"You look tired," Mrs. Banashevsky said. "Come back inside and have a cool drink."

Strangely, Carrie thought, Mrs. Banashevsky suggested they sit in the dining room to drink their iced tea. The heavy curtains on the windows facing the street were closed, and the room was nearly dark. A walnut breakfront crammed full of mementos and framed pictures of her sons' families took up most of one wall. Carrie wasn't sure she'd ever been in this room before.

Mrs. Banashevsky seemed uneasy. She stood beside the table, fidgeting with a lock of hair that had escaped from the neat bun she always wore. Finally, she opened a drawer in the breakfront and took out a large tan envelope.

"This is something I want you to have," she said, handing it to Carrie. "A photograph of your uncle Theo."

Inside the envelope, which was soft with age and handling, Carrie found a studio folder containing a black-and-white picture. The picture had not been taken in a studio, though. It was Theo at eighteen or nineteen, standing on the ferry dock, dapper in white trousers and a dark shirt. He seemed to be absorbed by something to one side of the camera. Or possibly someone. With his hands in his pockets and the hint of a grin on his face, he appeared at ease but hopeful too.

Mrs. Banashevsky sat down and took the picture from Carrie's hands for one last look. "Oh," she said, her eyes glistening. She closed the flimsy cardboard flaps over the image and handed it back.

"When was this taken?" Carrie asked her.

"The beginning of summer, his first summer home from college." Mrs. Banashevsky drew a line in the beaded moisture on the outside of her glass with her fingertip. That summer, she told Carrie, her father hadn't been able to work because he'd injured his shoulder at the mine. That was in the days before unions, and by then Mira had seven brothers and sisters. Friends of the family, including Theo and Marian's parents, helped out by bringing produce from their gardens and milk from their cows, but still her older brother's paycheck from his job as assistant weighmaster wasn't enough.

So when Mrs. Mackenzie came down with lumbago around the middle of June, Mira took her place at Mackenzie's Dry Goods. Six days a week, she worked in the back of the store, measuring torsos and inseams, cutting cloth from the heavy bolts, counting out buttons and hooks, matching thread.

"The men would tease me because I was shy when they came in for a new pair of overalls," she recalled. "They never remembered their size, and they'd say, 'Go on, get it all the way up there, won't bite you,' if I didn't go far enough with the tape when I measured their inseams. Then if I happened to bump their balls, they'd giggle like schoolgirls."

Carrie smiled at her. She'd never heard a woman her grandmother's age mention male anatomy. The work was exhausting, Mrs. Banashevsky went on. At night her ankles were swollen from standing all day. On Sundays, she helped her mother at home and washed and pressed her two blouses and polished her shoes to get ready for work the next day. By the Fourth of July, when she went to a picnic and fireworks with Marian and Theo and some of their friends, she already felt much older than the others.

"Once again, I was the outsider," Mrs. Banashevsky said matter-of-factly. "I was grown up, and they weren't."

The Sunday before he returned to school, Theo invited her on an outing, just the two of them. He and a friend had spent the summer restoring a boat, and he wanted to take her rowing. She was flattered. She hadn't reckoned on rowing across the river, though.

"It was a beautiful boat," Mrs. Banashevsky said. "Still smelled of new varnish, and Theo was very proud of it. But I was afraid. In a little boat, the river looks so wide. And then I got angry. At everything—the way my family never had enough money, the way Theo could decide about his own life and I couldn't. We lived in different worlds; I could see that as we got older. So before we went very far, I told him to take me back. When we reached the shore, I jumped out

230

and waded up to the bank, soaking my good shoes. Then I kept walking, I never even said good-bye."

"He let you go?"

"A few weeks after he went back to college, he sent me a letter. I never answered it."

"What did he say?"

Mrs. Banashevsky patted Carrie's hand. "That was a long time ago." She sat up straighter in her chair. "I've decided, though. One time before I die, I am going to row across the river. You'll come with me."

In *The Messenger* that Thursday, Carrie's story took up the entire front page of Section C and two inside columns. It ran with three black-and-white photos of Mrs. Banashevsky— one of them the high school graduation picture, one taken by her husband on their tenth anniversary, one Carrie had taken in the garden—and a file photo of Main Street in 1947. Theo was mentioned only in passing as a childhood friend, the brother of Marian Kramer. Through Mrs. Banashevsky's eyes, Tenney's Landing emerged as a mostly benign, hardworking town. In her recollections, immigration, the Depression, the wars played out alongside quilt raffles, chicken suppers, her sons' measles, the occasional sensation, such as the night blind Evan Sayers dove into the river and saved four boys. "History will come and find you, even in your little town" was the quotation Carrie's father ran under the headline.

When customers at Paula's Café stopped by their table to tell Carrie how much they liked the story, her father beamed at them. "This is exactly the sort of thing we need more of," he insisted three or four times.

"My phone has been ringing," Mrs. Banashevsky said,

kissing her wetly on the cheek when Carrie appeared at the door with extra copies of the paper. "And I don't mind telling you, I like being Queen for a Day."

Alone in the newsroom in the early evening, Carrie tidied up her desk. It was hardly surprising that Nick hadn't called again. Carrie had sent him an e-mail asking him to cancel her health insurance, and then a letter saying she needed more time away from him. She didn't blame Gerald for not calling her either, but she knew it would be awkward to see him at the next council meeting. The prospect of being in the same room with him made her feel light-headed. Next thing she knew, she was making a list of phrases that started with his initials. Good Dog. Get Down. Good Day. Galaxy Destroyer. God Damn.

"Do you want to go fishing tonight?" Gerald asked when he finally called the following Monday morning.

"Fishing? I don't know." Carrie looked at the faded yellow bruise on her wrist, wondering why he never called her on the weekend. "I mean, I don't have a rod or reel or anything."

"I have everything you need. It's just pond fishing, anyway. Chess and I like to catch a mess of bluegills, and then we fry them up over a fire. It's fun. Come with us."

"What about Chess's mother?"

"No, she hates fishing." Gerald laughed, and when Carrie didn't reply, he said, "Really, it's all right. And besides, I have a surprise for you, so I hope you'll come." He gave her directions to a turnout at the end of a dirt road near Sweetwater Pond.

As Carrie approached the pickup, she saw Gerald and Chess leaning against the hood. Except that Chess was a foot taller, they looked like a father and son. Both stood with their arms crossed, chins up, waiting. Gerald had turned his truck around so that it faced out. He had something tied onto the bed, and when she reached them, Carrie realized it was a boat.

"What do you think?" Gerald said, opening her door before she'd even switched off the ignition. "It needs work, but they say it floats."

"Well find out," Chess said, unfolding himself and grinning at Carrie. "It looks better right side up," he added.

Carrie was looking at the boat doubtfully. She knew she should say something.

"Once we get it sanded and repainted, it's going to be a terrific little boat," Gerald assured her. "Really, you'll see."

The three of them got into his truck, Carrie in the middle. She braced herself with her hands so as not to bump against either one as Gerald turned the truck around and started off down the overgrown trail to the pond. For some reason, she was thinking of Nick. What might he say if he could see her at this moment? What would her parents say, for that matter? She'd lied, telling them she was going to a poetry reading at McClelland College, a few miles down the river, and then she'd stopped at a gas station restroom to change out of her skirt and sandals into cutoffs and sneakers. Her fishing clothes. What if someone saw her car parked at the end of the road, conspicuous with its Illinois plates? They'd think she'd been kidnapped.

"When was the last time you went fishing?" Chess asked her.

"You think the answer is 'never,'" Carrie said. "But when we were kids, my grandfather took us fishing all the time. After lunch we'd go down to the creek and fish for trout."

"That's the worst time," Gerald said. "Heat of the day."

"Maybe that's why we never caught anything." There was an edge to her voice she hadn't intended.

Gerald nudged her with his elbow. "I'm just giving you a hard time."

He stopped the truck at the bottom of the hill below the pond and got out to untie the ropes holding the boat in place. When they lifted it out of the truck and righted it, Carrie admitted to herself that it had potential. They put their gear inside, and then Chess and Gerald hoisted it onto their shoulders and carried it up the incline. Carrie followed them, empty-handed, and in a few minutes she could hear the sound of bullfrogs splashing into the water as the boat settled on the pond.

Gerald handed her the end of the line attached to a metal ring in the bow. "It's going to leak some, but don't worry about it. The boat's been in a shed for a couple of years, so the wood's dried out."

Carrie noticed that he wasn't looking at her.

"All right," Gerald said to Chess. "I'm going to go back and get the cooler. And I'll look for something to bail with. You get the poles set up."

Chess shook his head as they watched Gerald walk down the hill toward the truck. "Poor guy," he said.

"What?" Carrie was gauging the amount of water seeping into the bottom.

"You wouldn't believe all the trouble he went to, finding this boat."

"Seriously," Carrie said, "don't you feel disloyal, considering that you're related to his girlfriend? Isn't she your mother or something?" She was trying to pass it off as a joke.

Chess held a fishing pole between his feet and concentrated on fastening tiny lead weights, hardly bigger than tomato seeds, to the line. "If you're looking for a reason not to hook up with Gerald, you'll have to do better than my mom," he said after a minute or two.

Carrie watched his slim fingers at work. She understood that Chess's life could not be easy. She also understood that he loved Gerald and his mother did not.

"Do you and your mother live with Gerald?"

"We have our own place." Chess lay the pole down and started on another one. "I stay at Gerald's sometimes, when things are weird with my mom. And she likes to go pick on him once in a while. But she's not really his girlfriend anymore."

"You know I'm married," she said.

"He mentioned it." Chess looked up and nodded at Gerald, who was cresting the hill with a cooler in one hand and a rusty coffee can in the other.

"It's not leaking that much," Carrie called out.

"Give it time," Gerald answered.

He and Chess sorted out the gear, leaving some on the bank. Gerald took three beers out of the cooler and set it down in the center of the boat. "You can use it for a seat," he told Carrie. "And you might want to take your shoes off. So they don't get wet."

Carrie sat facing Chess, who was in the bow, as Gerald rowed. She felt awkward, sitting up high on the cooler. The two of them would be having a better time, she guessed, if she hadn't come along.

"It's called a pulling boat," Gerald said eventually. "They're good for a long haul—see how far one stroke moves it forward?"

Carrie turned to look at him and felt the boat surge ahead as he leaned back on the oars. She picked up the coffee can and started to bail.

When they reached the middle of the pond, Gerald brought the oars in and laid them in the bottom of the boat. He showed Carrie how to cast her line so that the fly would dip just below the surface. Chess opened the beers and handed them around. For a long time, no one said anything. There was only the sound of the reels clicking as they cast the lines out and reeled them in, the soft splashes as the weighted nylon hit the water, the occasional croak of a frog.

Sweetwater Pond was a basin set into the top of the hill. If she threw a stone with all her might, Carrie calculated, it would make it about a third of the way across. Cattails grew at one end, and red-winged blackbirds perched on the dry stalks, swaying as they called out their hoarse *check* and high-trilling *tee-err* before darting off into the nearby hayfields. Carrie could feel herself relax as they drifted. The boat rocked gently with their movements, as the hills around them slipped off into the dusk.

"It's like we're riding on a cloud," Chess said.

And just then the fish started striking. Gerald pulled in the first one, deftly removing the hook and holding the squirming silver body in his two hands until he got it into the bucket of water at Carrie's feet. Carrie felt a sudden, swift pull at her line and started reeling in. All at once, the surface of the pond was shattered by fish hunger, dozens of tiny mouths lunging for a bit of feather on a string. Inside the boat, the three of them were caught up in it too. They whooped and laughed and made quite a racket, bringing in fish after fish.

"Stop!" Chess yelled after a while. "How many fish can we eat?"

"I've never seen anything like it," Gerald said. "Maybe Carrie brings us good luck."

"I think it's the boat," Chess replied, winking at Carrie. "We usually fish from the bank."

They drifted quietly in the near-dark for a few minutes, listening to the pond settle. A cricket chirped from the nearby hayfield, and another joined in. As Gerald began rowing them back, Carrie noticed a sliver of moon hanging in the sky. She closed her eyes, concentrating on the dip and splash of the oars.

Too soon the boat bumped up against the weedy bank. They scrambled out, pulling it up onto the sand beach where children played during the day. She helped Chess gather twigs while Gerald got his cooking things together—a large black skillet, a long-handled fork, and two sticks of butter.

"This is how it works," Gerald told her. "Bluegills are so small we just cook 'em whole. You have to pick the bones out of your teeth—and any other parts you don't like."

"Because we're real men," Chess said, laughing as the fire flared inside the smoke-darkened circle of stones.

The fish were amazingly bony, but Gerald cooked them until the skin was crisp and the white flesh tender and sweet. Carrie soon found herself, like the men, biting off the heads and tossing them in the fire, collecting the tiny bones in one hand and then tossing them in too. It was a tasty combination—cold beer, crispy little fish, a smoky fire.

When they had finished eating, they sat back and watched the fire gradually die down. The air felt cool as soon as Chess doused the embers, and even chillier as Carrie led the way down the hill with a flashlight. Although it seemed much later, the clock on Gerald's dashboard read 9:35. In the short drive to her car, Chess fell asleep with his head against the passenger window, so Carrie slid out Gerald's side.

"Did you bring anything?" Gerald asked, giving her a hand down.

"A bad attitude, maybe," Carrie said.

"I noticed. But you got over it."

"Well, it's hard to take yourself too seriously when you're sitting on a cooler in the middle of a pond. Anyway, I had a good time." They were standing beside her car, and she was reluctant to leave him.

Putting his hands on her shoulders, as if to steady her, Gerald said, "We'll work on this boat together, right?"

When Carrie nodded, he leaned forward to kiss her. His lips tasted of butter and salt, and when he put his arms around her, she could smell campfire smoke in his hair, pond water and silver fish on his clothes. "See you soon," he said, stepping back.

In her room, Carrie took the picture of Uncle Theo out of its envelope and propped it up on her dresser. He must have found life impossibly unfair, she considered, studying the young face—losing first Mira and then his boy, Paul. And yet he had always seemed content. Maybe he really did love Grace Llewellyn, his second choice. Maybe the steady repetition of his days gave him comfort: the back and forth of the ferry, the long walks with his dogs, the careful tending of his gardens, a pipe smoked on the back steps after supper.

Carrie lay down on her bed with a sigh, remembering a game she and her cousins used to play when she was ten or eleven, a game they called Choose. They played it at night, after they'd gone to bed in the big open room their parents referred to as the dormitory, on the third floor of the farmhouse. The dormitory had a girls' side and a boys' side with a partition between that didn't quite reach the ceiling. Someone would call out a question, and each child had to answer. The first few would be merely stomach turning, questions like "Which would you rather eat, an earthworm or a maggot?" But they soon got more difficult: "Which would you rather lose, an eye or a hand?" By the end of the game, they would have to make choices like which of the cousins should be kidnapped or which of their parents should die in a car crash. Answering immediately was a point of honor, no wishy-washiness allowed. It was funniest when an aunt or uncle who had just been killed off would come to the top of the stairs and tell them to be quiet and go to sleep. They laughed, Carrie thought, because they were relieved, because the game always went too far.

Which would she rather do, go back to Chicago and resume her life with Nick or stay here and take her chances on Gerald—with his schemes and his skinny girlfriend? Former girlfriend. She did want to kiss Gerald again, that was certain. She set her alarm clock; tomorrow was going to be a long day, interview with Mr. Lenhart first thing in the morning and a town council meeting in the evening.

She liked the way Gerald nodded at her and smiled when she went into the council room above the post office. He was surrounded by a knot of townspeople trying to get a word in before the meeting started. The main topic of discussion that night was whether or not to pave Cindy's Creek Road, a six-mile stretch between two of the main county roads and a favorite shortcut. Like many of the back roads, it was still dirt. In the old days, most of the roads had been covered with red dog, the hard, reddish pink residue left over from processing coal. Her grandparents' farm, now owned by weekend people from Pittsburgh, overlooked Cindy's Creek, and Carrie had always loved the sound of car tires on red dog, the wet stone smell of the creek that ran beside the road. It used to mean they would soon be on their way up the rutted lane, leaning forward to catch the first glimpse of the house and listening for the bang of the oil pan on the hard-packed yellow clay.

Gerald, all business now, brought the meeting to order. Carrie took a seat at the back of the room and opened her notebook. Sometimes the strangest things got people riled up, she reflected. There were only seven houses along the road, four owned by longtime county residents, who wanted to get the road paved. The others—weekenders, as they were called with a whiff of contempt—wanted to keep the dirt road, "in order to preserve its rural character." None of the weekenders attended the meeting, but as a group they had sent in a written statement. Gerald read it aloud, ignoring the guffaws from the crowd of thirty or more who had come out to support the road paving.

"Those people don't come around when the weather's bad," Pete Harding said, getting to his feet when Gerald had finished. "They don't know what it's like, driving a sick child to the doctor in the middle of winter. I mean, a dirt road's fine in the summer, but get a little snow and ice, it's slick as hell."

Carrie knew Pete Harding from the days when his father and her grandfather hayed together. Back then, Pete was a teenager with a serious expression and a bare, suntanned back who drove the tractor around and around the fields. One of the first families to settle in the area, the Hardings all spoke with the distinctive county accent, their northern consonants softened by a southern Appalachia twang. Certain *l*'s wanted to become *w*'s, and their nearby *i*'s gravitated toward *o*'s, so that "child" came out "chowd." "They don't know what it's like, driving a sick chowd to the doctor." It gave their voices a gentle cast, even when they were angry about dirt roads.

After the meeting ended, Gerald got swamped again. There wasn't enough money in the current budget for paving the road, he'd explained, but the town could vote on it as a special referendum in the next election. He had a way, Carrie had noticed, of letting people speak their minds and making them feel that something was about to happen. This seemed a perfect job for him: countless proposals to be weighed and discussed, money to be found, precedents overturned. At least twice during the meeting, she'd caught herself staring at him and had to look away. She'd been thinking of their brief, fishy kiss, their secret.

Her mind had also wandered to her talk with Mr. Lenhart that morning. He was, as she had guessed, a widower, alone now for almost three years. In a long conversation, his mind wandered in and out of focus, but he had thoughtfully made a pot of coffee, and his memories of things that had happened forty or fifty years ago were still keen. He lit up, remembering a trained dog that escaped from a passing showboat and lived in the store for several weeks, until its owner came back and got it.

"Rosco, his name was. We knew because it said so on his collar. Little bitty thing, jumped right off the deck and swam to shore. I saw it with my own eyes." He glanced at Carrie, maybe checking to see if she believed him. "My kids were crazy about him, everybody was. He could do a backflip like nobody's business. He'd jump right up into my arms when I unlocked the store in the morning. It was hard to say good-bye to that fellow."

At the door, as she was leaving, Carrie mentioned how kind Mrs. Lenhart had been to her once.

"I can tell you this much, she was not an easy woman to live with," Mr. Lenhart said, bracing himself against the sofa back. "You know why I stayed with her, don't you?" he continued. "So we could be buried together. We have a stone up in the cemetery, her name and mine. And that's the way it is."

Carrie asked him how long they'd been married.

"I don't remember," Mr. Lenhart said. "Fifty years at least." He sat down unsteadily on the arm of the sofa. "That last part, that's not for the newspaper."

When Carrie pulled up to Gerald's house the next Saturday afternoon, his truck wasn't there. Except for a bicycle propped against a tree near the back door, the place looked deserted. She was standing by her car, listening for sounds of life, when Chess and a girl about his age appeared in front of the garage.

"Oh, good," he said. "We were having trouble because my

friend here has no muscles to speak of. So, Carrie," he added, gesturing in her direction, "this is Stephanie. Steph."

"Hey," said Stephanie Steph with a jaunty wave. She was nearly as tall as Chess and nearly as thin as his mother.

Carrie followed them into the garage, where the boat sat on the floor next to a quartet of brand-new sawhorses, its many layers of paint scaling off, dried pondweed plastered to the inside.

"See?" Chess said. "Gerald made these sawhorses to hold the boat. Now we need to turn it over and lift it up. You two get on the end down there."

Once they had the boat in place, Chess handed each of them a paint scraper. "You need to get all this old paint off," he said. "Take it right down to the wood."

"Oh yeah?" Steph remarked. "And what are *you* planning to do?"

"The hard part. This nasty stuff here, dried caulk." He demonstrated with a hammer and chisel, dislodging tiny chips with each stroke. "Unless you'd rather," he said, offering the hammer to Steph.

She stuck her tongue out at him and started scraping.

"Music would be good," Steph suggested after about ten minutes.

"Gerald's got this crappy radio," Chess said. "It's all staticky."

"By the way," Carrie said. "Where is Gerald?" He had called her at the newspaper two days ago and proposed getting started on the boat. "Saturday around one," he'd said. "Maybe you could stay for supper."

"He's dealing with a situation," Chess said, looking down the length of the hull.

"An Agnes situation," Steph added.

They seemed to think this was an adequate explanation, until they noticed Carrie looking at them expectantly.

"That's my mom, in case you don't know," Chess told her.

"When Gerald told her you were coming over, she had some kind of meltdown," Steph explained, arching her eyebrows dramatically. "She tore out of here and nearly ran me down. I was coming up the driveway on my bicycle."

"Gerald followed her," Chess said, "but he'll be back any minute now."

"When did this happen?" Carrie asked him.

"About two hours ago."

Carrie concentrated on an especially stubborn patch of paint. Two hours was a long time.

When Chess got tired of the silence in the garage and went to get the unsatisfactory radio, Steph put down her scraper and whispered to Carrie, "She's such an amazing bitch. Even though I don't like to use that word."

"Agnes?"

"She is, like, so possessive," Steph went on. "And she really hates me." Then, dropping her voice even more, "I'm not kidding, she has kind of an alcohol problem."

Chess came back with the radio and found an oldies station playing the Doors' first album. As he kept the hammer moving and swayed in time to the music, Steph watched him through the bangs that kept falling in her eyes.

"Those guys," she said at last, tossing her hair back, "are such druggy losers."

Without missing a beat, Chess looked up and smiled at her. "And you are such a pain," he said. Steph smiled back.

It occurred to Carrie that the two of them might be doing any number of things on a summer afternoon, but they seemed happy to keep her company, to chip away at the old boat. She was glad Gerald had rescued it. Boats, like houses, seemed especially forlorn when they'd been abandoned. It pained her to think of her grandparents' farm standing there unoccupied most of the time: the tall, narrow house, the two barns, the stone springhouse, the hayfields growing wild. Mice in the kitchen cupboards, spiders in the pantry, a big new lock on the door. She wondered how much it would cost to buy it back.

When they heard Gerald's truck, at last, all three of them kept working, heads down.

"Sounds like a party," Gerald said, joining them in the garage. He took off his green Dibbs Motors cap and wiped his forehead with his sleeve. He looked, Carrie thought, like the proverbial cat pulled backward through the wringer. His hair stood on end, and a trickle of sweat ran down one cheek. His eyes flicked from the radio to Chess to Steph and finally settled on Carrie.

"I need to get some water," he decided and headed for the house.

Carrie found him standing in the middle of the kitchen floor with an empty glass in his hand. "Start here," she said, taking the glass and filling it at the sink. She opened the freezer to get ice but found all the trays empty.

Gerald sat down, exhausted.

Taking the seat across from him, Carrie noticed that the glass had little green and yellow dinosaurs all over it. "Yours?" she asked him.

Gerald drank the water down in long, steady gulps and held the glass up to the light. "Chess's. We got it at a service station, I think, when Chess was about five."

"We?"

"Chess and I." He got up and refilled it and leaned against the sink. "That was the year his dad left. Agnes got herself a boyfriend in about two minutes flat, and she was always leaving Chess with us when she had a date. Kind of ironic, I guess."

"Ironic because Agnes ended up being your girlfriend?"

"No, because my wife ended up moving to Arizona to live with Chess's dad." Gerald was staring out the window.

Carrie tried not to let the shock show on her face. "So what happened just now with Agnes?" she asked.

Gerald sat down at the table again, glanced at Carrie, then looked away. "Agnes needs a lot of help, that's the way she is. And when she gets upset, which is fairly often, she drinks." He picked up the empty glass and moved it slightly. "So I'm trying to get her to go to AA, but she's putting up a hell of a fight."

"You were talking about AA for three hours?"

"Your name came up, too." Gerald tried to laugh, but it sounded more like a groan. "I can't expect you to understand. You don't know her."

"How did my name come up, though?"

"Basically, Agnes told me I'd be a fool to get involved with you."

"Because?"

"It's not like I haven't thought of that myself," Gerald said, shifting in his chair. "Someone like you, I can see you living in the city, married to a lawyer or a banker."

"I tried that once. It wasn't so hot."

"You know that story you wrote for the paper, the one about Mrs. Banashevsky?" Gerald finally looked at her. "It was really good. I saved it, and I didn't tell you."

"I just assumed you didn't like it."

"Are you kidding? I couldn't write something like that in a million years."

"Well, why would you?" Even as the words came out, she wished she'd said something else.

Gerald got up and stood by the door. Carrie could hear the radio playing in the garage. She wished she could reassure Gerald that everything would be fine. "I'm going to go now," she said.

At the last minute, as she was getting into her car, Gerald said, "If I were your husband, I'd be down here. I'd win you back." In the rearview mirror, Carrie saw him standing outside the garage, hesitating.

It was lonely in the car. Carrie decided to drive out Cindy's Creek Road; at least she could see the lane that led up the hill to the farm. She discovered that the chain was up across the bottom, which meant the new owners were probably not there. To be safe, Carrie parked at the pull-off by the swimming hole and walked back the quarter mile or so, the distance that had seemed so far when she was a child. Ducking under the chain, she turned and swung it angrily until it clanked against the iron posts.

The house appeared just as she reached the steepest part of the lane. It looked like an old friend in disguise, the white clapboards painted light gray and the black shutters now eggplant purple. The front door and the trim around the windows had been painted a dark, dusky green.

"Don't you look cute?" Carrie said, as if the house should be ashamed of itself.

Resisting the temptation to peer in the windows, she continued up the hill, past the cow barn, where a shiny new Kubota sat in the tractor shed, and higher, until she reached the flat rock above the bank barn. Seated on the warm, familiar stone, she could see across the valley to the Allegheny Mountains, the mountains that had been tunneled through to build the Pennsylvania Turnpike. Traveling over the turnpike once or twice a year, Carrie and her brothers had memorized the names of the mountains. "Tuscarora!" they'd call out, after reminding their father to remove his sunglasses and turn on the headlights, and then, after the brief stretch of sunlight between the twin tunnels, "Blue Mountain!" That was the sad direction, heading back to Philadelphia. But after Blue Mountain, her father would pull into the Howard Johnson rest area, and Carrie and her brothers would buy ice cream with the five-dollar bill her grandmother always slipped into her hand when she said good-bye. By then the money would be crumpled and sweaty, having been folded in Carrie's palm all those miles.

Bees, Carrie was thinking, noticing how the red clover bloomed in the fields. She and Gerald could keep bees, once she got the farm back. They would plow the vegetable garden and plant it again and build bee boxes. Gerald and Chess could fish in the farm pond. At night they'd eat dinner in the kitchen, at the long enamel-topped table, she and Gerald and Chess. Steph too. It would be their own Home for Displaced Persons.

Now that they'd tarted the place up, the owners from Pittsburgh would want a pretty penny for it, though. Carrie got to her feet.

She walked slowly back down the hill, toward the springhouse. It was her favorite building on the farm, made of smooth tan fieldstone, with a narrow door in one wall and a window in the wall opposite. Her grandfather's father had built it for his wife so that she would have a place to store her milk and butter. A spring bubbled up on the north side and ran through, keeping it cool all summer. A house for a spring. A snake had lived in it too, a black snake her grandfather named Elmerita.

Brushing aside a massive cobweb, Carrie stooped to get through the door. The stone floor was cracked and uneven and dry, but she could hear the gurgle of water. The spring was still there. She knelt on the floor and watched the water bubble up. Instead of flowing through the springhouse, across the floor, it now trickled back into the rock. Carrie filled her hands and splashed herself with the icy water. She leaned closer and let it wash over her face and soak her hair.

"Gerald Dibbs called," her mother announced the next afternoon, when Carrie returned from her Sunday visit with Mrs. Banashevsky.

Her parents were sitting on the screened porch at the side of the house, reading the *Post-Gazette* and sharing a footrest.

"Why would he be calling you, Cee?" her father asked, peering over his glasses.

Carrie had hoped to escape into the house without explanations. Her father's calling her Cee, a childhood nickname, caused a momentary pang of guilt. "We're working on a project together, actually," she said. "A boat for Mrs. Banashevsky."

"That boat again," her mother said.

"What's Gerald Dibbs got to do with it?" her father wanted to know.

"He found a boat that we're fixing up," Carrie said, moving toward the door.

Her father frowned and went back to the newspaper. But then, after she had gone inside, he called out, "He knows you're married, I suppose?"

"Of course," Carrie called back, heading for the phone.

Gerald sounded relieved to hear Carrie's voice. Instead of rehashing the events of the day before, as they might have done, they settled into a friendly conversation. Carrie told him about visiting Mrs. Banashevsky. Gerald said he'd forgotten to tell her he'd sold Mr. Lenhart's car. They decided that Wednesday after work would be a good time to start on the boat again.

After that, they settled into a routine, Wednesday evenings and Saturday afternoons in Gerald's garage. Usually it was the four of them: Carrie, Gerald, Chess, and Steph. They ate pizza right from the box as they worked, or shared the turkey and ham sandwiches Carrie sometimes brought. On Saturday nights, they sat down at the table for "Gerald's famous spaghetti," made with a spicy sauce that simmered in the Crock-Pot all day. After spaghetti, Carrie and Gerald might walk up to the top of the hill behind Gerald's house with his glow-in-the-dark star guide or squeeze into the front seat of his pickup and drive around the back roads while Gerald explained the history of every house they passed. There were times when she felt perfectly happy, holding Gerald's right hand as he drove with his left, leaning into him as they took the curves.

Carrie was aware of Gerald's leg draped over hers and the delicious warmth in the bed before she fully woke in the morning. She was also aware of an unpleasant pounding sound from below.

"It's Agnes," Gerald said, coming awake in a split second. He fumbled his pants on and pulled the sheet back over Carrie. "Stay here. I'll deal with it."

She listened to him going down the stairs two at a time. It was barely light, about six o'clock Carrie guessed. The instant she heard the door open, she also heard Agnes's voice.

"The goddamned door was locked. You never lock the door."

"Well, now it's open," Gerald said calmly.

"What the hell?" It sounded as if Agnes had stumbled against the table.

Carrie got up and gathered her clothes. She dressed quickly, deciding to wear Gerald's shirt when she couldn't locate her own.

"Well, well. Here comes Sleeping Beauty," Agnes said as Carrie entered the kitchen.

Carrie looked at her and thought about heading straight out the door. "I'll make coffee," she said.

"That's a myth, coffee. Tell her, Gerald."

Gerald, ignoring Agnes now, was rummaging in the cupboard. "I've got one of those old percolators. I hope that's all right."

By the time Chess came downstairs, yawning and rubbing

his eyes, Gerald was scrambling a skillet full of eggs. Agnes was sitting at the table, her head propped up with one hand, a steaming cup in the other.

"Hey, Mom," Chess said. "Thanks for waking us up."

So this is how it's going to be, Carrie thought as she watched Agnes drenching her eggs in ketchup. Gerald tried to make small talk about the new cars they were getting in at the dealership. The unusually hot weather, he said, had been keeping customers away. Carrie had been touched the night before to find clean sheets on the bed, fresh towels and new soap in the bathroom. It was the first time she'd stayed at his house.

"These eggs," she said, "are so good."

"He can cook, all right." Agnes pushed her plate away and got unsteadily to her feet. "Have a nice day, everyone," she called over her shoulder on her way out.

"That was special," Chess said when she'd gone.

"I've seen a lot worse," Carrie said as she got up to wash the dishes.

An odd thing to say, she reflected, driving home, and now it seemed laughable.

The nearly identical expressions on her parents' faces reminded Carrie that she was still wearing Gerald's shirt. They were finishing their own Sunday breakfast when Carrie went in the house, and they looked truly alarmed, both of them taking in the green-and-blue plaid shirt as Carrie stood in the doorway.

"It's weird, I know," she said, holding up her hands to fend off questions. "But we are not going to discuss it." She went upstairs and took a long, hot shower.

After that, Agnes showed up occasionally, in the evening. She would perch on the workbench and smoke a cigarette as they scraped and sanded, ignoring Chess's complaints about secondhand smoke. From time to time, she would contribute some caustic remark. "That's a hell of a looking thing," she said early on, nodding in the direction of the boat, and Carrie was pretty certain Agnes meant to include her in the comment.

Beyond offering her a slice of pizza, which Agnes always refused, the others hardly seemed to notice her, except that Chess did turn the radio up louder when his mother was there. Sometimes they listened to Pirates games or the country station Gerald favored. Agnes knew the words to most of the songs and would sing along in her scratchy voice, emphasizing certain lines of the "you done me wrong" variety.

One evening, not long after their scrambled egg breakfast, Carrie could smell whiskey on Agnes's breath, and she sensed Agnes watching her closely. "Hey, tell me something," Agnes said after a while, exhaling a great cloud of smoke. "You went to college, am I right?"

"Yes," Carrie said. "I did." The others had stopped what they were doing, and in the sudden quiet she braced herself for an insult.

"Well," Agnes said, "you're supposedly smart then, aren't you? Which makes me wonder what you're doing here."

"Agnes," Gerald said, taking a step toward her. "You're welcome to stay, so long as you don't harass my workers." Gerald's hands were shaking, Carrie noticed, but his voice sounded cheerful.

"Harass? That's a good one," Agnes replied, turning her head and drawing on her cigarette.

"All right, then," Gerald said, turning back to the boat. "Remember."

Steph, catching Carrie's eye, bumped Chess with her hip. "Hey, buddy, move over. Give me some room here." She grabbed his belt loop as he obliged and pulled him partway back. "Not that much room."

Although Agnes smoked another cigarette, staying long enough to prove she couldn't be intimidated, she left without Carrie noticing.

"How do you do it?" Carrie asked Gerald a few days later. It was a silent Sunday morning, and Gerald had wakened her by running his hand lightly up and down her back.

"Drive women crazy, you mean?"

"Sorry to change the subject," Carrie said, turning to face him, "but I meant Agnes. You never lose your temper with her."

Gerald rolled onto his back with a groan. "Could we talk about something else?"

"In a minute. I'm really curious—how do you stay so calm when she starts acting up? I'd be nuts."

"I had to learn the hard way," Gerald said, closing his eyes. "I hit her once, slapped her really—but hard. Right in front of Chess. It was a bad scene."

"What happened?"

"Oh, one of her boyfriends dumped her," Gerald said reluctantly. "She got tanked up and then drove over here with Chess in the car. He was about seven at the time, and pretty scared. She was really out of her mind that night. She was standing outside, yelling at me, calling me every name in the book, like I was the guy who'd left her. Anyway, when I went out and saw Chess sitting in the front seat and realized she'd been driving around like that, I lost it."

"So you smacked her?"

"Yeah."

"Well, you had to do *something*." Carrie placed her palm flat on Gerald's chest and felt his heart beating.

"It was the wrong thing," he said, covering her hand with his. "She took off with Chess before I could get him out of the car. It was lucky they made it home that night."

By August, when the boat on the sawhorses was a clean shell, ready for caulking and finishing, Mrs. Banashevsky seemed resigned to the fact that Gerald Dibbs was involved. "If that's the way it has to be," she'd said at last.

Her parents kept up a general frostiness at home, since Carrie now refused to discuss either Gerald or Nick with them. Things were going well at the newspaper, though, which pleased her father. Her piece on Mr. Lenhart had come out, and now people called to suggest others she might interview. The weeks her Elders series appeared, they sold every copy of the paper. At dinner one night, her mother mentioned—as if it were a minor miracle—that a friend of hers had bought a car from Gerald and had liked doing business with him.

And then a card arrived from Nick. On the outside was a photograph of two elderly men, both wearing berets, sitting at an outdoor chess table and concentrating on the game as pigeons pecked at crumbs around their feet. On the inside, he had written, "C, I miss you." He'd signed it "N." The picture was a scene from the park near their apartment in Chicago. Late Sunday mornings, when it was warm enough, they liked to go out for coffee and a bag of croissants. They had a favorite bench, close to the chess players, where they would camp out with the newspaper for a couple of hours, reading out loud to each other, dropping flakes of croissant to the pigeons strutting by on the sidewalk.

It shook her, the pleasure of the memory. Carrie had grown so accustomed to thinking of Nick as cold and silent that she'd forgotten their times of happiness. Later in the day, as she was organizing the events calendar in the newsroom, she remembered her friend Leigh explaining the dangers of "wrong thinking." Leigh attended seminars on spirituality and practiced meditation, and she was someone Carrie admired, even if her ideas were, as Nick said, "a little spooky." Wrong thinking, of course, always disguised itself as right thinking and would get you into quite a tangle and cause you to make all sorts of bad decisions. To avoid wrong thinking, Leigh said, it was important to get in touch with your spiritual side and also to check in with more enlightened beings from time to time. Who might she check in with, Carrie wondered. Her mother? Mrs. Banashevsky? Agnes?

At the thought of sitting down for a heart-to-heart with Agnes, Carrie started to laugh. The truth was, she'd begun to feel sorry for Agnes. But she had a vision of joining her on the workbench in Gerald's garage, of taking a cigarette from her pack and lighting up, of saying, "There's this guy in Chicago . . ." Carrie couldn't stop laughing. Tears ran down her cheeks, and people at nearby desks looked up. She hurried to the bathroom, where she turned the water on full blast, hoping to cover up the sound, and held her sides, walking up and down in front of the stalls.

Eventually, she returned to her desk as if nothing had happened, feeling exhilarated in an unhinged, unhelpful way. The shock of hearing from Nick had done it. She'd expected him to fade sulkily into the background, getting on with his own life—whatever that might be. Before they were married, Carrie remembered, her father had observed that Nick was a manipulative person. She had dismissed the remark at the time.

Nick called the following week, although—or maybe because—Carrie hadn't responded to his card. "You've been gone twelve weeks," he pointed out.

Twelve? Carrie hadn't been counting, but it seemed longer.

After mentioning that she'd been away nearly the entire summer, Nick sounded unexpectedly friendly. He asked about her family, her job at *The Messenger*, which he mistakenly called *The Herald*. It was easy to talk to him about her work once she got started. In fact, his apparent fascination with everything she said had been very attractive in the early days, before it vanished. She remembered dancing with him at the wedding where they met, flustered that such an elegant man was impressed by her journalism degree. Working at a newspaper seemed to her so inky and earnest, especially compared to the clean, crisp world of investment banking.

Nick had been doing a number of things Carrie liked, going to readings and outdoor concerts, poking around in used book stores. He'd also been getting up early to jog along the lake and was now running six or seven miles a day. In her head, Carrie ticked off her own list of summer activities: fishing, sanding a boat, driving around back roads in a pickup, standing on a hilltop looking at stars, sleeping with a car salesman, fending off his alcoholic ex-girlfriend.

"I owe you an apology," Nick said at last. "Many apologies." He could see how unfair he'd been, taking his job anxieties out on her. He was, he added, prepared to make changes.

"Nick," Carrie reminded him, "this went on for years."

"I would really like to see you," Nick said, ignoring her remark. "I want you to come home."

When Carrie didn't reply, he said, "If you do, I'm willing to reconsider the child question."

"The child question," Carrie repeated.

"I don't expect you to make up your mind right this minute," Nick went on, "although I do feel compelled to tell you that a woman in my office is showing real interest in me. A very attractive woman."

"That would explain the outdoor concerts, et cetera."

"I would prefer it if you came back, Carrie. But I need to know if you will. Soon."

"And what, in your opinion, is soon?"

"Why don't you sleep on it? Give me a call tomorrow."

Gerald had finished caulking the boat, and the day after Nick's call they started to varnish it. Finding the wood in good shape, they'd all agreed it would be a shame to cover it up with paint again. Besides, Carrie said, a varnished boat would be more like her uncle Theo's.

"Maybe it's the same boat," Steph said. "This might be the very boat Mrs. B got scared in."

"You are such a romantic little twerp," Chess replied, saluting her with a half-empty bottle of Rolling Rock.

"You never know," Gerald said, looking at Carrie. "It could be."

The comment struck her as silly. It annoyed her, too, that Gerald let Chess drink beer. Encouraged it, really, by keeping an endless supply in the refrigerator. Even if Chess never had more than one or two, Gerald should know better.

The boat took the varnish well, and when they'd covered the fourteen-foot hull, they all stood back to admire it. On Saturday they would give it another coat. Gerald said he thought they could have it ready by Labor Day.

"How sweet is that?" Steph said, smiling at Carrie, but she was too preoccupied to respond.

Gerald told Chess he could take the truck to drive Steph home and then turned to Carrie as soon as they heard the engine start. "What's up?" he said.

"It's Nick," she told him, recounting their phone conversation. "So it's over and done with. I told him to piss off—not in so many words." They were standing on opposite sides of the boat. Carrie still had a brush in her hand.

"And you think you did the wrong thing?"

"Not where Nick's concerned. But far from sleeping on anything, I was awake all night. I was thinking about you, about falling in love with you."

"Is that what you're doing? Because if you are, you might be a little happier about it."

"It's a huge mistake. You know it, too—you practically said so yourself, at the beginning. I mean, we could hardly be more different."

"I don't care about that. I thought I might, but I don't."

"You will, sooner or later," Carrie said. "And I will too. That's the way people are."

"So you're breaking up with me."

"Yes, I am."

"Give me that," Gerald said, reaching for her paintbrush. He took it to the workbench and wiped it with a rag soaked in turpentine. "Well," he said at last, folding the rag carefully as he turned back, "I think you are dead wrong. But I guess you know your own heart."

Carrie thought about that on Saturday, when she didn't go to his house. He gave her too much credit. She could see him standing in the warm, brightly lit garage, the smell of varnish heavy in the air, a chaos of pizza boxes and rusted paint cans behind him. It made her sad to think of the lovely, half-varnished boat.

When she next saw him, at a council meeting, Carrie wanted to smooth down his hair, which stood up like a turkey's tail when he pulled his cap off. Instead she took her usual seat in the back of the room. She couldn't understand why so many people were at the meeting, since there was nothing of real interest on the agenda. The council approved a request from the volunteer fire department to have a new door built for the station house and a request from the town clerk to cut back on her Saturday hours. Gerald went through the list in an efficient, lackluster way. He sounded tired when he got to the end and asked if there was any new business. There rarely was, but tonight Pete Harding got up to speak, and it was clear that most people present knew why.

"Some of us," Pete said, "want to get back to this ferry business."

Carrie could see nods of approval around the room as he went on. "Now it's a nice idea, and I even signed the petition myself. But I'll be damned if I can see how we might pay for it. I mean, if this town hasn't got enough money to pave the roads, how in hell can we afford to run a ferry? Me and some others would like to know."

Gerald seemed stunned for a moment. "Like I said before,

it would take a bond issue to raise the money. To start it up, I mean." He paused to write something on the pad of paper in front of him, a stalling tactic, he'd once confided to Carrie, that helped him get his bearings. "No way we could do that out of the annual budget, you're right. Once it was up and running, though, it would be a moneymaker."

"For who?" someone asked.

"The way it used to be," Gerald said, "the town owned the ferry and paid somebody to run it. So any profits went to the town. Or we could sell it to a private owner and pay off the bond faster."

"A private owner named Dibbs?" another voice called out.

There was laughter in the room, and Carrie noticed a blush creeping up Gerald's neck. She wished she could stand up and take his side.

"Seriously, how much do you figure this is going to cost?" Pete asked when the laughter had died down.

"We're still looking into that." Gerald picked up his pen and studied it, cleared his throat. "There's a firm in West Virginia and one in Ohio going to give us bids on a ferry."

"Why not use a Pennsylvania company?" Pete's cousin Sam Moffat got to his feet now, removing the unlit cigar he kept in the corner of his mouth. "Why send our money out of state?"

"Because . . . ," Gerald began.

"Because the whole thing's a joke," Sam said, looking around for confirmation. "It's about as cockamamie an idea as I ever heard. I mean, why don't we bring back the horse and buggy?" He turned to Carrie. "Why don't we take the vote away from women?"

It occurred to Carrie for the first time that everyone in

town probably knew she was sleeping with Gerald. Or had been. Gerald glanced at her with a worried expression, as if he'd just thought of the same thing.

"Hold on," he said, looking at his watch. "It's getting late, and this discussion is going off track. Here's what we'll do: we'll put the ferry at the top of the agenda for the next meeting. I should have more information by then, and we'll have plenty of time to talk about it."

"We'll be here, don't worry." Sam stuck his cigar back in his mouth, tapped Carrie's notebook with one of his fat fingers, as if commanding her to get everything down, and stalked out the door.

Pete Harding and the others followed after him in a noisy, satisfied bunch. Carrie wanted to say something to Gerald, but he was huddled with the other council members. She now understood what he meant about being a new guy in town. The old guys had roughed him up a bit because they didn't get their road paved. She decided to wait for him outside.

"Hey," he said, surprised to see her. "That should make an interesting story for your paper."

"What a pack of stinkers, huh?"

"That's the way it goes." He took her by the arm and started walking down the street.

"I have to say I'm impressed at how you handled them. It's like all your training with Agnes paid off. Well, I don't mean 'training' exactly . . ."

"Don't worry about it." They walked another block in silence.

"I still think the ferry's a wonderful idea." Carrie could see Gerald's truck parked on the next corner, and she came to a halt. "I'm headed this way," she said, pointing up the side street that led to her parents' house.

"Let me give you a ride at least."

"I'd better walk."

"Ah, Carrie." Gerald gave her arm a squeeze and pushed her gently away.

Going up the steep sidewalk, Carrie listened for the sound of Gerald's truck starting. When the street remained quiet, she knew he was still standing there, watching her. She couldn't turn around, though, and go back to him, no matter how much she wanted to. It was important to keep moving. One day she would be glad.

Mrs. Banashevsky looked stricken when Carrie told her things weren't going to work out with the boat. "Maybe we can find another one," she said doubtfully.

Although Carrie had never said much about Gerald, she now told her about the phone conversation with Nick, and Mrs. Banashevsky unexpectedly hugged her. Enfolded in Mrs. Banashevsky's generous bosom, she cried at the smell of Coty talcum powder. It was the same powder her grandmother had used, and it was the smell of their good-bye hugs, when her grandmother would hold her tight for a moment and slip the five-dollar bill into her hand.

The last week of August, Carrie received in the mail a cream-colored envelope that looked as if it might contain a wedding invitation. There was no return address, but it was postmarked Tenney's Landing. On the front of the handmade card was a pencil drawing of the finished boat, oars resting in the oarlocks, the initials "CW" at the bottom. On the back, in neat, careful lettering, it said, "Please meet me at the ferry landing on Labor Day, Monday, Sept. 3, at 11:00 in the morning. Bring Mrs. B." It wasn't signed.

That night she dreamed of the farm. Again, she slipped under the chain at the bottom of the lane and made her way up the hill. She stood on tiptoe and looked in the downstairs windows of the house, but all the rooms were empty. Finally, through the kitchen window she could see her grandmother's washing machine next to the sink. A basket full of sheets sat next to it on the floor. Her grandmother, she decided, had gone to the springhouse to get water because the well was dry. Sure enough, the small wooden door was standing open, and Carrie rushed down the slope, eager to help with the heavy water buckets. When she got there, the springhouse was empty, too. She placed a hand on the sun-warmed outer stones and looked through the door, searching for a sign—even a dried-up snakeskin. But there was only the sound of water running beneath the floor. In the dream, Carrie understood that she had come to say good-bye. She rested her cheek against the rough stone and listened to the spring as it came and went beneath its house.

In her waking life, Carrie was making plans to leave. Nick had started divorce proceedings, as she discovered when she received some papers his lawyer asked her to sign. After she'd sent them off, she called an old friend in Philadelphia who told Carrie she was welcome to share her apartment while she looked for a job. Her father asked her to consider staying on at *The Messenger*, and for a few days Carrie thought hard about her work there. She was finishing up a piece on Aggie and Jasper Moffat, at ninety-five two of the town's oldest residents, and was especially pleased with the picture she'd taken of them, standing arm in arm in the doorway of their house. It would be sad not to be around when that issue of the paper came out.

And then there was her hope of buying back the farm. But the fact was she had no money, and she wouldn't be making any as a part-time reporter. What sort of life would she have in Tenney's Landing, anyway, where there was always the chance she'd run into Gerald around the next corner? How would she ever get over him?

On Labor Day morning, a steady rain was falling. As she fixed her toast and coffee, Carrie looked out at the gray, dripping backyard, sorry on Mrs. Banashevsky's account. There would be no river-crossing today. And in another week she would be gone, a dreary thought on such a morning. She lingered in her bathrobe, watching the rain.

At ten-thirty the phone rang. "It's letting up," Mrs. Banashevsky said. "The sky is brightening. Are you ready to go?"

"Almost," Carrie assured her. She ran upstairs to dress, grabbing the jeans and T-shirt she'd dropped beside her bed the night before.

Half an hour later, as they approached the ferry landing, Mrs. Banashevsky raised her umbrella. "I told you it would stop raining," she said.

She looked like a lady who had stepped out of a painting, in her long skirt and white ruffled blouse, her faded orange umbrella shielding her from a hint of sunlight behind the clouds. When Carrie saw Gerald, she wished she had gotten more into the spirit of the occasion. He was wearing dark slacks and a white shirt and had a straw boater perched on the back of his head. Her own hasty choice of clothes seemed inadequate.

"Oh!" Mrs. Banashevsky exclaimed. "This is exactly right. It looks just like Theo's boat."

It was hard to believe this was the same boat they'd taken out on Sweetwater Pond. Varnished inside and out, fitted with three seats and new oarlocks Gerald had carved by hand, it was sleek and elegant, rocking gently on the water at the end of the line Gerald had tied to the rusty green railing. On Mrs. Banashevsky's seat, the one in the middle, he'd placed a cushion.

"We'll start out rowing along the shore here, until you get used to it," Gerald told Mrs. Banashevsky as he took her hand and helped her in. "There's a coffee can under your seat, just in case," he said to Carrie.

"And you might need this," he added, once he'd settled Mrs. Banashevsky. He was handing Carrie a familiar sweatshirt. "It's going to be chilly out on the water."

"I thought of that, too," Mrs. Banashevsky said, untying the shawl around her waist and retying it over her shoulders. Then she said, "My heavens," as Carrie gave the boat a shove and hopped into her seat in the bow.

The river was still choppy from the rainstorm, and Mrs. Banashevsky kept saying "Oh" every time a little wave slapped the boat.

"Once we get out a ways, it will be much smoother," Gerald assured her, turning the boat around. "You tell me when you're ready to go."

"All right," she said. "Not yet."

"Where's your truck?" Carrie asked him. "How'd you get here?"

"My truck's on the other side, over in Lynchtown. It's got lunch in it."

"You mean you parked in Lynchtown and rowed over?"

"No, Chess helped me. We dropped the boat here and drove around, across the bridge. Then Steph and her mom came by to pick Chess up and brought me back over. They left to do some errand a few minutes ago, but they were planning to come and see us off."

"Such a lot of trouble you went to," Mrs. Banashevsky said, obviously pleased.

"You were doing all this in the rain?" Carrie asked him.

"Sure," Gerald said. "I knew it would stop."

"So did I," Mrs. Banashevsky said. "And now, I think, I'm ready to go." She gripped her umbrella firmly with one hand and the edge of her seat with the other.

"Nothing to worry about," Gerald said. "This is a very stable boat."

Sitting in the bow this time, facing Mrs. Banashevsky and Gerald, Carrie watched Tenney's Landing fall back, the houses appearing to tilt for a moment before righting themselves. Then she saw Chess and Steph on the landing, waving.

Carrie waved back, a little ashamed that they had carried on without her. And then there came a sliver of fear. She hadn't been out on the river since she was a child and then only on the ferry. It was true, the river seemed much bigger from a small boat.

Mrs. Banashevsky looked terrified and delighted at the same time, turning her head cautiously when Gerald pointed out a cormorant floating nearby. "Watch out!" she cried suddenly, shaking her umbrella in the air. "Here comes a tidal wave!"

The wake from a powerboat was heading their way, looking as if it meant to wash over them.

"I see it," Gerald said, positioning the boat to meet it head-on. "We're going to ride over it, so hold on. We'll be fine."

Carrie felt her stomach slide as they went up the crest. Mrs. Banashevsky dropped her umbrella into the bottom of the boat and held on with both hands. Gerald shouted something she couldn't make out and lifted the oars out of the water as they went over the top. They seemed to hover before dropping down to meet the next wave. He gave a mighty pull as they started up, and then lifted the oars again.

"I don't mind telling you, that was more excitement than I bargained for," Mrs. Banashevsky said when they reached calm water again. She picked up her umbrella and dusted it off. "You must know what you're doing," she said to Gerald, who had stopped rowing for a minute to catch his breath.

"You lost your hat," Carrie told him. She could see it swirling in the wake they'd come through.

"Doesn't matter," he said. "It was only a cheap thing, left over from our Fourth of July promotion."

Carrie preferred not to think about Gerald in a goofy hat, hawking cars.

"At least the sun is coming out," Mrs. Banashevsky said, raising her umbrella again.

"We should be all right the rest of the way," Gerald said, checking up and down the river.

As she got used to the motion of the boat, Mrs. Banashevsky really did look like a queen, regal on her cushion, steadily watching ahead. Behind her, Gerald was working hard against the current so that they would be a little upriver of Lynchtown when they reached the other side. He could then let the current carry them into the cove where the ferry landing had been. Carrie remembered her uncle Theo, who had the help of a motor, doing the same thing. He would make an arc across the river, cutting the motor at the last minute and drifting right up to the dock. Each time, it had seemed to Carrie that they might miss, and she would hold her breath, waiting for the moment when her uncle tossed the mooring line over the piling. It was always the same sensation—held breath, line looping out across the water, the reassuring backward tug as the ferry was caught and held.

They were near the middle now, where the current was strongest. Carrie tried to imagine how deep the river was beneath them, what creatures might be swimming there. From either bank, their boat would look about the size of a pencil box bobbing on the water. Mrs. Banashevsky pointed with her umbrella, and they looked up to see a blue heron gliding overhead, wings motionless, its long legs trailing behind. Unlikely flier.

Even more extraordinary, perhaps, the three of them in the boat, rewriting history. As she took in the long sweep of river, the rain clouds breaking up and sailing off to the east, Carrie watched Gerald rowing, the rhythmic forward and back of his body that kept them moving. A gust of wind ruffled his hair and made his shirt billow, and there was that tug at the heart. Love, Carrie had decided, was not to be trusted. She hadn't considered devotion—its power to catch and hold her before she slipped away.

Acknowledgments

I am deeply grateful to the Vermont Studio Center for the gift of time, which enabled me, finally, to complete a draft of this book; to my wonderful agent, Nat Sobel, for seeing what it could become; and to my editors Nan Graham and Alexis Gargagliano for bringing it into the world with such generous enthusiasm. Through the years of writing these stories, I was sustained by dear friends old and new, who provided me with advice, encouragement, and diversions of every kind. Thanks to all of you, particularly to Mary Hays and Steve Long for reading and commenting on the manuscript—more than once. And thanks especially to my family, Pete, Anne, and Kevin Tudish, for their unstinting support and unbending optimism.

About the Author

Born into an air force family, CATHERINE TUDISH spent her childhood moving from one place to the next—England, France, and all across America. She taught writing and literature at Harvard for eight years before moving to Vermont to work as a journalist. She now lives in Strafford, Vermont.